Love and Money

By Edith Konecky

Love and Money

By Edith Konecky

Hamilton Stone Editions

Hamilton Stone Editions

Copyright 2011
by Edith Konecky
Library of Congress
Cataloging-in-Publication Data
Konecky, Edith.
Love and money / by Edith Konecky.
p.   cm.
ISBN-13: 978-0-9714873-6-9 (alk. paper)
ISBN-10: 0-9714873-6-7 (alk. Paper)
1. Inheritance and succession--
Fiction. I. Title.
PS3561.O457L68 2009
813'.54--dc22
2005028190

Hamilton Stone Editions
P.O. Box 32
Maplewood, NJ 07040
Web Site: http://www.hamiltonstone.org
Email: Hstone@hamiltonstone.org

Cover Design by Kat Llewellyn

Other Books by Edith Konecky

Allegra Maud Goldman

A Place at the Table

Past Sorrows and Coming Attractions

View to the North

Love and Money

CHAPTER ONE

Augusta had neglected to bring a book. The waiting room was pristinely empty of words, as if so many were needed within the offices beyond the closed doors that there wasn't one to spare. You could tell this was the office of lawyers. It had been made familiar by films, plays, even novels. Walnut paneled walls, gleaming maroon leather wing chairs studded with brass nails, thick carved carpeting, English hunting prints. Somber and masculine. Historically, law is the good right arm of patriarchs, but she, a feminist by instinct, was not intimidated.

With nothing to read, she thought, instead, about a piece she'd been meaning to do by splicing a tape she'd made last summer when, finding herself in a swamp, she had recorded its night sounds, frogs and crickets pleading for mates, all low, rhythmical, guttural, insistent and mysteriously seductive, overlaid a few times by the mournful hoot of an owl and the occasional swishing of something unidentifiable. She'd stayed until the trumpeting of fowl and the chorus of a multitude of birds announced that dawn had come, bringing the new day. It was almost a piece already, but she needed to shorten it and she wanted to carpet it with something flamenco, because flamenco was emotional and unexpectedly sad and demanding, like night, night in a swamp.

Mysteriously, her greeting by the receptionist, who reappeared now, had been humbly effusive, as though she were famous, an actress or a rock star. In fact, Augusta had no idea why she was there.

"You may go in now," the young woman said, poised to lead her there. Augusta rose and followed her guide the few

9

steps to Oswald Summerville's office. (A matter of "the utmost importance," his letter had said). She walked past the door held ajar by the young woman, which then quietly and discreetly closed behind her. It took a moment to locate the rumpled figure behind the massive tooled-leather-top desk. It was his voice that focussed him for her, a slightly reedy voice.

"Miss March? Augusta Juliette March?" He smiled, motioning her toward yet another polished leather wing-chair, this one somber brown, one of two that flanked his desk. Half rising, he leaned to shake her hand. He had the pallor of someone who has spent a long time beneath a rock, but his hand was warm and dry.

"I suppose you know who I am?" he said. "Oswald T. Summerville?"

"Your name was on the letter," she reminded him. "It's also on the door."

"The 'T' stands for Theocritus, can you believe it?" He grinned at her. He was so homely that she checked an impulse to console him. "It's quite a name to be saddled with. The whole package, I mean. The compulsion to live up to it is probably the only reason for what modest success I can claim." He shuffled some papers on his desk. "But enough about me. Let's talk about you. I imagine you're anxious to learn why you're here."

"Of course, "she said. "It can't have anything to do with my job, and I don't think my landlord could afford you."

"What is your job?"

"I teach at City College. Electronic composition"

"Music?"

"In the music department, yes. There are those who debate whether it's music."

"And you?"

"Of course it's music. All sound is music."

10

"Is that so?" He smiled at her. "Well, then, let's get on with it. Tell me, how well did you know Alfred Nickleby?"

"Who? Oh. Alfred Nickleby. Uncle Freddy."

"Uncle?"

"I called him that, though he wasn't. He was a friend of my father's. I knew him as one knows the friends of one's parents. Peripherally. I was sad when he died."

"It was a great loss."

Lost at sea on some kind of yachting expedition. Time had blurred the details. So this had to do with him.

"It's been seven years since his disappearance," the lawyer said. "He's now, at least legally, presumed to be dead." He looked at her quizzically. "You're extremely attractive, Miss March."

She raised her eyebrows, puzzled by this non sequitur.

"I'm looking for a reason," he explained, sighing, "though obviously that can't be it."

"A reason for what?"

"For the startling news I'm about to give you. Better brace yourself."

"Bad?"

"No, I don't think so. Maybe. It depends. You see, he left you all his money. Virtually all."

"Who did?"

"Nickleby."

"His money? Why would he do that?"

"I don't know. I was hoping you did."

"I can't imagine. I mean, I hardly knew him. I haven't thought about him in years."

"It's a lot of money."

"Could you be more specific?"

"I could be somewhere in the neighborhood. It's not easy to be specific. You see, the money's invested in various ways by a management firm and it keeps growing." He said this with annoyance, as though he were speaking of a

11

fungus. "It's probably more than doubled since Nickleby's death, though of course with what's happened to money . . . I mean, money isn't what it used to be, is it?"

"I don't know what money used to be. I hardly know what it is now. Things cost more, I suppose."

"Still, it's an awful lot."

"Awful?"

"I would say so. Roughly, it seems to be something like sixty million dollars."

She could think of nothing to say. Sixty million of anything was beyond her comprehension. But dollars? When she went out in the morning, she checked her billfold and if it held forty of them she felt more than safe. A few hundred dollars left in her account after paying her monthly bills made her feel virtuous.

"Sixty million? What does that mean?"

"Mean?"

"In real language, I mean. I mean I don't know what I mean." She burst into tears. "What would anyone do with all that money?" she sobbed.

"Look here, there's no need to cry."

"I can't help it. I'm not much of a crier, but this is insane. There must be some mistake. Why would he do that? To me?"

"I suspect he thought he was doing it for you."   "But why?" she moaned.

"I suspect he was . . . fond of you?"

"Sixty million dollars for fondness?"

Had he been fond of her? In any special way? She searched her memory. It was true that he had never come to dinner without bringing her a delightfully imaginative gift that she invariably wondered how she had ever lived without. That must have required some thought, some knowledge of her, maybe even fondness.

12

"But I haven't seen him since I was . . . seventeen? Eighteen?"

"Who knows why people do the things they do, even Fred. Especially Fred."

"Maybe he wasn't in his right mind."

"He was in his right mind. Nobody's going to contest it."

"That's not what I meant."

"Of course it isn't. Anyone can see you're a decent person, a perfectly lovely person. I haven't known you very long but I have the feeling that I've always known you."

The hell you do, she thought. "Thanks, Mr. Summerville."

"Call me Oswald, why don't you. And that's enough crying. Please stop it."

"It's the shock." She blew her nose and stopped crying.

"I understand," he said gently. "You know, I was his friend as well as his attorney. With Fred it would have been impossible to have been one without the other. I mean, obviously you could have been a friend and not been his attorney. What was I saying?"

"That you were his friend."

"Right. And I know he was sane, though I'm as much at sea as you are. Oh, unfortunate choice of words, that. I never could understand what made him go off alone in that small boat of his."

"He was alone?"

"His plan was to go around the world by himself, circumnavigate the globe. But he wasn't that kind of man. It was as though he'd fallen under a spell. You see, he'd always been surrounded by people and I never considered him particularly adventuresome, except perhaps in business. There he had guts. And in marriage, too, I suppose. He did have five wives."

"Was it five? He mustn't have been very dependable, must he?"

13

"He was, though, paradoxically. Dependable as a rock. I never understood about his wives any more than I understood about that yacht. Part of your inheritance, by the way, is the other yacht, the big one."

"What on earth would I do with a big yacht?"

"Sail it, I suppose, or sell it; there's not much else you can do with a yacht. You've plenty of time to decide." He rooted among the papers on his desk. "There's a letter here for you," he said. "Somewhere. It was left along with the will. Maybe it will give us some answers. Ah, here it is." He handed a sealed envelope across the desk. "Go ahead, read it."

She tore open the envelope. There were four pages densely covered in a strong angular hand. "It's long," she said.

"We've got time. Unless you'd rather I didn't watch you read?"

"I'll read it aloud," she said. She paused to summon up some picture of the man whose letter she held, trying to imagine him sitting somewhere, all those years ago, thinking of her while penning this letter. Had he had a moustache? She didn't think so. Was his hair white? No, it was dark. His eyes? Oddly, she remembered his eyes. They were bluish gray, yet of surprising depth and intensity. That she remembered. "'My dear astonished Augusta;'" she read. "'I am imagining you, who knows how many years before the event, seated in Ozzie Summerville's deceptively austere chambers with your mouth pursed in bewilderment. Since I can't tell at what age you will be reading this, I'm unable to picture you with precision. Are you eighteen? Twenty-five? Forty? And what are you wearing? That would depend on the season, wouldn't it? Let's say it's almost spring and you're wearing blue. You always favored blue. Because of your eyes. But whatever age you are, I'm confident of your loveliness.'"

14

It was April. She was wearing a navy suit with a pale blue silk blouse. She looked across at Oswald Summerville and laughed, then went on with the letter.

"'You'll want to know why you're the beneficiary of this accumulation, the detritus not so much of the sweat of my brow and the brilliance of my mind as of my happening to have stumbled into the right industry at the right time.'" He had made his fortune in synthetics. "'Factories all over the world spew out sheets and bolts of this stuff that more and more people are finding uses for. And it is useful, no matter how nature may abhor it.

"'Nonetheless,'" continued Uncle Freddy in Augusta's voice, "the game, for that's what business is, has long since ceased to intrigue me. While initially of some interest, synthetics, chemicals, having revealed their ersatz secrets, eventually become a bore, except perhaps to chemists. This is probably true of all business. As for the money, Emerson wrote that it 'represents the prose of life, hardly spoken of in parlors without apology, but which is, in its effects, as beautiful as roses.' Money has often seemed sweet to me, opening doors that would otherwise remain closed, but its excessiveness has been incidental and sometimes burdensome. Having more money than you need isn't an unmixed blessing, as you'll no doubt discover, but I hope you'll be on your guard. I know that the strong spine of your character will protect you.'"

She looked up, puzzled. "What could he have known of my character?" she mumbled.

"You have a lovely reading voice," Oswald said. "Do go on."

"'In a few days I set off on a much more ambitious journey than any I've ever had the time or inclination to undertake, a journey, I hope, of discovery --- self-discovery. I'll be circling the globe, a distance of some 33,000 miles, but I intend to detour as the fancy strikes. Perhaps I'll climb

15

Mt. Everest, or become a Hindu and go naked in the dusty countryside with a begging bowl, maybe find some island where it's still possible to comb a beach, or become a Jainite and never swat another mosquito or sit carelessly on a living rock. My options are unlimited; for the first time in my life I feel deliriously free. Still, I can't help having premonitions, probably because of the guilt that accompanies this unfamiliar delight, but premonitions, nonetheless, that impel me to make provisions. I've left each of my ex-wives enough money to insure their inability to contest my will, except in one case where there will always be need (to her I've left enough to keep her comfortable and free of worry). Since I'm descended of people notoriously parsimonious in the propagation department, my nearest living relative is a maiden aunt once removed who, at age 87, happily and prosperously runs a Taco Villa franchise somewhere on the outskirts of Eugene, Oregon. She would want nothing of me.

"'And so, my dear, we arrive at the point of this letter: why you.

"'When you were a child, Augusta, I fantasized that you were my child. When you were almost grown and I saw more clearly the shape of your becoming, my foolish fantasy was that I was a younger man and that in a few years you would fall in love with me and become my wife. For one reason or another, all my marriages were wrong. My own stupidity, as well as circumstances beyond my control. But you, Augusta, unformed though you were, seemed utterly right to me. Maybe I made you up. Maybe I needed to make you up. Still, you had, and I've no doubt even more abundantly have, strength and intelligence, beauty and wit . . .'

"Oh, embarrassing," Augusta said, looking up. Oswald smiled at her sweetly and urged her to go on.

"'... beauty and wit, grace and loveliness, and, above all, the capacity for happiness." She stifled a sob. "I've seen

16

delight and joy and wonder on your charming face and I can think of no one more likely to put this money to its best possible use: to give you the ability to make choices, to give you the life you deserve, the life I want you to have. I've every faith that you'll not only survive this inheritance but will take the utmost pleasure in it.

"'I've written and hope to go on writing other letters to you that I expect will turn up from time to time in other places.

"'Your loving and, in death as in life, always devoted Uncle Fred.'"

She sat with her eyes cast down. "Ohhh. Poor man," she said, tears again threatening. "I had no idea he was so romantic. How lonely he must have been."

"Never! He was never lonely. He was surrounded by adoring women, admiring men, respectful and faithful employees."

Still, something must have been missing. How she regretted that she'd never given him the attention she now saw that he had deserved. She sighed.

"Ah, tears and sighs," Oswald said. "I'm sorry the news I've brought you hasn't made you happier. It would certainly delight almost anyone else on earth."

"Don't apologize. It hasn't made me unhappy. Perhaps in a little while it will make me happy."

He glanced at his watch, then leaped to his feet. He was taller than he had appeared, slumped behind that desk, and twice as thin.

"Can I get you something to drink?" he asked.

"No, thank you."

"Coffee? Tea? Sherry? A martini?"

"Nothing, thanks."

He sat down again and shuffled through the papers on his desk. "There are a few other things. Yes. As I've said, until now the proceeds from the estate have been reinvested,

17

but I've taken the liberty of opening a bank account in your name with the first month's income."

"Income?"

"Yes, of course. The sixty or so millions are capital, principal. It has to be somewhere, you see. Even if it sat in a bank it would be earning interest, at least a million a year. But most of it isn't sitting in a bank. It's invested and it's earning much more than that."

"You mean that even if I never spend any of the money, I'd have to spend, say, three million a year in order to keep that sixty million from increasing?"

He beamed at her. "How quick you are," he said.

She groaned. A lot of money was like a cancer.

"This is the firm that manages your portfolio," he said, handing her a card. "They're an old reliable house. Nickleby's instructions to them were to continue to invest your capital safely and conservatively. Henceforth, however, you're to receive the income monthly. Though it's probably more income than you can use, you're free to invade the capital without any limitations. Except one. There is one restriction in the will."

"And that?"

"It states that under no circumstances are you to give any of this inheritance to your father."

"My father? Marco?" She was astounded. "But he was Uncle Freddy's friend. Why would Uncle Freddy do that?"

"I don't know. There's no provision, though, for any action to be taken should you disobey this injunction, so I guess it's enforceable only by your sense of honor. Here's the bankbook," he said, passing it to her. "And the signature cards for the bank. There'll be other papers for you to sign. I'll have them ready for you in a few days."

Without looking at it, she slid the bankbook into her purse, then signed the signature cards and handed them back.

"I'll send one of the secretaries down with these this afternoon. You can start using the account tomorrow."

Tomorrow. Good God. In the morning, when she awoke, she would be a . . . millionaire. Millionairess? Millionaire.

"I think for now that's about it, except for me. I mean, we're going to have this continuing professional relationship, but I hope, well, you know, that you'll find other uses for me in your life. I mean, I hope we can be friends, as well."

"Of course we can be friends, Oswald," she said.

"I've neglected to ask if you're married, Miss March. Augusta."

"Is there a contingency in the will about marriage?"

"No, no. That was a personal question, not a professional one."

"I'm engaged," she said. "Sort of."

"Sort of?" he asked.

"We're not thinking about marriage right now. I'm not nearly ready,"

She stood to leave, and he rose, too. She reached to shake his hand, thanked him, and turned to go.

"Oh, the keys, Augusta."

"Keys?"

He was holding them out to her. "To the house. On Sixty-eighth Street. The address is on the key chain. He sold all the others before he sailed off. He sold the cars, too."

"There's a house? Mine? Has it been sitting there empty all these years?"

"No, there's Mrs. Corcoran, the housekeeper. She's been getting, I think it's five hundred dollars a week to live there and take care of it."

"Five hundred dollars a week!" she cried, thinking of her own salary. She was only an adjunct. "To mind an empty house? Isn't that a little excessive?"

19

He smiled. "I'm glad to see that you're already making the adjustment," he said.

She took the keys from him and departed.

CHAPTER TWO

On Eighty-second Street between Central Park West and Columbus, three flights up (no elevator), Augusta, groping in her purse for her keys, her fingers stumbling over the other, newer keys, paused in front of the door to the apartment she shared with Camilla Strong, her closest friend. The aroma of a roasting chicken, garlicked and herbed, drifted under the door. It was Camilla's night to cook. Camilla was a terrific cook.

After leaving Oswald Summerville's office, Augusta had walked up Fifth Avenue to Sixty-eighth and stood on the sidewalk contemplating the house that had just become hers. For a long time she stared at it, trying to convince herself that it was her house, that if she chose it might even be her home. It was impressive, large, limestone-solid and beautiful. It could easily have housed an embassy for any respectable mid-sized country.

She made no attempt to go inside. Instead, she walked home through the park, trying to clear her head. She was not a mystic, although she was far too respectful of the not-yet-known to shut her mind entirely, and she now found herself thinking of Fate and wondering if, had she consulted a psychic, an astrologer, a tea-leaf reader, or the I Ching, some hint of what had happened to her today might have been foretold. She had never considered herself in any way set apart from others, although when she was twelve a gypsy fortune-teller at a fair had told her that she would have an interesting and romantic life. For a few months she waited for it to begin but when nothing happened she had put it out of her mind.

She let herself into the apartment. It was April and the windows were open wide to the soft air and the late afternoon sun slanting through the ailanthus tree whose topmost branches were beginning to show a green fuzz. If you reached out the window, you could touch a branch of the tree and imagine that you felt the throbbing of the sap in the nerve endings of your fingers. It was a pleasant two-bedroom apartment, though small and unavoidably cluttered, but she and Camilla had done what they could to make it bright and cheerful with lots of cushions and throw pillows in exotic prints.

"Hi! Have I got news for you!" Camilla called, popping her head out of the kitchen doorway.

"You have news for me?"

"Listen to this! In the entire biological kingdom, guess among what the most intimate form of cohabitation takes place. You'll never believe it." Camilla had recently stumbled on a new passion, the sexual life of everything up to but not including homo sapiens.

"Octogenarians?" Augusta guessed.

"It's a worm!" Camilla said triumphantly. "No one-night stands for them, no ships that pass in the night. These worms mean business. They're inseparable for life."

"Good"

"They're trematodes. Called . . . oh something long and Latin, Schisto something. He's built with a hollowed-out side which she fits into. She literally spends her life in his embrace."

"You're anthropomorphizing again. I'm sure there's some disgusting reason. Where does this go on, in mud?"

"In human blood vessels. They're parasites."

"There you are! Sexy parasites! Now sit down, Camilla, because I have something to tell you."

Camilla came all the way into the room, wiping her hands on a dishtowel. She knew that Augusta had gone to

22

see a lawyer. "It's that bastard Kingston, isn't it?" Kingston was their landlord. He could get twice the rent they paid if he could dislodge them. They had endured every kind of inconvenience. "We're going to have to move, aren't we?"

"It wasn't Kingston," Augusta said, flopping onto a corner of the sofa. Her purse slid off her arm onto the floor, where it clanked to rest.

"Why is your purse clanking?" Camilla asked.

"Because it's filled with heavy metal keys," Augusta said, frowning. "Let me begin at the beginning." But Augusta did not begin. She sat staring out the window, sighing. Fearfully, Camilla sat and waited, though sitting and waiting weren't easy for her. Dark and pretty, smaller than Augusta, she had unlimited energy, manifested not in perpetual nervous activity but in a contained intensity that occasionally erupted into spasms of enthusiasm, indignation, impatience, or wild humor. Of the two, she was the more practical, less romantic than Augusta, who was apt to disappear into dreamy silences, as she was doing now.

"It's, believe it or not, money," Augusta said, finally, her voice no more than a whisper. "Someone left me money."

"Oh, is that all!'" Camilla said, relieved. "Who died?"

"Nobody died. That is, a friend of Marco's, a long time ago. Someone I hardly knew."

"So much the better."

Augusta fished the letter out of her bag and gave it to Camilla. "Read it," she said, and while Camilla did, Augusta leaned back and discovered that she was trembling, beginning to feel the enormity of what had happened. Alfred Nickleby. Uncle Freddy. What could he possibly have known about her to imagine that her character was strongspined? Was it? How could he have been so enamored of her and she never the least bit aware of it, young though she was? Who had Uncle Freddy really been?

She was going to have to call Marco soon and tell him the news. No, she must give it to him in person.

Finished reading the letter, Camilla looked up, her face radiant. "God, Augusta," she breathed. "It's like a romance novel. What will you do with it?"

"I don't know." Money! It was something Marco was forever thinking about and desperately scrambling after, not out of mere bread-and-butter need (that part was easy), but out of some far more profound necessity. Whereas Ben, the man, as she had told Summerville she was "sort of engaged" to, seemed completely bewildered by money. When the time came to pay for something, he would reach into a trouser pocket and draw out a handful of crumpled bills, surprised to find them there, and pick through them, frowning. She herself hardly thought about money. She put her salary check in the bank and when bills came she wrote out checks and sent them off, and she always had a vaguely accurate idea of how much was left. Perfectly normal. She had never seen anything complicated about money, nothing that deserved Marco's extreme dedication to it, or Ben's utter indifference to it, or Uncle Freddy's extravagant possession of it. Never, until now.

"By itself, money doesn't really mean anything," she said to reassure herself. "It's only paper and promises, symbols."

"For God's sake, Augusta, it means plenty!" Camilla howled, "It's negotiable!"

"Yes, it's a means. To what end depends, I suppose, entirely on who's got it. I can do anything I like, can't I? It's a question of finding out, now, what I like. What would you do with it, Camilla?"

"Me?" She looked flustered.

"You'd buy shoes."

"Oh, eventually, shoes," Camilla conceded. She loved shoes. She had quite a collection of them. "But I resent the implication that I'm such an airhead, that given a passport to anywhere the first thing I'd think of was shoes."

"I'm sorry, Camilla. I haven't even got a first thing I'd think of. If at least I had shoes!"

"I think the first thing would be to give money to one of the anti-nuclear organizations."

"Of course! Why not to all of them? Say a thousand a year to each, the scientists, the physicians against, Sane, there must be at least thirty or forty organizations opposed to nuclear weapons."

"The environmental organizations," Camilla said, warming up. "Sierra, Greenpeace, Wildlife..."

"Oceans, lakes, acid rain, climate."

"The arts. What about them?"

"Naturally. The 92nd Street Y. The New York Public Library, artist colonies, the opera, the Philharm..."

"Disasters. Famine. Earthquakes. Floods. Leaks." Each worthy cause lifted their spirits higher.

"Leaks?"

"Civil liberties. Political action. The League of Women Voters. NOW. ERA." The money wasn't going to be a burden at all; she could easily get rid of it. There might not be enough of it!

"We mustn't neglect diseases," Camilla said.

"Of course. Aids, Alzheimer's, heart, cancer..."

"Multiple sclerosis, muscular dystrophy, cystic fibrosis ..."

"Oh, lovely, there are so many diseases. Let's make a list."

"Not now, Augusta. You'll have to hire people to write out all those checks."

"Of course I'll hire people," she said cheerfully. "Gun control. Mothers Against Drunken Driving. What about fathers? What are they against?"

25

"We haven't even mentioned native Americans, the NAACP, civil rights, saving the children." A thousand times a thousand, she reckoned, was . . . her heart sank . . . merely a million. Hardly a dent. She was never going to be able to make ends meet. She would have to give them all more.

"What about you, Gus? Aren't you going to spend anything on yourself?"

"We were talking about you," Augusta said. "We never got past your shoes. What else?"

"Well, clothes to go with the shoes." It wasn't as though Camilla had two sensible skirts and four blouses to mix and match. Although, like Augusta, she worked for a living (she was a dental technician, but she was also a sculptor and might yet be a biological sexologist), she had impeccable taste and was unfailingly chic. "Then I'd buy a Ford Fairlane."

"You're so eccentric, Camilla. I don't think they make them any more. Why not a Honda?"

"I'd quit my lousy job. God, I'm sick of teeth. I'd take piano lessons. I'd get a huge studio and poke around Vermont and Italy for slabs of marble. Maybe I'd get a place in Vermont and grow herbs and vegetables and keep chickens and pigs."

Augusta laughed. "I can see you in Vermont with your two dozen pairs of shoes, knee deep in mud and pig slops. You're not the back-to-nature type, Camilla."

"I am, though, I think. I'd spend long hard winters there, surviving. And observing the sexual practices of whatever happens along, though vertebrates aren't all that interesting. My own lovers would be aging hippies with beards and sweaty headbands who help out with the chickens."

"You're in a whole other era, Camilla."

"I'd bake strawberry rhubarb pies."

26

"I'm going to make this money over to you, Camilla. Your plans for it go way beyond mine."

"It's a very hard question, Augusta, what you'd do if you had lots of money. Nobody but Marco could give you a quick answer. By the way, just how much money are we talking about?"

I thought you'd never ask." She felt her face grow hot. Shame? Embarrassment? Well, it wasn't her doing. "After expenses --- taxes, lawyers, accountants,--- something like sixty million."

"Sixty million what, Gus?"

"Dollars, of course. What did you think?"

"You don't have to snap at me. It's not my fault."

"I'm sorry."

"Sixty million dollars, Good God," Camilla said. "I didn't know anyone but a government could have that kind of money. You could buy a country, Gus."

"Do you have one in mind?"

"Biafra. Ruanda. Some poor oppressed one. You could run it properly, fatten everyone up, stop them killing each other.. You could probably get one cheap." "You could bring your rhubarb pies."

They looked at each other and began to laugh because it was all so strange and serious and scary, Soon, they were laughing uncontrollably.

"My chicken!" Camilla remembered. Tears streamed down her cheeks. She leaped to her feet. "Do you think you can eat?"

"Of course I can eat. There's nothing wrong with my appetite. The first thing we'll do is move. Part of the inheritance is a house on Sixty-Eighth Street, near Fifth. I think it might be nice to live in it."

"A house? We?"

"We'll go see it tomorrow. Of course, we. You can quit that lousy job. I'm going to need you."

27

"I'm not going to quit teeth to write checks to charities. Anyhow, I couldn't work for you, Gus. I'd hate it."

"I don't want you to write checks. And you won't be working for me. I need you with me."

Augusta and Camilla had met when they were six at the 63rd Street playground in Central Park. Unlike most of their peers, they were accompanied not by mothers (Camilla's worked, Augusta's was dead), but by nursemaids who, upon discovering that they were both Hungarian, became fast bench pals, thereby bringing their young charges together. When Camilla, whose father was dead, learned that a father was all Augusta had, she proposed, in her practical way, that they become sisters so that their parents would marry.

"That way we'd only need one nursemaid," Camilla said. "Two of them is so wasteful." While Augusta considered, Camilla expanded. "And one apartment. And one set of everything except sheets and towels." She was sure that when their parents were advised of this plan they would find it irresistible.

"I'd have to meet your mother first," Augusta said. "She might not be right for me."

Camilla was hurt. "What difference would that make? Who says she's right for me?"

They spent many afternoons in many weathers discussing the good and bad points of their respective parents, determining which of the nursemaids to keep (not an easy choice; they would have liked to dispense with both), and which of their apartments would best contain the four of them. It was a game that caused them to examine and question the circumstances of their lives minutely, an enlightening pastime for both. They plotted and giggled and planned and disagreed and fought and nodded their heads sagely and compromised and whispered and giggled some more and counted the pillowcases when they got home at night. Talking was more fun than the swings and jungle

28

gym. They understood and appreciated each other perfectly, forging bonds of friendship strong enough to last forever.

As far as they could arrange it, they were inseparable, so it was inevitable that Marco and Camilla's mother would meet. There was a brief, polite flirtation, but it was Camilla who fell in love with Marco. She was relieved when nothing developed between Marco and her mother. She wanted him for herself, although she would share him as graciously as she could with Augusta. Camilla had fallen out of love with Marco by the time she reached her full height, but she and Augusta remained closer than sisters.

It had been Camilla's suggestion that they share an apartment. Augusta had completed graduate school and Camilla had just begun to work at the Blavitksy Laboratory for Dental Enhancement. They hadn't much money so, again, practical considerations were paramount. Augusta had no intention of leaving Marco's apartment to move into Ben's, and Camilla had just terminated a painful love affair (all her love affairs were painful; with the help of group therapy, she was hoping to find out why). What more natural than that they live together since they were together so much anyway. In their three years in the apartment there had been no friction between them, no need even to discuss any of the arrangements of their cohabitation. Now, perhaps, all that would change.

Remembering the bankbook, Augusta extracted it from her purse and allowed herself to look inside it. She groaned. The sum on deposit, merely part of the initial monthly deposit, was far more than she'd ever hoped to accumulate in her whole life. She must arrange things so that it would be impossible for Camilla ever to feel employed by her. They would go tomorrow afternoon to see the house together. She told Camilla about Mrs. Corcoran.

"$500 a week! We'll have to let her go, of course. She's probably drunk up all the wine."

29

"What are you talking about, Augusta? What wine?"

"There must be a wine cellar."

"Anyhow, what's $500 a week to you now?"

Augusta shook her head, trying to clear it. "Oh, God, you're right," she moaned. "Let's eat."

When Augusta returned from washing up, the chicken was on the table lying on its platter as chickens do, with its feet up, like a ready whore. There was salad and a chilled white wine. Augusta felt a surge of pleasure. Maybe they wouldn't move into the house. They were perfectly comfortable here, except for the paucity of closet space, though it would be nice to have two bathrooms and no landlord and a room just for her equipment. Speakers and wires were draped all over the living room walls so that there was hardly any room for pictures. She could soundproof a room in the house and turn everything up as loud as she pleased. She had a plan for an elaborate synthesizer; she'd hire an engineer and have it built and installed. It was nearly the end of term. She could take a year off and spend all her time composing, what luxury!

But first.

She had a nagging feeling that something else must come first.

"Have you told Ben yet?" Camilla asked, midway through their meal. "I wonder how he'll take this. He's so peculiar about money."

Augusta sighed. "It will disgust him to hear how much of it I have."

"He won't give it a second thought. If he does, he'll be amused. "

Ben taught art history at Columbia College. They had been dating since her senior year in high school, although she was still only fifteen. He took her to look at pictures and helped her to really see them, and she took him to obscure lofts and halls to listen to the new music and watched him

30

out of the corner of her eye, struggling not to hate it. Most of their time was spent side by side, little of it vis-à-vis or tête-a-tête. Each was part of the other's education, but in her last year of college, in an offhand way, Ben had begun proposing marriage. While she believed she loved him, she was far from ready. He and Marco, though entirely different, were alike in some way that made her feel, toward them, tender and protective and angry.

"When we've moved into the house," Augusta said, "I think the next thing may be to bury Uncle Freddy properly."

"What do you mean? Is there a body?"

"Not literally, Camilla. I think I owe it to him ... to myself ... to find out more about him. Who he really was, what he was really like." She had, naturally, been thinking about him on her walk home. "I want to piece together his life, find out about his wives, find out where he went in those last months, what he was looking for, how he died."

"How will you do that?"

"I don't know. We'll figure it out. Step by step. We'll travel. Maybe in his... my... our yacht. We'll follow his trail."

"We have a yacht?" Camilla asked, already at the point where nothing surprised her. "Did he leave a trail?"

"He must have. Everyone leaves a trail." Augusta's face, which had been closed in thought, now cleared. "I'll take equipment along. I'll collect sounds. You can find rocks, Camilla, and marble, and ship it all home. Chunks of exotic trees. Fig. Baobab." Her face reflected her excitement.

"You know I don't work in wood," Camilla said.

"Damn. I'm going to have to tell Marco," Augusta said, the brightness fading from her face. They ate in silence for a while. "Oh, God, thinking about money is exhausting."

31

CHAPTER THREE

"What do you mean, left it to you?" Marco sputtered, his handsome graying moustache quivering. He was a man of high color, but the hue of his face had turned dangerously higher. "Why should he have left it to you? You were little more than a child."

"Precisely my own reaction," Augusta said soothingly, she hoped. "Why are you so angry?" He was a man who rarely lost his temper, certainly never with Augusta. He prided himself on his civilized behavior.

"Because obviously there was something between you. What did he do to you? How many times did he do it? If he were alive I'd tear him to shreds!"

"Are you asking if Uncle Freddy molested me?"

"That's precisely what I'm asking, and I expect the truth."

Her laughter trilled across the dining room. "Marco, he was your friend." She put down her fork. The peach tart was inedible; canned peach embedded in library paste in a fluted cardboard crust. It had been baked by a bookbinder. "You should know better than I that he was always a perfect gentleman."

"True, I did know him better than you. What a devious son-of-a-bitch he must have been to have had me so bamboozled."

"He didn't have you bamboozled, Marco. There was nothing like that."

"I knew he was mad about you. But I never suspected."

"There was nothing to suspect. Was he mad about me?"

"Why shouldn't he have been? You were adorable and special. And he didn't have children of his own."

32

"I never noticed that he was mad about me."

"Your unselfconsciousness, Augusta, was always one of your more endearing traits. You were never one of those show-offy brats. You always seemed to know who you were."

"I did? Even without a mother? A role model?"

"But I should have been more careful. I blame myself. After all, Fred was a womanizer."

"What a quaint word, Marco, but I don't think so." Marco had a tendency to dramatize. His observations were often more interesting than the truth. His unreliability was part of his charm.

"Anyone who's had five wives and no children in twenty years is ipso facto a womanizer," Marco said firmly. "He could hardly be described as a family man."

"He wouldn't have married all those women if he were what you call a womanizer," Augusta said. "He was probably romantic and idealistic but with unfortunate taste in women." It was more likely that Marco was the womanizer, else why hadn't he remarried in all the years since her mother's death? Marco claimed it was because no one could replace her mother, a paragon, but he was much too happy in his unsettled life for that to be more than a fraction of the truth. She saw now that his color was returning to normal She dreaded what was coming, having to tell him the other part of her news.

"Then you swear it? It's true? There was never anything irregular between you?"

"Of course I swear it," she said. "He was never anything but the proper uncle."

The danger past, Marco's face brightened. He now had the leisure to realize that his dearly beloved daughter, his only child, was probably one of the wealthiest women in the world. How wonderful for her, what a miracle. All sorts of

33

things would now be within his grasp. He might never again be compelled to use his wits. Good old Freddy.

"Well, then, that's all right, isn't it? He beamed at her, reaching across the table to pat her hand. "Good girl," he said.

"What the hell do you mean, good girl?" she said, angrily. "It's not as if I'd done anything. "

Marco scarcely heard her. His mind had leaped ahead. "There's no reason now," he murmured, "that I can't make that deal with Julius."

"You mean Corned Beef & Cabbage?" she asked, alarmed. The moment was at hand. "Marco, you're too old to start running a dance club." It was his fondest dream. He had talked about little else for months.

"Too old?" he said, stung. "What's age got to do with it?"

"You only want it because you're so gregarious. Why don't you just give parties?"

"It's a fantastic business," he said. "It mints money."

"It was a fantastic business," she reminded him. "It's no longer the in club. You've told me yourself that Marilyn is now the in place."

"I can bring it back," he said. "I could do it in a month."

"Marco," she said, "I haven't told you everything."

"What do you mean?"

"The will. I'm not allowed to give you any money. The will forbids it."

Stabbed, Marco fell back in his chair, clutching the heart side of his chest.

"The will says that? Naming me?"

"Yes, I'm sorry, Marco."

"I feel as if I've been stabbed."

"I wish it were otherwise."

34

"It's not your fault," he said, deep in thought. "I suppose there's nothing to prevent you from buying it and then letting me run it? It could be in your name?"

"Who would we be fooling, Marco?"

"What a cruel thing for Nickleby to have done. I can't think why it should have occurred to him to do such a vicious, cruel, painful thing to me, a loyal old friend. My God! And how I've wasted my time missing him!"

He looked so forlorn that Augusta's heart turned with pity. Unreliable he may have been in many ways, but he had always indulged her. She had never doubted his love and pride in her.

"I can imagine how you must feel," Augusta said. "But considering Uncle Freddy's enormous generosity, I don't see how I can fail to respect the one restriction he's placed on me. It must have been important to him. It must mean something I can't even guess at."

"My God, such a waste," Marco mourned. "My best friend. My only child." Tears came to his eyes. "All. That. Money."

CHAPTER FOUR

The house on Sixty-Eighth Street had four broad stone steps leading up to its vaulted portico. It resembled a small cathedral, designed to contain the cathedra, the seat of authority, but the familiar figure on the topmost step sprawled in tweedy dejection.

"Ben!" Augusta said, charging up the walk. "What are you doing here?" At the sight of her he straightened up and grinned.

"I called this morning and got Camilla. She told me you were meeting her here." He looked at his watch. "You're both late. Watch out for that pile of dogshit."

She stepped nimbly over it and climbed the steps to sit beside him, not entirely pleased that he was there. Simultaneously impelled by habit, they leaned to kiss each other. She was always surprised at the tug of feeling his presence evoked, a contradictory mix of the sexual and maternal. He was a large man, her own age almost exactly, with big hands and feet, but until the day he died she knew she would see in him the boy he had been. His nose was splashed with freckles and his straw-colored hair, rebelling against all efforts to tame it, sprang up in random thickets in back and flopped across his brow. Recently, he had tried letting it grow in the vain hope that a unisex stylist could find some modish solution to its waywardness. Now, weeks later, it was its usual shaggy mess. Although occasionally given to bouts of gloom and pessimism, at this moment, he was twitching with excitement and impatience.

"What is it you can't wait to tell me?" Augusta asked.

"I'm an open book to you, aren't I, darling?" he said happily. "Such a clever reader you are. It's one of the infinite number of things I adore about you." Not that he had ever actually ticked off the things he loved about her. From the moment she had crystallized for him, he had never questioned his love for her any more than he would have questioned his love for Vuillard or Monet or Matisse. She was serenely symmetrical, her colors good, her voice in no way jarring. She fit into any background. She made him see things as though they were not framed, separate and discrete.

"Well?" she asked, spying Camilla rounding the corner.

"I've been offered the Parker Festerson Chair in Art History at Santa Cruz," he said.

"Oh, Ben!"

"It means full professorship, tenure, and, at last, a respectable salary."

"That's wonderful, Ben. It's a tremendous honor at your age."

"Or any age," he said, ducking his head modestly. She squeezed his hand.

"I'm so happy for you."

"For me? For us." His face turned serious. "There's no reason now, Augusta, not to get married. You know I wouldn't dream of going there without you."

She frowned. "Here's Camilla," she said. They both rose to greet Camilla, who was standing at the foot of the steps, looking past them at the house.

"If possible, it's even grander than I imagined," she said.

Ben turned, noticing the house for the first time. "This house? Why were you imagining it?" he asked. "What are we doing here? Do you have a doctor's appointment?" The thought alarmed him. "What's wrong, Gus?" Then, with a new thought, his face brightened. "Gus, are you preg..."

"No, no," she said, pressing the doorbell. "Nothing's wrong."

Heavy though the door was, they could hear the chimes Augusta had set off reverberating through what sounded like

37

an empty house. Although she had the keys, she would not have dreamed of using them this first time. Mrs. Corcoran. She would be tall, gaunt, darkly mysterious, forbidding, a woman who had spent solitary years guarding this empty cathedral, Gloomy, perhaps mad. She would resent Augusta's intrusion. Worse, she would hate her; she would brood in the shadows, plotting. Augusta felt a moment of fear, then reminded herself that she was extremely wealthy and also that there was no reason to keep this Mrs. Corcoran.

They heard the solid sound of locks being sprung and then, as though unaccustomed to such exertions, the broad door groaned open. A tall black woman filled the doorway, beaming at them. Although she wore a purple silk dress of excellent cut instead of gingham, and no handkerchief bound her splendid halo of hair, and she was more amazonian than rotund, there was something ineffable about her that made Augusta feel that she might have stepped off a box of pancake mix. Perhaps it was the rush of warmth she projected.

"Come right on in," she said in a rich contralto, stepping back to let them through. "One of you must be Ms. March?"

"I am," Augusta admitted, extending her hand, which the woman clasped, "and these are my friends Camilla Strong and Ben Stillman."

"I surely am glad to meet you, honey. Mr. Nickleby's lawyer called to say you'd be coming round soon."

"You're Mrs. Corcoran?" Augusta asked.

"Yes indeedy. But you just call me Aurora, hear? Now I expect you want to look the place over instead of standing in the vestibule, so come on in and help yourself while I go fix the tea."

"Look it over?" Ben said. "Why?"

"Feel right at home," Aurora said, smiling. "Which is where you are, and a good thing for this poor old place. If you want me for anything, just pull that wall thing, there's

38

one in every room, and I'll come find you. Why don't you start in here with the living room." She opened a wide double door off the foyer. "The next to last Mrs. Nickleby, or maybe it was the two from last, she called it the drawing room, beats me why."

Discreetly, she withdrew, leaving them in a small puddle of silence.

"Ooooh!" Camilla at last said.

"It's beautiful."

"Not at all what I expected."

"Why were you expecting?" Ben's back was to them; he was facing a wall. "These paintings are real!"

"Of course they're real."

"My God, this is a Cezanne! The genuine thing. And here's a Seurat. And over here ... I'm not sure ... the trompe l'oeil. Harnet? No, my God, it's Peto. These people knew what they were doing."

"Of course they did."

"It's elegant."

"Yet somehow so contemporary."

"Without being austere."

"Comfortable."

"Warm."

"Picasso, this plate. Not one, but two."

"Naturally, two."

"With such a feeling of space and light."

"I wish someone would throw a little light my way."

"Oh Ben." Augusta put a hand on his arm.

"Well? Enlighten me."

"This is my house, Ben. A family friend, a man named Alfred Nickleby, who died some years ago, left it to me. The estate was just cleared, or whatever it is that estates are."

"Probated."

"I just learned of it yesterday."

39

"Yours!" Ben said, looking stunned. "But places like this cost a lot to run. Taxes and insurance, things like that. Though I suppose if you sold the Cezanne."

"He left me money, too."

"A lot of money," Camilla purred.

"But surely you're not thinking ..."

"Right. I'm not thinking. Why don't we look at it?"

Her voice trembled with her rising excitement. It was as if she had been given a marvelous new toy, one of those enchanting presents Uncle Freddy used to bring her, only this one was bottomless, endless, this huge box filled with boxes filled with treasures. It exactly matched a dream she had had several times, one from which she always awoke feeling happy, although she knew the dream wasn't really about things but about her life, her body, her mind.

"It's hard to believe no one has lived here in all these years," Augusta said.

"It's immaculate."

"Yet not unlived-in."

"Full of character and charm."

"Do you suppose the fireplaces work?"

"Of course they work."

"The study."

"The library. All those books!"

"Is this the master bedroom, do you think?" They had mounted a wide, curving staircase to the second floor.

"Hard to say. They're all master bedrooms."

"So many bathrooms. I've lost count."

"Seven, so far."

"With bidets."

"I've always wanted a bidet, haven't you?"

"I've never really thought about it."

"These fixtures aren't chrome."

"They look like silver."

"They are silver."

40

"Not sterling, surely?"

"I love it. Don't you love it, Augusta?"

"Of course I love it. How could we not love it?"

"Not me. I don't love it."

"Oh, Ben."

Mrs. Corcoran appeared as they were about to mount the stairs to the top floor.

"Tea's ready," she said. "I've laid it in the garden sitting room."

"Oh, thanks, Aurora. We'll just have a quick look at the top floor first."

"That's the servant's quarters. Nothing to see up there except some small bedrooms and the help's sitting room."

"I'd like to see it, if it's not an intrusion. I want to see it all."

"Course you do, honey." Aurora said, reluctantly leading them on. "It's a bit of a mess. Tell the truth, this big old house empty all these years, I let my nephew Marshall stay here time to time. He's in NYU. Says it's too noisy to study up to home, all those babies his mama keeps having. Seem like every year she have a new one, nine last I counted. Marshall's the oldest."

"Oh, well, then, we'd better not go up," Augusta said, halting. "We don't want to disturb him."

Obviously relieved, Aurora wheeled and began to descend. "He's probably still sleeping," she said. "Up all night, sleep all day, these young ones. Some kind of animal instinct, I reckon."

"I'm not asleep," a voice called from the top of the stairs. A tall and very handsome young black man stood there, tucking an old army shirt into even older khaki pants. "Come right on up, Aurora, and bring your friends."

They turned again and climbed to the hallway at the top of the stairs, shaking hands with Marshall and introducing themselves.

41

"This the lady whose house it is," Mrs. Corcoran explained. "Miss March."

"Well, thanks for the use of it, Miss March," Marshall said. "It's been a great convenience. Hope you don't mind."

"How could I mind? It wasn't even my house until yesterday," Augusta said, glancing through the doorway into the room Marshall had been using. It was small, and contrary to Mrs. Corcoran's warning, tidy. The walls were hung with old posters of Che, Angela, and Huey, and she thought how quaint to be back in that time, how sentimental this Marshall must be. At that moment, a door across the hall opened to reveal a pretty young woman with a magnificent afro haloing her head.

"This is my neice's girl, Star Rising," Aurora said, looking surprised. "I didn't know you were here, Star honey."

"Malden's here, too," the girl said. "We got in late. I'm glad we didn't wake you. Oh, and Caleb's in the end room."

"Why don't we have that tea now?" Augusta said.

Tripping down the stairs behind Augusta, Camilla whispered, "For an empty house, it's a beehive of what looks like an army of subversives."

"I didn't notice any books in Marshall's room, did you?" Augusta whispered back.

"No, but I think I saw a rifle under the bed."

"Camilla! It was probably a boot."

"I don't think boots can be mistaken for rifles. Or vice versa."

"I hope they're not making bombs in the basement."

The tea spread before them was splendid, especially since Aurora could have had only the shortest notice of their coming. There were little sandwiches of smoked salmon and cucumber and watercress, and a magnificent raspberry walnut torte. The tea service was delicate translucent English bone china, a lovely floral pattern. Uncle Freddy must have

42

had remarkably good taste, or more likely it was one of those wives. How little Augusta knew about him.

"Thank you, Aurora, it's a beautiful tea," she said.

Beaming, Aurora withdrew, leaving them to it.

"This was probably meant to be breakfast for the top floor cadre," Ben said, helping himself to a plateful of sandwiches. "Okay, Augusta, fill me in. Why has someone left you this house with all these priceless paintings and a regiment of guerillas?"

Already tired of telling it, she told him in as few words as possible. "As for Marshall and Star Rising and the others, I don't know any more than you do. I'm sure it's all very innocent. It's a big house, after all, and virtually empty all these years."

"And such a convenient location," Camilla added.

"The FBI probably has the place staked out," Ben muttered. "I hope you're not planning to move into it."

"Of course I am," Augusta said. "Camilla too."

"Have you tasted the raspberry torte?" Camilla said. "It's extraordinary."

"Then you're not coming with me." Ben said, sagging. "You can hardly live on two coasts at the same time. Damn it, Augusta, how long am I supposed to wait for you?"

"I know," she moaned, but she was thinking of Uncle Freddy again. Everything that had been his had become hers; how odd; how like a marriage. "But you do see, Ben, that it's out of the question right now, don't you, Ben?"

"Why doesn't Ben move in, too?" Camilla said. "There's loads of room."

"It's nice of you to offer," Ben said glumly.

43

CHAPTER FIVE

"I've never actually seen a man wearing those," Lynda said. "They're really bizarre!"

Marco finished attaching them to his black silk hose. The garters, black, red, and gold, girdled his legs at mid-calf. He'd had them forever. When this pair went, it might be impossible to find another. They were an anachronism; the socks were elasticized and stayed up perfectly well on their own. Still, the garters were insurance and they accentuated the strength and shapeliness of his legs.

"I've never seen a woman wearing garters, either, come to think of it," Lynda said. She giggled. "Except in movies with can-can dancers. When you were young, were they still considered sexy?"

When he was young! He looked across the room at Lynda sitting on the bed in her perfect skin and smiled what he hoped was a patient smile.

"Yes, they were considered sexy," he said, crossing the room in his socks, garters, underwear. He sat beside her. "Because they were worn here, on the lovely upper thigh." The palm of his hand curved around the inside of one of her lovely upper thighs. "Provocatively near, well en route yet not quite there." He slid off the bed and knelt on the floor, burrowing his head between her legs. He kissed the thigh where his hand had just lain, then slowly slid his mouth inward until it came to rest upon the even lovelier place he had so recently vacated, still moist and plump from the pleasure of his visit. He felt her become even more pleased. Above his head, Lynda sighed, her fingers winding through his hair. She had already had three orgasms this morning and he had meant to kiss her only as illustration, but it was already too late. She had begun to undulate and her hands were over his ears, locking his head in place. They had danced half the night, made love, fallen asleep, awakened, and made love again and again. It was now noon. Surely this was more sex than was necessary. Perhaps she was, as she suggested in the beginning, too young for him.

His mouth, gratified by her responsiveness, continued its work, while his hands busied themselves elsewhere. Her sighs now descended into the moans that so heightened his own excitement. She was a wonderful young machine; all her parts worked so well. He would have to shampoo his moustache again.

When he felt she was nearly ready, he rode his mouth slowly up to hers, pausing to graze along the way, and by the time he entered her she came almost at once, in great grasping throbs, crying out into his mouth. It would have been impossible for him not to respond in kind.

"Oh, Marco," she said, when she got her breath. "You're such a good lover! Even with those garters."

He stroked her arms and kissed her eyes, grateful for her gratitude as well as for her ripe young body. He was going to be late for his lunch with Erwinna. He'd have to take a taxi. He could charge lunch, but you never knew what might turn up in the course of the day, and he had no more than six dollars in his wallet. How disgusting that a man of his stature should have to think about money so much. Damn Freddy Nickleby. They had been good friends. Marco still missed him.

"I've got to run, love," he said, rising from the bed with feigned reluctance.

"I'm sitting here in a puddle of you and me, which is growing cold," she said happily, stretching. "Will I see you tonight?"

Hunched over the bathroom sink, he stifled a groan. He spent at least three afternoons a week at his health club

45

keeping in shape, but since the news of Augusta's inheritance, although there hadn't been time for disappointment, he was awash in it. His energy had begun to flag, and with it his libido. He was pretty sure he wasn't going to feel like dancing by ten o'clock tonight, and even surer that he wasn't going to be able to make love again.

"I've got a business meeting tonight," he said through his foaming mouth. "No telling what time I'll be through."

He was meeting Julius at his office at six o'clock; he must convince Julius to sell him Corned Beef & Cabbage. He'd come close at their last meeting, with Julius almost agreeing to retain a fifty-one percent interest for a year if Marco could put up two hundred and fifty thousand dollars. After the impossible million Julius had been asking, a fourth of that was a bargain, a sum Marco convinced himself he could wheedle out of Erwinna without risk of matrimony. Julius would never be able to get a million for the place; it had been operating in the red ever since everyone had switched to Marilyn. Even Marco had been dancing at Marilyn all month, scouting the competition and keeping close to his friends whom he was confident of wooing back once Corned Beef & Cabbage was his.

He had met Lynda at Marilyn a few weeks earlier. Lost in a swoon induced by the loud pumping beat of the music and whatever she had been drinking and smoking and sniffing, she gyrated into him. When she bumped into him the second time without noticing, Marco, challenged, put his arms around her and his cheek to hers and said, "Let's dance kinky," and swept her across the floor in an old-fashioned ballroom foxtrot. It woke her up, more or less.

"I've seen this kind of dancing," she said, thrilled. "On television. The late show."

She was delightful. He spirited her away from the animal she had come with, a tanned square-jawed ape, his tight pink shirt open to the elaborately clunky belt buckle of

46

his hip-huggers, revealing a wide swathe of fur, damp and matted from his abandoned exertions.

"Your place or mine?" Marco asked over a nightcap and hamburgers at Rusty's. He hoped she would say hers. His place was rent-controlled and no matter how hard he worked to give it that air of subdued money that would reflect his self-image, it smelled rent-controlled. There was nothing he could do about the lobby or the elevator, though he had certainly tried.

"Yours, of course," she said. "When Ricky discovers I'm gone, he'll come straight to my place. God! If he found you there!"

"Ricky! Of course he'd be named Ricky." he said with contempt. "What does Ricky do?"

"Well, you know, this and that. Plus he has a regular job as a space salesman."

"Space? How do they sell it? By the cubic acre?"

"Advertising space!" she said, giggling. Later, she confessed that she had not made love with just one person since she was thirteen. "At a time, I mean. We're always at least three, but four is best."

"Then you'll hardly be missed," Marco said, smiling benignly. He thought of himself as romantic, if not sentimental. He had never been able to divorce sex from the person with whom he was having it. He had tried the more gregarious versions on several occasions and, though they offered their own pleasures, these were not the kind that particularly interested him. The choreography itself was distracting and besides, although confident that he was devoid of any trace of latent homosexuality, he hated having another man in his bed.

"It's different with just one," Lynda said, stroking his arm. "Old fashioned, but I kind of like it."

Now, barely two weeks later, she was sitting on his bed, obviously mad about him.

47

"Do you have any cash on you, love?" he asked, knotting his tie. "I won't have time to get to the bank."

She motioned toward the bureau. "In my bag," she said. Then, in a smaller voice, as he dipped into her billfold which was, as always, generously stuffed, "I'm seeing Ricky later. I'm going to tell him to get another fourth." He took three twenties and replaced the billfold in her purse. He glanced at her. She looked shy and embarrassed and a little coy. "I'm going to tell him I'm out for good."

He went over to her and pecked her cheek, barely breaking his stride toward the door.

"I took sixty dollars," he said. "Put it on my tab."

"Take more, darling. That's hardly enough to get you from the door to the street."

A Jewish mother, he thought, smiling fondly at her. "Call you later, darling." he said, closing the door.

CHAPTER SIX

"My dear Augusta:

"I hope you've found the house to your liking and are comfortably settled. If you're married, my hopes embrace your husband, and as well, if they exist, your children. That's a lie. My selfishness can't allow for a husband. I know it's unrealistic, but I can't imagine that you would be married. Since I don't believe in an afterlife, it pleases me to fancy that I'm creating some sort of one in you, at least for a while, and my imagination balks at including a husband of yours in my afterlife. Sorry. For the purposes of my extended fantasy I'm going to deny you that."

She was annoyed and amused. What right had he, even in his imagination, even years before the fact, especially years before the fact, to meddle in her personal life? She could easily have been married to Ben by this time. In fact, it was hard to explain, even to herself, why she wasn't. She was not passionately in love with Ben, but she loved him nonetheless. They were so comfortable together, like brother and sister, though she couldn't be sure, never having had either. It wasn't really odd that she, who lived in her ears, should have been drawn to him, who lived so much through his eyes. They brought each other not new dimensions, but a heightened experience of them, and a refreshing respite from their own intense pursuits.

In the beginning, they had argued fiercely about which was the nobler language, music or painting, smashing quotations back and forth as if they were tennis balls.

"Painting is the intermediate somewhat between a thought and a thing."

"Who said that?"

49

"Coleridge."

"Music is nothing between. It's absolute. 'Music is a thing of the soul --- a rose-lipped shell that murmurs of the eternal sea --- a strange bird singing the songs of another shore.'"

"Who?"

"I forget."

"The eye, the brain, the brush, the paint."

"The ear, the soul, the sound, the tone."

"Painting is silent poetry."

"That's Plutarch. Simonides," she said. "There's more: 'And poetry is painting with the gift of speech.'"

"What a silly argument," he said, hugging her. "It's all art."

"And art is science in the flesh. Cocteau."

"Art is the conveyance of spirit by means of matter. de Madariaga."

"Who's that? Never heard of him. Or her."

"Art is an instant arrested in eternity. Huneker."

"Art is not a thing; it is a way. Elbert Hubbard."

"Elbert Hubbard! Art is as irrational as great music. It is mad with its own loveliness. George Jean Nathan."

"George Jean Nathan! All arts are one, all fingers on one hand."

"Nature is everything man is born to, and art is the difference he makes in it. John Erskine."

"This is childish."

"Huneker also said, 'Scratch an artist and you surprise a child.'"

"Enough! You win."

"Never forget it."

She returned to Uncle Freddy's letter. She had found it in her new house in the desk of what had been his study, sealed in an envelope addressed only "Augusta." Both Oswald Summerville and Aurora had told her that their

50

instructions in the event of his death, were that everything in the house be left exactly as it was until his heirs took possession. Aurora had assured Augusta that, except for the fifth floor which she considered her domain, as it had been during Uncle Freddy's tenure, she had meticulously observed his instructions. Her eyes had filled with tears when she told Augusta this, and Augusta was moved by the obviously sincere affection Aurora still felt for her former employer. "Poor Mr. Nickleby," she said. "I never met a better man. He was like my own brother." That she had said brother and not father struck Augusta as significant. "Well, we all pass on, but it's a pity a man like that had to pass in his prime."

She looked across the room at the portrait of Uncle Freddy that hung above the fireplace. He couldn't have been more than thirty-five when the portrait was painted. What kind of man, she wondered, sat for his portrait at that age? The answer came at once: an egotistical man, a man without a shred of doubt about his worth. Unless, of course, one of his wives had been responsible.

In the portrait, he was nearly her contemporary, an attractive man with dark hair and those intense gray eyes under thick black brows, good bones, though his nose was slightly crooked. His mouth was set, determined, but as she studied it she saw that there was something sensual about the lower lip, just as the strong line of his jaw was somewhat mollified by the faintly cleft chin. If she were to meet him now as he was then, she would probably be attracted to him. The thought chilled her, as though not his portrait but his ghost hung there in the room with her.

Ghosts. She thought of her dead mother. Sometimes she thought she remembered her, but what she remembered was ephemeral, a feeling, what the infant must have felt: a comfortable presence, a painful absence. Peace and safety. Then yearning, like pain. There had been nursemaids, some

51

of them loving and all of them attentive, but she had gone on missing her mother in an increasingly vague, undefined way. Later, when she was more grown up and her thinking more ordered, she missed her mother more abstractly, yet with more curiosity. Marco told her that she was like her mother, and she knew from photographs that she resembled her, so that gradually her mother began to seem like a self she had lost, the self she would attain but must grope towards in the dark. "My mother would have loved me," she sometimes thought, "but she died." Not that she felt self pity or had really missed being loved. She was the kind of child, self-sufficient and undemanding, to whom adults responded with lavish displays of affection, sometimes more than she needed or wanted. She knew her mother's death had left a void, but she was never sure what it was she was missing, perhaps that ease she sometimes thought she discerned between one of her friends and her mother, that unspoken acceptance, or whatever it was, that exists between two people who know each other best.

Ghosts. It was in pursuing her mother's ghost that she had found music. Music was a divine revelation, coming from a realm that was so much more explicit than words. There was, after all, more to life than could be found in books, in rational discourse, in the imagination that requires words and pictures. There was this sphere of pure sound, another language entirely, one where emotion dwelled, and feeling, and perhaps her lost mother. Why else would it be, as it was, the universal tongue?

Once she had found music, she knew she could never again be lonely; it would always fill her solitude. She would learn not only to listen to it, but to play it, to make it, and how it was made, its arithmetic, its elements, the speech of tones and melody, that absolute language. "God has a few of us," Browning wrote, "whom he whispers in the ear." She felt that she was one of those, one of the elect. It was only

52

when she found music that she set about the real business of her education.

She turned back to the letter she held in her hand, the letter written by that other ghost.

"Since I can't imagine that you've settled into being a housewife and mother, I also can't help wondering what you've done, are doing, with your life. You were interested in so many things. I remember you coming home one day after a softball game. You were flushed and excited and you wore a T-shirt that said "The Medusas," which I suspect was the fanciful name of your team." (It was; she had named them). "You were punching the pocket of your glove. Your team had won and you had batted in three runs. You were swaggering a bit, but beneath your T-shirt your breasts had just begun to bud. You were adorable." She felt herself redden, furious again. How macho he was, and patronizing. She had been deadly serious about softball and genuinely good at it.

"And then there was your cello. You played for me one night, do you remember? It was part of the Mozart E-flat Sonata. You sat beside the hearth. There was firelight in your hair, and I was amazed at your professionalism. Every note was pure and clear and discrete, nothing indistinct or muddied, and the cello sang for you as though it were your own voice, part of your body. You really understood music. I hope you have continued with it and will all your life."

She had, of course, though he would be surprised and probably appalled at the turn her interest had taken. How Ben had hated her conversion to electronic music! He hoped it was only a phase.

"That which takes effect by chance," he quoted Seneca to her, "is not art."

"Everything can be said to take effect by chance," she countered. "The artist seizes chance and bends it to his educated will."

53

She had never really wanted to perform music, except for her own pleasure. The real excitement lay in creating it and though she had begun conventionally enough, she soon found that there was no point composing Mozart since Mozart had already done that, and she, Augusta, would hardly be able to do it better. Besides, technology had opened up new frontiers of sound that Mozart could not have dreamed of and that she could happily spend the rest of her years exploring. She felt as if she was explaining this to Uncle Freddy and thought: how odd. Perhaps he wasn't dead. Perhaps when she and Camilla set out on their odyssey in the wake of his wanderings they would come upon him sitting naked in the lotus position on some Himalayan peak. Would she recognize him? The sun would have burned him the color of a walnut, and fasting would have made him thin and bony, and he would have a long gray beard. When he spied her and Camilla struggling up the mountain, he would scramble for his loincloth or dhoti or whatever. Meditation and vegetarianism would have kept him nimble for his age. Then she remembered that he would not be so very old. Marco, who was fifty-six, had told her that Uncle Freddy had been almost ten years younger. That would make him a mere two decades her senior. It would once have seemed a staggering age difference but she had begun to observe that as she herself grew older, older people seemed to grow younger --- which was, she supposed, the kindness of time, letting you grow accustomed to its cruelty.

"By now," the letter continued, "you will no doubt have come to know some of the cast of characters in my late life. Aurora Corcoran will doubtless have stayed on in the house." How could he know this? Well, of course, he had arranged it so that she could hardly have done better than to stay on. "Although I doubt if she is precisely what she seems, it amused me to allow her to play the role in which she cast herself. She's an extraordinary housekeeper and

54

cook and can be entrusted with every detail of the management of your establishment. I hope you've given her a free hand in rounding out the household staff."

The household staff, my God! Augusta thought. It hadn't occurred to her to round out any such thing. They had been in residence more than two weeks (although Augusta had been away a lot of that time) and Aurora still reigned in solitary supremacy. How stupid and unthinking she, Augusta, was! She would rectify that as soon as she came to the end of this letter.

"It also occurs to me that you may have met some or all of my former wives." Augusta gasped again. How could it have occurred to him all those years ago that this was exactly what she would do? She had spent ten days doing little else, had even flown to Los Angeles to see Gloria, number 3, with a stopover in Chicago for poor Peggy, number 5. She looked wildly around the room, almost expecting to find him grinning at her from behind the draperies, but there was only his portrait, serious and somehow official, not even looking at her but staring, instead, at something in the middle distance. A farsighted man. A man of vision. But not a dreamer, no, a man with practical, attainable goals.

"Percipient as I know you must be," he now, or then, said, "summing up my wives may be redundant, so I'll be brief. We'll take them chronologically. Marcia, first. We were high school classmates, childhood sweethearts. We grew up in Nutley, New Jersey, where my father was a physician, hers what they nowadays call a custodial engineer, at the high school. She was a "nice" girl, very pretty and trim, and she was crazy about me. I was usually class president and I was also an athlete. She was a cheer leader. It was that way in our marriage, too. We married when we were twenty. I was in my junior year at Harvard and she had gone to secretarial school (her sole ambition was to be my wife), and she worked to help put me through school, since

55

by this time my father had died and left surprisingly little money. (He'd had a working class practice and often neglected to send out bills). Marcia helped me through graduate school, too, where I took two masters degrees, one in chemistry and one in business administration. She wasn't the kind of woman who would have grown with me, though I was too busy to give it much thought or even to care. But she wanted babies and I wasn't ready for them."

Later, after Freddy, Marcia had had her babies, six of them.

"Neither Fred nor I knew what we wanted, though we thought we did," she said to Augusta one recent bright afternoon over coffee. They were sitting in the kitchen of Marcia's split-level home in New Rochelle. She had gray hair and the babies had robbed her of her figure, but Marcia was still pretty. "We were young. In those days, twenty was young."

"Isn't it still?" Augusta asked.

"Oh, no! Think what kids today have done and know by the time they're twenty." She gazed across the kitchen table through the picture window. Her forsythia was just beginning to bloom. "Of course I was hurt at the time, but Fred was right, it was all for the best." She smiled placidly, looking around her shining kitchen with its ranks of major and minor appliances, as though it proved what she said. "It was sweet of him to leave me that money, though. Not that we need it. Bert has a terrific practice."

Her outfit: vinyl boots, a voluminous felt skirt with appliqued pears and apples, a peasant blouse from some Central American sweatshop, and an abundance of jewelry that looked homemade, constituted her token rejection of the suburban world she had obviously so ardently embraced. Her house gleamed. She looked, if not exactly smug, entirely contented.

56

"We'd been married six years," the letter continued, "when I met and fell in love with Hadley, but I had no intention of divorcing Marcia. Hadley was twelve years my senior, and famous, and as far as marriage went, she didn't care one way or the other. Marcia found out, though, and divorced me and almost immediately remarried some nice young dentist she met on the plane to Juarez where he, too, was flying to rectify a mistake. Her recovery from me was so instantaneous that rather than relief at being spared guilt, I suffered shame and self-doubt at finding myself so easily replaced.

"But how my life changed with Hadley! She wasn't beautiful, as you must know, but she had so much wit and style that beauty was beside the point. She taught me so much! She taught me how to dress and how to behave and how to make love, but most important, she taught me what my strengths were. You might say she sophisticated me. Our three years together were wonderful. If you've seen Hadley, you'll understand that."

Augusta hadn't seen Hadley. Hadley had been dead for two years.

"The stage took her away for long stretches of time and I was busier and busier, working long hours at building my empire. Our worlds hardly overlapped so the logistics were impossible and our drift away from each other inevitable. Men adored her and some of them had the advantage of being there. We remained good friends.

"Enter Gloria. I don't know how to account for Gloria except to think of her as a lapse, like an illness, nothing serious, perhaps a head cold. She was nineteen, a perfect beauty, and brainless, but she had a smart, managing mother who knew a good thing when she saw it, and she assumed I was it. What a peculiar time in my life that was! I think success must have momentarily unbalanced me. It went not to my head but to my groin and filled me with lust. I'm

57

ashamed to say it, but I didn't have time to get Gloria to bed any other way (if I had, she'd have been a one-night event; hate me if you must) so I married her. Gloria wanted to be a starlet. I'm sure nobody else in this world has ever said, 'I want to be a starlet,' but Gloria said it over and over. That marriage ran its course for three months and then I sent her to a friend in Hollywood who made a starlet of her."

Gloria had never grown up into a star, though she was in her forties now.

"Alfred who?" she'd said on the phone. "Oh yeah, him." She lived with her mother in an apartment that embraced at its heart, like a pearl in an oyster, a swimming pool around which tenants gathered, occasionally pairing off to disappear into one of the units. "I never went for his lifestyle," she told Augusta. "Except for the first week, he was more interested in Formica than in fucking, if you'll pardon my saying so. It was embarrassing." She shook her head ruefully. "He should've left me more money than that!"

"Denise was old money. She was like the wives I was beginning to meet through the men who were more and more my associates. I was by now at least halfway up my ladder ... far enough up so that I knew I was going to make it all the way. Denise was the kind of woman I could take anywhere (I was becoming a snob, you see). She bred Labradors, jumped horses, played a smashing game of tennis, and had her picture on the society page almost weekly. She was known by all the important maîtres de, and she also knew how to keep herself busy in worthwhile ways."

Augusta was on enough mailing lists to have seen Denise's name often in the column of sponsors running down the left margin of letters of appeal. "With Denise I began to acquire my houses, including the one in which you are now presumably sitting, although she had execrable taste and it was I who took the time to choose not only the houses but their contents, my chief recreation in those years apart from

58

squash and deep-sea fishing. I loved doing it. Also, I knew Denise would make a good mother and I was ready, now, for a family. Alas, she was unable to conceive. Still, she was as ambitious for me as I was for myself, and a distinct asset, a woman to respect and admire but, though I tried for six years, not an easy one to love."

Denise now lived in a house not unlike this one. She was a handsome, self-possessed woman with admirable posture, the wife of the president of Axioma, a huge conglomerate.

"So you're the heiress to Alfred's estate," she said, pouring tea, which they were taking in Denise's bedroom, a chamber all costly mauve and puce. Denise was recovering from measles contracted at a Children's Aid Society birthday party where she'd helped serve the ice cream and cake. "I never had a childhood disease," she told Augusta. "They didn't have them at the schools I was sent to." Augusta had liked her. "It was silly of Freddy to leave me that hundred thousand dollars, though I suppose it was a gesture of some sort, fond remembrance, perhaps. I'll give it away, of course. Poor Fred. He had such a peculiar romantic streak, always did. I knew it would do him in. Were you and he lovers?" Augusta assured her that they were not. "Oh, you're Marco's daughter," Denise said. "I knew Marco a little in those days. I'm no longer sure, but I think I didn't approve of him. There was something unsavory about him?"

"Oh, not Marco!" Augusta said, laughing.

"Well, in any case, you're nothing like him." They were almost friends when she and Denise parted.

"Last, but certainly not least, Peggy. She was far and away the most fun, the most inventive, the most outrageous and exciting. Alas, she drank. She was always scraped or banged up somewhere on her body, or with a limb in a cast. Bruises leaped at her from everywhere. `Attacked by furniture,' she used to say. `Felled by floors.' She was a poet

59

when she could manage it. We were married for three intense, unmanageable years."

Augusta had found her in a halfway house, haggard and dull-eyed, obviously unsuited to the wagon she was riding. "What you see before you," she told Augusta, "is the merest shadow of my former self. Among other things, my energy has dribbled away."

An overstuffed dachshund waddled across the floor on its tiny legs, its stomach nearly scraping the rug.

"Sit, Sasha," Peggy pleaded. "Give up walking." She shook her head sadly. "If her belly sags any further, I'll have to get her high heels. The Germans are so cruel. I don't know how I acquired Sasha or why I keep her. Oh, Freddy. Freddy sent her to me. I imagine he thought she'd be therapeutic, but as you can see, she depresses me. What a splendid man Freddy was. I was mad about him." Tears filled her eyes. "How I miss him."

They sat in silence for a while, Peggy remembering, Augusta waiting. Outside, rain fell steadily, relentlessly. Of course with Peggy there would be rain. The room they sat in was dreary, a room for transients, nobody's home. Twisted cigarette butts, impatiently stamped to death, filled the ashtrays. The floor was littered with newspapers, paperback books, crumpled tissues.

"I was a terrible wife, but when Freddy had time for it, we did have fun. We played." The tears vanished from her eyes; she hadn't permitted herself to cry. "One moonless night, oh, it must have been two in the morning, we went to Coney Island and took off our clothes and swam in the black sea and then for more than an hour we couldn't find our clothes. It was a wonder we didn't drown, though we had stomach cramps for days. The water was polluted then. I suppose it still is."

She lit another cigarette. "It's so long since I've had anyone to talk to about Freddy. Do you mind?"

"It's what I've come for," Augusta said.

"Sometimes after theater or a party, we'd break into a school playground on our way home and we'd ride the swings for hours. We celebrated our first anniversary in a subway train, the Lexington Avenue Local to Pelham Bay Park and back again. We brought a huge picnic hamper packed with goodies, and an ice chest filled with bottles of champagne and glasses, and we invited everyone in our car to join us and most of them did and rode the whole way with us." She smiled, cigarette ash falling to the floor.

"Once, I was foolishly persuaded to give a poetry reading at the 92nd Street Y. I had a dreadful cold and had to keep blowing my nose and toward the end of the ghastly evening I was knee deep in balled-up Kleenex that had rolled off the lectern, and at last when I was finally blessedly finished and the audience, who hadn't been able to make out a word I said, was applauding feebly, six midgets in tuxedos tripped onstage and solemnly presented me with huge bouquets of flowers." Laughter rumbled in her throat and broke like thunder into the room. Augusta, too, imagining the scene, laughed and laughed and soon they were both helpless, tears flowing down their faces.

"This," Peggy gasped, "is exactly what I did then. I laughed so hard that I had to lie down on the floor of the stage, clutching my stomach, surrounded by flowers and used Kleenex, though thank God the midgets scrambled off the stage and disappeared, or I'd never have stopped. And thank God the audience began to laugh, too. The place was in an uproar, the evening saved." Freshened by memory, her laughter rose again. "One of those bouquets," she said, the words emerging slowly, with difficulty, "was in the shape of ... the shape of a ... horseshoe, my God ... and it had a shining silver message. It said ... oh, I can't ... it said Good Luck in Your... oh, help!... in Your New Store."

When they were finally able to stop laughing, Peggy sighed, cigarette smoke curling out of her mouth and nostrils. "That Freddy," she said. "I loved him. He thought he could save me. I can't imagine what I'm doing here in Chicago. Did you love him, too?"

"I hardly knew him," Augusta said.

"We were married three years," Peggy said, "but even after the divorce, and even after he was lost, the money kept coming. I never had to worry about that."

Augusta left reluctantly to catch her plane, but not before extracting Peggy's promise to come stay at the 68th Street house if she ever got to New York.

"So there it is," Uncle Freddy's letter continued. "A depressing recital, five little failed pas de deux. Not that I ever for one moment felt sorry for myself."

He'd had so much, Augusta thought, surprised at her anger. "Let him stay dead," she muttered aloud, prepared to call off all further plumbing into his life. He was a selfish man. At least four women had loved him, but had he ever really loved anyone? How dared he have made of her, Augusta, what he had, invented her, used her this way? She could scarcely bring herself to finish his letter, but as she was forcing herself to go on with it, the phone rang. It was Ben.

"I've been thinking," he said. "I'm usually thinking, of course, that's my livelihood. What I mean is that I've been thinking obsessively, while really not thinking. In circles. And sleeping badly."

"Oh, Ben."

"Maybe I should turn down Santa Cruz."

"You can't do that, Ben."

"I know I can't," he said. "I don't know what to do. I'm so depressed. I think that's what I am. I've never been depressed before."

What could she tell him? She was really so fond of him. But he knew that.

"I'm so fond of you, Ben," she said.

"Fuck fond!"

"Oh, Ben, I don't want to get married now. And I don't want you to be unhappy. And you have, too, been depressed before. Often."

"I have? Well, not like this!"

"I'm sorry. What can I do?"

"You know what you can do."

"Darling, my whole life has just changed. I've got to get a little used to it. I can't begin to think about anything else now."

"If you really loved me ...," he sighed. "Okay, I'll give it another year. Maybe I'll get over you, fat chance. Can I see you later?"

"Come to dinner."

"Can we go to bed?"

"Of course. Spend the night."

"I don't mean instead of dinner. I'm sure I'll want dinner first. My appetite doesn't seem to be affected."

"It never is, thank God," she said, laughing. "Ben?" She wasn't sure what she wanted to say and was amazed to hear herself ask, "Do you have enough money, Ben?"

"Money? Of course I have enough money. What an odd question."

It was an odd impulse, too, wanting to give him money. Was she trying to substitute it for love, or was it a way to be generous that hadn't been available to her until now? She would have to think about it. Money. They exchanged goodbyes and rang off, and she forced herself to finish with Uncle Freddy ... no, she could no longer think of him as Uncle ... with Alfred Nickleby's letter.

"Summing up my personal life, I see now that instead of having been in control, as I believed, I was a kind of victim

63

of the American dream, playing out all those stupid cliché roles one after another ... the perfect conformist. Well, at least I'm finally able to recognize this and, with shame but no bitterness, renounce the life I've led. I hope I'm being honest, but I imagine now I'll have time to really think about those things I know are important. I believe your center is solider than mine, lovely Augusta, and your eye less blinking. I think you'll be safe."

There the letter ended, unsigned. She sat for a long time staring at his portrait, wondering if perhaps he had been a little crazy. Then she picked up the phone to call her office at school for messages, feeling dutiful since there so rarely were messages. The phone was in use.

"As for the bilingual issue," she heard, her curiosity warring with the impulse to hang up immediately. It was a woman's voice. "The answer is an absolute and unequivocal no. They'll simply have to learn English." "Ees a question of pride," a soft Hispanic male voice said. "Bullshit. Every ethnic group that has settled in this country, and they've nearly all been ethnic, has learned English. Even the Poles." "Ees a Polish joke?" the man asked, tittering nervously. "Your people are culturally more prepared to learn the language of the adopted country than we were, fresh out of the jungle. You chose to come here."

Softly, Augusta replaced the receiver. She had a good enough ear to know that the woman on the phone was Aurora, and without a trace of southern accent. How odd that she would not have her own telephone. Well, it had been her own for years. But what had that conversation meant? What could she be up to? How mysterious that she should be discussing the bilingual issue. She waited a few minutes to give Aurora time to complete her call, then made her own useless one. When she had hung up, she rang for Aurora. She wanted to apologize for her stupidity in assuming that Aurora would run the household unassisted.

"I'm not used to having money, to living like this," Augusta explained. "You'll have to tell me things. What do we need? A chambermaid? Cook? Butler? Are there butlers in America?"

"You've hardly been here," Aurora said, "and soon you be going away. The children help me out time to time. Star Rising does the dusting."

"When I get back we'll organize things better. Meanwhile, you're sure you can manage this way?"

"Yes, Ma'am."

"And Aurora?" But she could think of no way to ask about the telephone conversation. "Ben is coming to dinner," she said, instead.

Aurora nodded and turned to go.

"One more thing, Aurora."

"Yes'm?"

"Could you please not call me ma'am? Could you just call me Augusta?"

CHAPTER SEVEN

"We would be equal partners, of course," Marco said. "You could be silent or not, as you choose." They were behind a huge silver bullet of a truck, keeping a respectable distance. He was a careful driver, not only out of self-respect, but respect for Erwinna's beautiful white Mercedes. What a pleasure to drive it. "Flammable!" it said aggressively on the rear of the bullet.

"Think what a lark it will be, Erwinna. Ahhh." Her face was in his lap, his cock in her mouth. Were flammable and inflammable interchangeable? And why? Her mouth was a soft wet cave, her tongue a sinuous grotto creature, flicking, teasing. The speedometer hung steadily at sixty-eight, the speed of the bullet ahead. He hoped there was no taste of Lynda on him.

"Ohhh, that's awfully good, Erwinna. If you wanted to have an active part you could give up that silly job." She was headmistress of an expensive girls' school in Duchess County. Bored, she'd taken the position a few years earlier and found that she was good at it. She was an excellent administrator. Recognizing her as their social equal, affluent parents entrusted their daughters to her with such zeal that the school, for the first time in its seventy-seven-year existence, was forced to turn down an increasing number of applicants in spite of its annual tuition increases. She would be an asset to Corned Beef & Cabbage, no doubt of it. "Though I know how attached you've grown to the school. Darling. That's so good."

But she hated dancing and she considered disco music savage, as of course it was. "All those tomtoms and restless natives," she'd said the one time he'd taken her to Marilyn.

66

She liked the lights, though. "You're not against primal screaming," he'd reminded her. She often screamed when she felt tension building (although at school only in the privacy of her office bathroom); it was good for her marginally high blood pressure. "Disco-ing is a form of primal screaming, but much more fun."

"Fun is not the point," she had snapped.

She was a striking woman in her forties (though just how many forties she hadn't confided), with the posture of a Prussian army officer and a high aggressive bosom that preceded her like the prow of a ship parting the ways. She was undeniably handsome, though her good looks owed less to the felicitous arrangement of her features than to the substratum of intelligence that informed them. She managed to be both haughty and attentive. In the beginning, Marco had found her intimidating. Kissing her, he imagined, would be like pressing one's mouth to the flyleaf of a library book, a classic ---Virgil, perhaps, or Tacitus. He was amazed and pleased to discover how wrong he was.

"What's the matter, Marco?" she now said, lifting her head from his lap. "Don't you love me anymore?" His budding erection had wilted and died.

"We're coming to another bloody toll," he said, accusingly. "It was your idea to take the turnpike instead of the Merritt."

"Damn," she said, sitting up and groping in her bag. It was the third toll. "I don't have exact change." She pressed a dollar into his window hand and threw her sweater across his lap. He navigated the Mercedes into one of the manned stalls. "I suppose it's sentimental and foolish," she said moodily, "going all this way for lunch. I'm not even hungry."

"On the contrary, Erwinna," he said, retrieving the change and pocketing it. "You've got a great sense of style; I've always said it." Their destination was an inn a few miles north of Westport where, exactly a year earlier they had had

67

their first "date." It was an anniversary. "I should have thought of it myself."

"Never," she said, removing the sweater from his lap and replacing it with her head. "Not in a million years would you have thought of it."

She was getting cranky.

"You really don't have to do that, darling," he said. "Though of course it's heaven."

"I know I don't have to do it," she snarled, her words muffled. "But it's such a boring drive. You were right; we should have taken the parkway."

He drove in silence for a while, trying to keep his mind on what she was doing. It was the least he could do for her considering what he was asking of her. So far, she had made no response at all to his proposition which, in his optimism, he took to mean that she was considering it. His erection rose with his hopes. She was extremely skilled. He had known few women who made as good use of their tongues, in whatever capacity. After his night and morning with Lynda, there was no one he would have credited with the ability to arouse him sexually, yet between the Stamford toll and their exit, with the barest minimum of concentration on his part, she had him not only standing fully at attention but quivering for release. They were coming to their exit; he flicked on the right-turn signal. As he made the turn off the turnpike, she did something exquisite with her tongue, the roof of her mouth, and her lips, and he gasped and came, slowing the car for the stop sign at the foot of the egress road and switching on the left-turn signal. By the time he had brought the car to a halt, she was sitting up, licking her lips and looking at him evilly. Gently, she tissued him off and tucked him back into his trousers.

"That's given me an appetite," she said, zipping up his fly.

68

Over lunch he made an effort to talk of many things but Corned Beef & Cabbage recurred like the subject in a fugue. He knew he should tell her about Augusta's inheritance, and sooner or later he would have to, but how under the circumstances could he explain why he should need money from Erwinna? How could he explain the implications of his being excluded from any share of Augusta's immense wealth when he himself had no idea what they were?

"You're obsessed, Marco," Erwinna told him when, during coffee, he suggested that the club might be a perfect legacy for her son, Paul, who was twenty-three and trying to find himself, though he was not looking very hard. "Paul is trembling on the brink of something," Erwinna said, "but I don't think it's a dance club."

"What do you think it is?" he asked politely, not really interested.

"Homosexuality, Coming out" she said.

Solicitously, he covered her hand with his. "Would you mind that very much?"

"If I thought he could be happy," she said, considering. "He always seems so tormented."

"And now, of course, the danger" Marco mumbled gloomily, regretting that he'd brought Paul into it; they were going to have to go on talking about him.

"He blames me for never having given him a proper father, though God knows I tried. And tried. And tried." She had had three husbands. Two had died, one by God's hand, one by his own. The first, Paul's father, had left her while Paul was still in utero. He was somewhere, perhaps along the Riviera, gambling. "Why isn't the father ever to blame?"

"You have to blame whoever is at hand."

"No, it's always cherchez la mère. If Daddy's a bastard, why didn't she leave him, or why did she marry him in the first place? If Daddy's not a bastard but leaves her, why

69

wasn't she lovable enough to keep him? If Daddy dies, why did she fail to keep him alive? And if Daddy kills himself, you can be sure she drove him to it."

"Does he hate you?"

"Of course Paul doesn't hate me. He adores me. But that doesn't stop him from blaming me."

"It's time he grew up. It's time he had some real responsibilities," Marco said, sternly. He was pretty certain that Erwinna's marital designs on him had nothing to do with her wanting another shot at a father for Paul. Paul was old enough now to find his own father. He must get her off the subject of Paul, who was depressing both of them. He glanced at his watch. It was nearly three.

"What do you think, Erwinna," he said. "Shall we join forces? My connections and boundless enthusiasm. Your administrative skills, good sense, and, dare I say it, money?"

"Are you proposing, Marco?"

"Of course I am, darling, though not a connubial partnership. A more intimate one than that."

She knew him well enough to understand that what he said was truer than he knew. If she bought him, she would indeed have him by the balls. Money, money! But she wanted more than that. A few days earlier she had turned forty-eight. Soon she would be fifty. The years had become frighteningly abbreviated; they now seemed to fly by in about three months. It was always either Christmas, summer, or her birthday.

"You want it so much, don't you, Marco?"

He smiled boyishly, ducking his head, and glanced again at his watch.

"Don't keep looking at your watch," she said, annoyed. I've reserved a room upstairs for the afternoon."

"Oh, no!" he groaned before he could stop himself. "The afternoon's almost gone. It can't be done!"

"Only for an hour, Marco. I know it's shabby to keep score, but you owe me one."

"I know, darling, but I've got a six o'clock appointment."

"You'll make it."

Yes, he could just about make his appointment with Julius, but sex again? She patted his hand reassuringly.

"Don't worry, Marco. You'll make it."

CHAPTER EIGHT

Camilla sat at her worktable contemplating the construction she had just completed, a lower plate, ten teeth curved to fit the somewhat pinched lower jaw of a man she would never know, whose name was on the card before her: Herbert Kalinsky. She tried, as she always did, to extrapolate the individual from her handiwork. He would be small, fine-boned, a non-smoker, probably finicky in his habits, and nervous. His soon-to-be-teeth grimaced at her cruelly, but it would be unfair to assume that he was sadistic, since all teeth, out of context, are cruel. Teeth are weapons, designed to tear, gash, pulverize. She had matched these to the specimen of his natural teeth included in the dentist's package of instructions, choosing the proper color, a white on the blue, rather than yellow or brown side, actually a number fourteen. She had made them slightly irregular, not only to fit the uppers, which were God-given and still anchored to his skull, but so that anyone who might care wouldn't readily assume them to be false. Though it was extra work, she felt that her artistic integrity demanded this, despite the deplorable odds that the plate would be returned to her for correction of the irregularities, assumed to be errors. Since they were paying for new teeth, why not perfect ones?

Would Herbert Kalinsky be one of those who understood? This mandibular accessory, the last she would ever make, she hoped, was perhaps her masterpiece. She ran a finger lightly over the ridge of the teeth, lingering on the rise of the canines, and thought that soon this denture would reside in the intimate recess of a stranger's body, moistened by his saliva, probed by his tongue, hiding bits of food, helping him to form words and to bite into peaches, giving strength to his collapsed face and making his smile bearable. Until he grew accustomed to them, he would curse them for their intrusiveness, their unrootedness, but at night he would remove them, precious as jewels, and lay them away in a plastic container filled with a cleansing solution. Teeth. What an inordinate amount of time and care and money and emotion is spent on them.

She heard approaching the slow heavy tread of her employer, Dr. Blavitsky, a short, stocky, seventyish woman who walked with a cane and looked a little like Gertrude Stein, perhaps by design, and who insisted on being called Doctor, a status she had earned, she said, at Koln, following her exile from Russia.

"Very nishe," she said, leaning against Camilla's worktable. For some reason having nothing to do with her own teeth, perfect pearls strung on healthy gums, she had a problem with sibilants, which she consistently spoonerized. She picked up the denture and held it against the mold of the upper jaw.

"Beautiful, beautiful," she said, carefully appraising the fit. "I could not have done better myshelf." Since being tendered Camilla's resignation, the doctor had been lavish in her attention and praise. She herself worked exclusively in metals and alloys. "Jusht yeshterday I wash shaying to my shishter I am loshing my finesht technissan, Mish Shtrong." She put down Mr. Kalinsky's teeth and took Camilla's hands in her own large powerful ones, examining first their backs then turning them palm upward. "Theshe golden handsh," she mourned. "Theshe magic fingersh. How can I pershuade you to change your mind?"

"Oh, Dr. Blavitsky, if I were two people, one of me would stay here forever," Camilla lied, her voice ringing with feigned passion.

"If it were for marriage, I could undershtand. Or for babiesh. But to shacrifishe your career becaushe of a friend'sh inheritansh? To be a paid companion?"

Stupidly, Camilla had told Dr. Blavitsky the truth. She had also emphasised, repeatedly, that she would now be in a position to do what she felt she was really meant to do, sculpture, but this the doctor had chosen not to hear. There was no point saying it again. Camilla sighed. The doctor's hands tightened over hers, imprisoning her.

"I will tell you shomething I sould have told you shooner, perhapsh. I am a shingle woman, ash you know, with only a shishter for family. Thish buishnesh, and you know it'sh reputason, ish mine alone. Shishter hash no interesht, and shertainly no talent." Her voice grew tender. "I am not a young woman. Shomeone sould inherit. It came into my mind I would gradually make you into a partner and finally, when I am ready to retire, it would become your bushinesh. Who better?"

"Oh, Dr. Blavitsky," Camilla cried, moved. "I am deeply moved."

"Sho why not reconshider?"

"I can't. I'm committed."

A few weeks earlier, the doctor's offer would have been irresistible. It was a lucrative and honest business, useful, filling a real need. She could easily recruit and train technicians, coming in only to check on their work and to see that the bills were sent out and paid. She could keep a studio nearby where she would spend most of her day. Perhaps she would buy a house in Sag Harbor for weekends and summers, where her larger pieces would be done and where she could play tennis and lie on the beach, turning bronze, meeting people. It had been two months since she and Jonas, who was never going to leave his wife, had finally broken up, driving her into group therapy where she'd begun to see that masochists require marriages made in hell and

74

that, in fact, she was helping to keep Jonas's marriage going by giving him the even greater torture of having at least the illusion of a choice between duty and happiness. A happy marriage, for Jonas, could never last; it would make him miserable. He would become catatonic. He would have to leave home in search of pain. She could have held onto him forever, given the arrangement as it was, since she had no doubt that Jonas truly loved her, but as soon as she understood that, no matter how perversely necessary, her role would always be adjunctive, she had completely and sanely lost all appetite for Jonas. How complex and devious, the mating behavior of humans, hung about as it was with that excessive emotional baggage that had so little to do with propagation. Only thinking animals, she imagined, were capable of such irrational behavior.

Only now, turning down Dr. Blavitsky's unexpected offer, was Camilla sure that she was really going with Augusta. She had discussed it with her therapy group and was nettled by their reaction, which was to accuse her of doing anything to postpone facing her own problems. "Anything?" she had screamed. "You call this anything? This is an adventure NO one could refuse. You're all jealous, and I don't blame you!" Really, they were all so dull and predictable. With the possible exception of that computer fellow, Michael Bell, who always understood exactly what she meant, even when she herself didn't.

"Committed, committed," the doctor said with disgust. "I think you are being fooliss." She heaved herself off Camilla's desk, onto which she had earlier settled, and reached for her cane. The doctor was in no way crippled; the cane was an affectation. Camilla had once asked her why she used it. "Does your cane make you more able?" she had asked. She was occasionally overwhelmed by a pun and then compelled to utter it. But the doctor had merely an-

75

swered, "Yesh, it shteadiesh me. The earth ish not flat, you know."

"Committed ish a word overworked by the young," she said. "You would think they had all been shent to inshtitushionsh, when it ish merely that they are doing what they want to do. Well, my child, if you ever change your mind. Or your commitment. Meanwhile, I hope you will shtay in touch."

"I'll shend poshtcardsh, er postcards," she said, and assured the doctor that she was grateful to her for having taught her everything she knew about dentures and for having considered her a possible heir, and said nothing about having been underpaid and overworked. None of it mattered now. Her worktable drawer was crammed with charts and maps. She had spent all of an overstretched lunch hour on this, her last day, with Captain Packer at the East River marina patronized by the late Alfred Nickleby. The larger of his yachts rested there in a state of perpetual care, like a well-tended grave. Captain Packer, who owned and ran the marina, seemed to have been expecting her.

"Someone was bound to show up once the will was probated," he explained. He was a stocky, sunburned man with the bluest eyes she had ever seen and curly graying hair cropped close to his skull. "The estate's been paying the bills but I've just received instructions to bill Miss March directly. You're Miss March?"

"I'm her assistant," Camilla said, and introduced herself. She asked if she might go aboard the yacht and he took her around to where it lay. She admired its lines; it was a beautiful piece of sculpture, all power and grace. She was surprised to see that it was named The Augusta.

"Has it always been named that?" she asked.

"She's been The Augusta since he bought her. That would be, let's see now, he's been gone a little over seven years? Then it would be close to ten years."

76

"How mysterious," she said, her eyes slowly traversing the yacht's length from the flying thrust of its bow to the gently rounded stern. It dwarfed the yachts berthed on either side of it. "It's awfully big."

"She's only a bit over 100 feet," he said, leading her across a short gangplank onto the deck. "The great yachts are at least twice that and as much as four times longer. But she is a beauty. I'm always getting offers for her. You can tell Miss March any time she wants to sell her to say the word."

"We're planning to use it," Camilla said, carefully eschewing the feminine pronoun. Ships were genderless. Men called ships "she and "her" because they manned them, rode them, mastered them, steered and directed them, and occasionally went down on them. "Will it make it across the Pacific?"

"Of course, but you'd have to get her to the Pacific first. Were you planning to fly her there?"

Camilla, who was not entirely ignorant of geography, blushed angrily. "I assumed we could sail it down the coast," she said, "and through the Panama Canal. That would bring us to the Pacific Ocean, I believe."

Her anger apparently amused him, for his eyes twinkled. Had she ever actually seen eyes twinkle? "You'd need a crew," he said.

"Yes."

"I'll take care of that for you when you're ready. Might even sign on myself," he said longingly. "I've skippered her before to the Mediterranean. Where were you planning to go?"

Camilla told him.

"Follow him?" Packer asked, astounded. "What an idea! After all these years his trail will be pretty cold. Still, we could try it." She took note of the "we." "I've got a record of the itinerary he planned to follow. I supplied him with a

77

complete set of charts. But judging from where the wreck washed up, I'm not sure he followed his original plans." He looked meditative. "Still, it might not be impossible. Most port masters keep pretty good records." They had circled the deck and he led her inside to the main salon, which was spacious and bright with deep plump sofas and armchairs covered in blues and greens with occasional gay splashes of yellow like Matisse cutouts. The dining salon, similarly decorated to reflect tropical sea, sky, and sunlight, was an extension of the main salon, separated by olivewood doors that could be thrown open to make one grand and festive room. There was a bar at one end, a glassed-in wall of books at the other. "What luxury," Camilla exclaimed.

"The whole point of yachts," Packer said, leading her down the companionway to the lower deck. He opened a door. "There are four double staterooms and smaller rooms for the crew. This was Nickleby's." They stepped inside. It was almost suffocatingly elegant, like a seraglio, or so she imagined. The adjoining bath was all marble and gold.

"He knew how to live," Packer agreed, seeing the expression on Camilla's face. "But he was a good man all the same. Not a hedonist. I've missed him."

She looked at him carefully, for the first time, startled by the implications of what he had just said, and by his having perceived her feelings. Strange how people were forever turning into people right before your eyes. That moment of crystallization. There was a thin gold ring on the fourth finger of his left hand. Idly, Camilla turned down a corner of the heavy brocade spread and saw that the oversized bed was carefully made up with crisp, white sheets, plump pillows. "So clean and inviting," she noted. "It's hard to believe it's been sitting here idle and unused all these years."

"Shipshape," he said. "We're paid to keep it that way. Ready to go at a moment's notice even though I knew it wouldn't be doing that." He ran the hand with the ringed finger lightly across the surface of a heavy marquetry desk, then looked at his palm. Not a speck of dust. Too bad about that ring, Camilla thought. He was undeniably attractive. Not since high school had she fallen in love with a man who wasn't, finally, unavailable. In therapy she had been forced to face the knowledge that this was not due to chance alone, though she had not yet figured out why.

"However, I haven't gone through the drawers," Packer said, sliding one open. "His things are still here. "For example, here's an unsent letter." He took from the drawer a fat white envelope. "Addressed to Augusta." He looked puzzled. "The ship?"

"Give it to me," Camilla said, laughing. "It's for Augusta March. He's left other letters. They seem to be springing up everywhere like wildflowers. I'll give it to her."

"Ah, then she's the Augusta the ship was named for. Surprising I never met her. I met most of his women at one time or another."

"She wasn't one of his women." She glanced at her watch. "I really must go."

"Come into the office first," he said. "I'll give you a set of the charts he had with him." Again, his sea-blue eyes twinkled at her. "I imagine you'll want to start studying them."

She couldn't wait to start studying them. The thought of them in her worktable drawer and the knowledge that her last day here at Dr. Blavitsky's Laboratory for Dental Enhancement was almost at an end, suffused her with joy. Captain Packer would decide on the course they would follow, at least to the point where he was almost certain Nickleby had foundered, but she knew she could spend hours dreaming over the maps with their seas and bays and gulfs and inlets and their exotic names and their latitudes and longitudes. What an adventure it would be! Packer had suggested that it might be appropriate to sail on the anniver-

79

sary of Nickleby's departure, only a few weeks off. He was confident that he could have everything ready by then. She could see that he himself had become more and more excited by the prospect, as though he had already made up his mind to captain The Augusta I. It would be reassuring to have him along; he was so obviously competent and knowledgeable, but she wondered how he could arrange to leave both his business and wife for such a long period and on such short notice.

Herbert Kalinsky's teeth were finished. There was really nothing more to keep her, early though it was, so she began to gather up the things she had accumulated in her worktable drawers, the tissues, the comb, the pocket mirror, the Life Savers, the Tampax, an apple, two chewed pencils with dry, dead erasers. She put all these items into a large shopping bag. Then, remembering that home was now the house on East 68th Street, she dropped the bag into a waste receptacle, took the charts and Augusta's letter and her final salary check, and glancing neither to right nor left, and certainly not behind her, trotted out to freedom.

CHAPTER NINE

"Dearest Augusta,"

Dearest!!

"What a tricky exercise, splitting myself off in this year from this present and living self into a projected time, unknown to me, when I am dead and you are reading these words. How do I see you? The only thing I can know with reasonable certainty is where you are: aboard The Augusta, in the Sultan Suite."

Wrong. She was in the third floor studio she had created for herself in the 68th Street house. Marshall had helped her install it, volunteered by Aurora. "He handy with wires," she had told Augusta, and he was. He also had an excellent ear. It occurred to her, watching him work, that it might be a good idea to invite him along on their trip, not only because he was strong and capable, but because of the possibility that his absence from New York might delay any disaster that might be brewing because of whatever he and Aurora and the others were up to. If they were up to anything.

She had not yet even set eyes on The Augusta, although Camilla, who an hour earlier had delivered the letter to her, had described the yacht in detail almost as glowing as her account of Captain Packer. Augusta, wavering in her plan to retrace Uncle Freddy's final months, was at work on a new piece, a collage of sounds she had taped at random from television commercials and was now splicing into wonderfully funny and musically grotesque juxtapositions. She was so engrossed that merely thinking about the trip was wrenching. Yet, as Camilla talked, her eyes dancing with excitement, the trip began to have concrete reality. Even the date was practically determined; the anniversary of Freddy's

81

departure was barely three weeks away. She began to imagine the sounds the sea would make during storms, and the wind, the thrumming pulse of the ship's engines, the squawks and cries of following seabirds, the hubbub of foreign cities and the babble of exotic tongues in teeming streets and marketplaces; the oxen, yaks, water buffaloes, elephants, camels, burros, goats, cows sacred and edible; the wagons, bicycles, vans, motorcycles, jeepneys, jitneys, tongas; the Kashmiri ghazals, the Ceylonese dances, the Ketjak dance in Bali, the Takarazuka All-Girls' Revue, the Barong at Tampaksiring. She was doing her homework, reading up, and it was endless, endless. The world was full of sound. Yes, they would go; how could they not go?

"I don't even know what tense to use. Present? Future? Future perfect? In these last half dozen years, I never dreamed in the future perfect a dream that did not hold you, Augusta, at its perfect heart. I hope you don't mind."

She was beginning to feel like a character in a nineteenth century novel. He had been a hard-headed businessman. His business was synthetics. How romantic he was! But while he dreamed of her, who had lain beside him in that sumptuous bed Camilla had described so eloquently?

"None of my wives," he wrote, answering her at once, "ever sailed with me on The Augusta. From the beginning, this was your ship, yours and mine, for my time and for yours. And so it pleases me more than you can imagine to think of you aboard her, dreaming where so often I dreamed. Perhaps once or twice you'll dream of me. You are my life in death."

Was that the price of her inheritance? Was she charged with the perpetuity of her benefactor? How presumptuous romantics are, bulling ahead without even asking your permission. And suppose she were reading this in that bed, on that ship, and had persuaded Ben to come along (as she had almost been tempted to do, at least for the summer months) and he was there beside her in that bed. She might even be reading this letter aloud to him. Or suppose she had married Jacob Warshawsky four years ago, as she might well have done during those months when she was so madly in love with him. There would have been a child by now, since Jacob had wanted one, and no thought of going off on The Augusta, though Jacob, a poet, would have appreciated Freddy and both his legacies.

Surely the reality of her own present was beside the point. What had really mattered to Nickleby all those years ago was what was inside his own head. The myth he had created of her was his myth, not hers. Still, she couldn't help thinking, she had not married Jacob, and Ben was not with her, and she would be sailing on The Augusta, and in a sense she was exactly what he'd wanted and expected her to be: single and susceptible, and, so far, reasonably acquiescent.

"You will probably think this presumptuous of me," he now, or then, wrote. It made her dizzy to think that all those years before any of this was happening, he was reading her mind. She was being manipulated by a ghost. "And manipulative." She nearly screamed. "As of course I am. But perhaps none of what I project, or imagine, will be at all as I imagine it. There are so many possibilities, even probabilities, which I refuse to take into account. Why should I? You are the Augusta I know and know will be, the Augusta I love. This love, in your now, will have been transmuted into something ethereal, but believe me, my darling, in my now, in the now of this penning, it's far from that. Should I not die, should you never read these words, you will long since have heard them from me directly. It makes me sad to contemplate this alternative, the one in which I will never have spoken words of love to you, or touched you, or kissed you, or seen your face in love. Still, there is happiness in knowing that right now, in my moment, we are both alive on the same earth, in the same time, separated not by many miles but merely by your youth (or my age). And there's even some happiness in knowing that in your moment the ghost of my voice will rise from these pages to you, and for that little time, at least, we'll be together."

She lifted her eyes from the page and wondered again if he was a madman. He had known so little of her, and she less of him, yet he had invested her with this monumental love.

She tried to recall her first memory of him. The circus? He and Marco had taken her there, perhaps on her birthday. The two men had sat happily eating peanuts and crackerjacks and hot dogs while she, between them, wept, eating nothing, hating the circus. She hated it that the animals were in cages, or, like wind-up toys, made to do stupid tricks that had nothing to do with their natures. She hated the acrobats because they were in danger, defying death, and you were supposed to applaud their miraculous survivals. She hated the sad, grotesque clowns, many of them midgets, tumbling on their little rubbery legs, trying to make you laugh at them. It had been Uncle Freddy who had lifted her onto his lap and helped her blow her nose.

"There are certain moments with you that I carry around with me like pictures in an album, and that I have looked at over and over. I think the earliest is a circus picture. You were six or seven. You hated the circus and cried. When I asked you why you hated it, you said, 'Because everything in it is hateful, even the music.' I asked you what you hated most and the question interested you so much that you stopped crying in order to think about it.

"'What I hate the most,' you said, 'the very most, is that there are three rings and I can only watch one ring at a time.'

"'And you don't know which to watch?'

"You giggled, and said which to watch, which to watch, witches' watches, wishy washy, and giggled some more. 'That's not why,' you said. 'It's that I feel sorry for the people

84

and animals doing things in the rings I'm not paying attention to. What if nobody is watching them? Why are they there and why are they doing those things?' It was such a profound philosophical worry for someone so small."

She remembered none of that. She remembered only that he had been kind, that, like Marco, his cheek was rough but smelled nice. She had been wishing she had a mother and not just Marco, because she knew a mother would understand and take her home and not make her sit there just because there were tickets that had been paid for, and then Uncle Freddy had said, "Let's go, then. If you hate it so far, you'll hate it even more when they shoot the man out of the cannon. Come on, Marco."

But Marco was enjoying himself and they had left him at the circus and gone walking in the park. She asked him if they really shot a man out of a cannon and he said yes, indeed, he was a human bullet, and she said that that was one thing she hoped she would never have to see in her whole life. And so far she had not.

"There's another memory from around that time, not more, really, than a snapshot, but one that moved me enormously. Your cousin Will had come down with his family from Toronto where they'd moved a year or two earlier."

Yes, Will. They had been so close, almost like brother and sister, and then Uncle Joe's firm had transferred him to Canada, breaking Augusta's heart.

"You and Will are about to go outside to play. He's holding your hand you're looking up at him, your face aglow with happiness and so incandescent with naked, unabashed, excited love that I can hardly bear it. I am amazed at the pain I feel and even more amazed to recognize that what I am feeling is actually *jealousy*. At the same time, although I knew that as you grew older you would learn to be less candid, more guarded, I also knew, and know, that you have that in you, that capacity, that heart, that fullness

85

and generosity. That's all there is to that snapshot, but it's among those I treasure most."

What had made the picture charming to him, she thought, was her unselfconsciousness, the very thing that might have been lost had she known with what careful and sensitive attention she was being observed and judged. But he had never let her know. And Will? She had adored him. He was two years older, tall and strong and gentle and handsome, and though they would always love each other and feel a special familial attachment, she had outgrown him. This is no way detracted from the fact that until she was ten, at least, he had been her knight in shining armor; she had had that. Time, again. That time should have altered her feelings didn't negate them or make them less real or meaningful. Or did it? Was endurance the measure? Then what of this strange "love" of poor Uncle Freddy's (oh, it was so hard even to know by what name to think of him!)? She truly had scarcely noticed him, though she remembered liking him when she did. She already had a father and had felt no need for another. It was a mother she'd missed and sought and occasionally found --- in her seventh grade English teacher, her second cello teacher, her Aunt Sarah, Will's mother.

Yet during most of the time she was growing up, even while marrying all those other women, he had loved her, or so he claimed, and now, years after his death, here was that love confessing itself to her in the angular strokes his pen had laid on these pages she held in her hand, beneath her eyes. You could certainly say that this was an enduring love. Did that give it more weight and power than, say, her love for Jacob Warshawsky, which had been so hectic and intense during the eleven months it lasted, before, knowing him better, she had willed it to die? She was suddenly impatient with herself. Why was she sitting here measuring the unmeasurable.?

For the first time, she wondered where he had sat when he wrote these letters to her. Had it been in the rooms, at the desks, where he had left them for her to find?

"There are so many treasures in my album, those brief glimpses I was allowed into your heart and your mind. I was a voyeur, but you mustn't imagine that I was always obsessed with you. My life was full and busy, as you know, and it was only this one part of me, though an important part, that was reserved for you. That part grew, has grown, and there are times when it consumes me and all the other parts of me vanish.

"This letter is already so long that if I go on with it you'll reach your destination without ever having time to emerge from this cabin to smell the changing air. What is your destination? I'd like to think that you're somewhere in the wake of The Divine Sara so that, in spite of the time warp, we'll be sharing whatever experiences, the happy ones, I mean, that lie ahead of me. If you are doing such a trip, I hope Avery Packer is around to captain it. You won't find a better skipper or a more decent man anywhere, and I'd rest easier knowing you were safe in his hands.

"Goodnight, my love."

Slowly, she folded the letter and put it away in its envelope. He knew she would be following him, just as he had known that she would look up his wives. She felt as though there were invisible strings connecting her to him and that he was pulling them, not only across the miles but across the years. When she slept, a little later, she dreamed of him. His hand was on her breast, his warm breath on her cheek.

87

CHAPTER TEN

Marco invited Erwinna to accompany him to his meeting with Julius, but she already had a date. She was allowing her son Paul to take her out to dinner for his birthday. She had not said yes to Marco's proposition, but neither had she said no. He had made very careful love to her after lunch at the inn, in spite of feeling so pressured for time and so uneager for sex, and had given her what she called "an uncommonly lovely fuck," so that now, confronting Julius, he felt relaxed and full of confidence.

"Your assurances are not legal tender," Julius said in his flat voice from behind his cigar. He was a squat, shapeless man with a bald head that gleamed with sweat most of the time. It was gleaming now, behind the big desk in his office on the floor above the almost defunct Corned Beef & Cabbage. Marco noticed --- it was the sort of thing Marco noticed --- that the huge diamond Julius always wore on his fat pinky was gone. "I'm going to level with you, March. I need the bucks and I need them fast. Promises mean zero. I could be dead tomorrow."

"Your heart?" Marco asked, concerned.

"Not my heart!" Julius said, drawing out the last word with disgust. "I owe, I owe."

"You mean someone's out to kill you?" Marco asked, appalled.

"Maybe not kill. Not yet. Maybe just maim for the time being. They know I'm trying. What's in it for them if I'm dead?"

"Them?"

"Listen, March, you're a grown-up adult person. You think you go into a business like this free as a bird, no uninvited partners? You think it's a candy store, just mom and pop? You got to pay off or they wreck you. My life is hanging on my fingernails, on credit."

Marco was relieved that Erwinna hadn't come with him. "Surely you exaggerate?" he said, hopefully. Julius made a sound of pure disgust, somewhere between a bark and a barf.

"The mob," he said. "The mob. You go to movies. You watch television."

"I've heard of the mob," Marco said. "Is there only one of them?"

Ignoring his question, Julius said, "I read in the papers where your daughter came into a whole lot of money."

"Forget it," Marco said. "She has nothing to do with this."

"A shame."

"Who in the mob? Give me a name. I'll go see him. Maybe I can make a deal."

"You crazy?" Julius said, then jumped halfway out of his chair when the door, with no warning knock, flew open. A woman strode in, eyes flashing.

"Oh, you. Janet," Julius said, his hand on his heart. "Take a seat a minute, doll. Marco March, my wife Janet."

"I'm starving to death," Janet said, barely glancing at Marco. She lit a cigarette. "You said you'd be through by seven and it's after eight. She slipped off her sable jacket to reveal a perfect figure sheathed in understated black silk, beautifully cut, tight across her breasts, a choker of huge pearls gleaming at her neck. Her face, half hidden by a broad-brimmed black straw hat angled across her right eye, revealed that she had once been a great beauty. She was still beautiful, but her beauty had begun to congeal a little. Nonetheless, Marco wondered how anyone as hideously unattractive as Julius had snagged her. Money, he supposed,

89

though plenty of men more appetizing than Julius had money. Alas.

"I got too much to do, Janet," Julius said, his voice a whine. He was scribbling something on a piece of paper when, struck by inspiration, he looked craftily at Marco. "You got a dinner date?" he asked.

"Well, I had thought you and I..."

"So why don't you take Janet? You'd be doing me a big favor. I'll probably be here half the night."

Janet crossed the room to where Marco sat and carefully looked him over out of lovely green eyes, dreamily myopic.

"You'd be doing me a big favor, too," she said, satisfied, "unless you chew with your mouth open."

Marco smiled. "I'd love to take Janet to dinner, he said.

"Take her to Pavanne and tell them to put it on my bill. Janet, you can sign."

Marco rose and held Janet's fur for her. "I'll call you tomorrow," he said to Julius, taking Janet's arm.

"Wait a minute," Julius said, folding a scrap of paper on which he had been writing. He handed it to Marco. "Here. Take this."

Marco took it. "Menelaus Talifiero," it said, "and then a phone number. "Not the big one, but the one to see first." Marco nodded at Julius and, bearing Julius's wife on his arm, exited, his heart beating just a little faster, not because of Janet but because of the scribbled name. An odd name. What was he getting himself into?

"Marco March," Janet said in the cab, trying out his name. "I like it. I have a feeling I'm going to be saying it a lot." She smiled at him. Her smile glittered.

"Janet Bloom," he said. "It sounds like a command. But you have bloomed."

"And am fading fast."

"Ah, no, in full and glorious bloom. How long have you and Julius been married?"

"Forever," she said gloomily, lighting a cigarette. She smoked so furiously that he had the impression that she was smoking two cigarettes, one with each hand. "You?" she said. "Married?"

"Widower," he said, with just the right note of sadness.

"I'm sorry," she said, happily.

"Oh, it's been a long time," he said. "Tell me about you and Julius. Is it a happy marriage?"

"Happy? Are you kidding? Listen, Marco, what do you say we skip Pavanne. All of a sudden I'm not in the mood for that whole rigamarole, the maître de and the wine and all that service with the cork-sniffing and presenting and turning over ashtrays after every Goddamn flick. Let's just whip over to the Carnegie and get a pastrami and a bowl of soup, okay? Get it over with?"

He leaned forward to give the driver revised instructions, mentally counting his cash. Would he have enough? Pastrami sandwiches were almost as expensive as the quail at Pavanne these days. Then he remembered that he'd spent very little of the money he'd taken from Lynda that morning (was it only this morning? The day had been going on for at least a week); Erwinna had paid the bill at the inn. Her idea, her treat, she'd insisted, although he had made no protest.

Lynda! He'd forgotten to call her!

"I'll have whatever you're having," he told Janet when they were shown to their table, excusing himself. The phone was next to the men's room.

"I was just going out," Lynda said. "I gave up on you."

"I'm sorry, darling. I got all tied up. Couldn't get to a phone a minute sooner."

"Are you through?"

"How I wish I were. It looks like we'll be going on into the wee hours."

"What about then? Those wee hours?"

91

"If I'm not too tired, though I expect to be. Otherwise, I'll call you in the morning. Maybe we can have breakfast."

"I love breakfast."

"Where are you going? To Marilyn?"

"No, I'm steering clear of Ricky for a while. He's been disgusting on the telephone. I'm going to the movies with Natalie."

"Who's Natalie?"

"My mother."

Since when did she have a mother? "That's nice, darling. What are you going to see?"

"'Murmur of the Heart' My mother's dying to see it."

"Awful title, but it's a wonderful film."

"It's not too intellectual for me? It's in French."

"I'm sure you'll enjoy it. It's about incest. Call you soon, darling."

"Good night. Oh, Marco?"

"Yes?"

"I miss you."

"Miss you too, sweetie."

A bowl of matzoth ball soup awaited him on his return to the table.

"This is what came forth from my mother's breasts," Janet said.

"Doesn't seem to have done you much harm."

"You can skip the flattery," she said. "I'm already yours."

He looked at her, alarmed, resting the spoon on the rim of the plate. "I think we should waste a little more time," he said.

"I'm not interested in appearances," she said. "When I lust, I lust."

"I couldn't do that," he said. "To Julius. I wouldn't want to risk his. Friendship."

"You wouldn't risk anything. In fact, it's his pleasure."

"What do you mean?"

"Waiter, bring me a celery tonic. You want a celery tonic, Marco? Make it two. And have you got a full sour pickle? This is practically a cucumber here. Marco, you're gonna love my body."

"I'm sure."

He watched her spread mustard on her sandwich. She did it slowly, sensuously, indecently.

"See, Julius is my frog," she said. "Only he's never gonna turn into a prince. If I couldn't do it, nobody could."

"What do you mean?"

"See, he's impotent. He can't get it up, never could. Never in his life. He's got this big fat doodad and it just hangs there idle."

Her vulgarity almost startled him. The corners of her mouth dimpled bewitchingly.

"You're thinking how coarse I am, right? Well, I say it like I think it."

"That can be dangerous."

"I'm not a hypocrite. And I'm not stupid, either. You probably won't believe this, but I was the smartest girl in my class. Always. And I couldn't even finish high school See, everybody kept trying to jump on me and I got knocked up, God knows who, and when the baby was born dead I just left town and came here and went to work. The first job I ever had was with Julius. He was a wholesale butcher then."

"What color is your hair?" Marco asked, not wanting to know this much about her life. She unpinned her hat and, not taking her eyes from his, took it off and put it on the empty seat between them. Her hair was flaming red, and he was pretty sure it was natural. She was stunning, all right.

"I thought Julius was the richest man in the whole world," she said. "He gave me everything I wanted. He gave me things I didn't even know I wanted. Actually, he taught me how to want." She shook her head sadly. "But he never gave me anything I really wanted."

93

"Why didn't you leave him?"

There was a speck of mustard on her lower lip. He checked an impulse to reach over and lick it off, and instead took the last bite of his sandwich.

"I can't leave him," she said, her head drooping. "He cries."

"I don't understand."

"I mean he cries. If I tell him I want to leave him, he cries and cries, like a baby, like his heart is breaking, and I just can't do it."

Marco was not a reflective man. He was an adventurer, and adventurers don't dwell on the past. The present is what engages them and the future only insofar as it pertains to the present. Only men of conscience live in all the tenses. Therefore, it never occurred to Marco to ask himself how, after his morning with Lynda and his afternoon with Erwinna, he could be swept off his feet in the evening by Janet. "What," he would have asked, if questioned, "has one thing to do with another?" He would have been only half-pretending since he had been enough in the world to know that such things existed as a deep and consuming love for one person, passion, commitment, even fidelity. But never, not even in his marriage to Betsy, though she was as close as he'd come, had he been bothered by any of these feelings. He considered himself a perfect gentleman, faithful to whomever he was with while he was with her. He was attentive and loving, and truly caring. But each moment was precious, to be lived as it presented itself.

"Come on," he therefore said to Janet, motioning to the waiter for the check. "Let's go."

They tore off their clothing and fell upon each other with the greed of teenagers. They didn't even make it to the bedroom, but fell onto the living room sofa and, when that proved too confining, to the floor where, within minutes, simultaneously, they exploded and subsided, gasping for

94

breath.

"You must've been without sex for a long time," Janet said, not unkindly. His impatience had more than flattered her. "It was like fucking a priest."

He wondered how she would have known what that would have been like. "But without the guilt," he said.

"How long has it been, if I'm not being too personal?"

"Not that long," he said, vaguely, slowly running his hand down the long line of her side from her rib cage into the valley of her waist and up again onto the hillock of her hip. She had a lovely well-tended body, not as munificent as Erwinna's nor as youthfully exuberant and texturally perfect as Lynda's, but exciting in its own knowing way. "You can take my haste as the sincerest form of flattery."

"I already did. Do you think if we go inside now and lie down on the bed, we could take it again a little slower?"

CHAPTER ELEVEN

There is little in life more thrilling than the beginning of a voyage with its promise of adventure, events, places, people, the unknown, that lie ahead, that can within limits be imagined but not known, but that are now surely going to be known and added like snapshots in an album to one's store of memories.

It was a sparkling early morning late in May. They stood at the rail, watching the city slowly glide by. The sun, slanting out of the east, turned the patches where it struck the filthy river from dross to diamonds. They had pulled anchor only minutes earlier and already they were rounding the battery and there, ahead, the green lady rose from the sea, brandishing her torch, not nearly as tall, somehow, as remembered.

"It really works," Camilla said, her face lit with excitement. She and Augusta and Marshall were all grinning uncontrollably. The Augusta moved smoothly, almost silently, except for an occasional exuberant blast of its horn. "This elaborate bath toy really works."

Echoing Liberty, Augusta held the wand of her tape recorder aloft, capturing the sounds of the harbor and of their departure. It was her plan to keep a journal of the voyage in sound, as Marshall would do in photographs and Camilla in words. She wasn't sure it would work; she had no idea if the sounds of one port or city would differ from those of another. She debated now whether the conversations around her were a legitimate part of the sound picture, or whether to turn off the recorder. She would leave it on; she could always edit the tape.

"Sinful. Decadent. Depraved. Debauched. Demoralizing," Marshall muttered through his grin. "This is goodbye to my innocence."

"What a lovely vocabulary you have," Augusta said. She had prevailed over his and Aurora's objections and persuaded Marshall to come along. The more she had seen of him, the more she liked him. He was intelligent and capable and as dashing as a prince. He was finished with school, she had argued, and the pay would be good, and since his major was foreign studies how could he resist seeing some of the world that was his concern? But he did resist. He would surely get seasick; he'd never sailed on anything but the Staten Island ferry. He knew nothing about ships or how to sail them; he wouldn't be able to earn his keep. Nonsense, she told him, most of the work on ships didn't require any special knowledge or skills; wasn't literature filled with adolescent lads running off to sea? Besides, he was strong and handy and good with tools. Still, he resisted. He didn't know if he should be away so long, though he didn't say from what. Finally, she took him to see The Augusta and to meet Captain Packer and she could see that she'd won; he was dying to go.

"Anyway, luxury isn't the sin," Augusta said. "Poverty is."

"Gross inequity is the sin," Marshall said, his smile fading. He turned his handsome face to her and she thought she saw rebuke on it. He was still so close to his childhood, no more than twenty-two. She wondered what his childhood had been.

"I'm not going to apologize," she said. "I didn't make this money off the backs of the poor. Why don't we just try to relax and enjoy it?"

"How would you define luxury?" Camilla said. "Anything in excess of mere comfort?"

97

"I'd have said anything unnecessary. But I'm willing to grant more than necessity, Marshall said. "I'll give you comfort; comfort doesn't seem too unreasonable."

Plunged into luxury, Augusta thought, hoping Marshall wasn't going to assume the role of her social conscience, since she already had one.

"Voltaire said that when it's a question of money, everyone is of the same religion."

"You know that's not true," Marshall said.

"I once sailed with my mother on what is called a luxury cruise," Camilla said, anxious to change the subject, or at least to alter it. "I was eleven."

"I remember," Augusta said. "I was so jealous. Tell Marshall about the widows."

"Who were not merry. And the divorcees who were not gay," Camilla said. There was a sudden blast from The Augusta's horn, E-flat below middle C, and they looked up to the bridge to where Captain Packer was at the wheel. He waved down at them, smiling. They waved back.

"It was an expensive trip," Camilla said, "and so the passengers were almost entirely wealthy elderly women, most of them considerably older than my mother."

The Verrezano Bridge lay ahead. A helicopter spun noisily overhead. Ellis Island lay to their right and a hundred yards ahead a fat beetle of a ferry buzzed across their path.

"Whenever a wind came up and the ship lurched, the elderly ladies would start falling down and breaking their limbs," Camilla said. "We hit some really heavy seas for a couple of days and the ship's doctor, possibly because he was so overworked, was drunk every night. By the time we left Lisbon, our first port, where a brace of orthopedists had been flown to join the ship, there were so many slings and splints and wheelchairs and crutches that we looked like a geriatric hospital ship."

The city receded behind them, diminishing. How different it looked from here, how compact. It was easy to imagine how one well-aimed mega-bomb could dispose of it all.

"At the cocktail hour, nonetheless, as if by magic, a flock of aging bachelors in tuxedos would appear and ask those widows still on their pins to dance. These men were hired for just that, to dance with the single women. It was a first class cruise."

"Luxury," Marshall said with disgust," is never having to sit one out."

"The men were not supposed to have two consecutive dances with the same woman. It was one of the rules. No favoritism, no hint of romantic temptation. But they were hard put to keep busy, what with all those women who were hors de combat. My young and intact mother was virtually tossed from one partner to the next, the belle of the ball."

"Or, tossed thus, the ball of the ball."

"Well, there are plenty of dance partners for you two belles on this cruise," Marshall said, encircling Augusta's waist with his arm and waltzing her three steps back and three forward. There was Avery Packer and his first mate, Bert, a dour lanky man, and Jacques, the chef, a tiny sprightly man with a waxed moustache. They would be taking on two more crew in Florida two days hence, and a final man in San Francisco. The other woman aboard was Rosetta, Jacques' wife and helper, who would also serve as stewardess. Marshall was crew, too, and should not have been rail-leaning like a passenger; he was supposed to be up on the bridge learning something.

The ship's whistle tooted (C-sharp) as they glided beneath the Verrezano Bridge. Soon they would be out in the open sea. A stiff breeze came up, causing them to hug jackets and sweaters closer. The air smelled of dead fish and salt and oil, but over or under these smells it smelled of air.

99

Ben had not come to see Augusta off. They had said their farewells last night, Augusta rather tearfully, because she suspected that between them things were changing and might never be the same. Ben was surprisingly cheerful, resigned to not seeing her for some time. He had his new life to arrange.

Minutes before they were to lift anchor, Michael Bell, one of the men in Camilla's therapy group, had appeared. How had he found out where they were docked and when they would be sailing?

"I never mentioned it in group, did I?" she asked.

"You should know as well as anyone how brilliant I am," he said.

"In mathematics."

"Brilliance has a way of spilling over," he assured her. He was tall and rangy, with a wild black beard and beautiful green eyes. He had started a computer programming business a year earlier that was already immensely successful. He invariably arrived at the group sessions late and breathless, as though coming there was a sudden, hysterical afterthought and he had run all the way. Some members had suggested that he not bother to come at all since he obviously no longer needed them, which was true, and came only because he was in love with Camilla, which was also true. Camilla had never taken him seriously, perhaps because before she even knew him she knew too much about him.

"He's too young," she told Augusta.

"He's only a year younger than you. What does that mean?"

"It means that when I'm eighty-seven, he'll only be eighty-six."

"He's interesting," Augusta said. "And intelligent. And I think he's sexy."

"You do? I can't see him objectively."

"That sweet sadness."

100

"It's because he had terrible acne as an adolescent."

"Oh, Camilla!"

"It's true. Imagine when you're so self-conscious and vulnerable just being an adolescent what an agony really violent acne must be. It could leave you scarred for life."

The ship was moments from casting off. Michael Bell pulled Camilla away from the group and, towering over her, though she was not short, said, "When you get back we're going to be married. I put all our data into the International Commander E Plotter and that's what it says to do."

"You programmed me?" Camilla sputtered. "You put me in your machine?"

"I processed you," he said. "Both of us. It's a smart machine. I've never known it to be wrong."

They were leaving. Bert called a warning and Michael leaned to kiss Camilla, a chaste, friendly kiss. "Have a good trip," he said, "but not too good. And try not to think about me every single minute, but do keep in mind our future together."

A small group of Augusta's students had surprised her by coming to see her off, and when they were gone and the anchor was grinding up, Oswald Summerville had come flying onto the deck. He grasped Augusta's hand.

"Late, late, late," he moaned. "Almost too late. Forgive me."

"Thanks for coming, but you'd better go," she said.

"Take care," he said, squeezing her hand. "Don't take any stupid chances. What I mean is, please come back safely."

"I intend to," she assured him.

"And don't worry about anything here."

"I won't."

"Send me a postcard."

She smiled, watching him lope off, his gait awkward and uncoordinated, his arms flapping at his sides like the wings of a large waterfowl preparing for take-off. He and Michael Bell walked off together, deep in conversation.

They had passed under the bridge, but Brooklyn still lay off the portside.

"It's too bad Ben couldn't come along," Camilla said, but Augusta was glad he hadn't.

"And Marco," she said. She had invited him, sure that he would leap at the chance, but he had declined. He couldn't risk losing Corned Beef & Cabbage now that it was, he felt sure, within his grasp. He had looked tired and Augusta thought a restful sea voyage might be just the thing, but he was not tired, he said, merely drained. Would he then, she asked, consider living in the house during their absence. "It would mean so much to me to know you were there keeping an eye on things," she said, seeing his struggle to mask his delight. "Just temporarily. You wouldn't need to give up your own place."

"I think I might be able to arrange that without too much trouble," he said.

Brooklyn had just dribbled into the past when Rosetta appeared bearing a tray with frosted glasses and a bottle of champagne. She was even shorter than Jacques, though plump. They made a charming couple; you could put them, Augusta thought, on top of a wedding cake.

"It is a tradition," Rosetta said, smiling, as she set the tray down on a cocktail table around which cushioned deck chairs squatted. They had not yet had breakfast; it was only eight-thirty. "To toast the voyage."

"Luxury is champagne before breakfast," Marshall said, though he didn't look unhappy.

"Wait for me," Captain Packer called down. They were well out of the harbor, now, with clear sailing ahead. He turned the wheel over to Bert and, solid and dazzling clean in his white uniform, trotted down to the deck to join them. He took the chilled bottle in its napkin and worked off the

102

cork, shooting it over the railing into the sea. "A one-gun salute," he said, filling the glasses and handing them around to everyone.

"To The Augusta ," he said, raising his glass.

"To a happy trip," Camilla said.

"To Alfred Nickleby," Augusta said.

"To Alfred Nickleby," they all agreed.

CHAPTER TWELVE

The deserted building, a lumbering square mass, was a hideous example of whatever its genre. Windowless, its facade was composed of large bricks of gray stone among which, at intervals, ugly blackened red bricks had been imposed in fanlike sequences, like eyebrows poised uselessly over nothing. There was a double doorway of painted wood, scarred and scored with graffiti, and above this, carved in the gray stone, as solemnly self-important as if the structure had been a government building, or a national museum, the words: TURKISH BATH.

Erwinna stood on the farthest reach of the sidewalk, contemplating this unprepossessing edifice in the first dark of evening. She could not imagine that anyone, even its perpetrator, an architect no matter how besotted with the age in which he'd lived, and champagne guzzled from his lady's slipper, could ever have thought it attractive. Now, additionally dingy with the years of its life and neglect, it was a positive horror. Just the thing; she would buy it.

Paul had brought it to her attention a few months ago. It had been scheduled for demolition and then, for no conceivable reason, spared. It could be bought, Paul said, for a song. It could be made, Paul said, into a terrific gallery. Paul wanted it. More explicitly, Paul wanted her to buy it for him. The spaces were perfect, or would be once the interior was gutted, and the absence of windows was an advantage. Furthermore, the location couldn't be better, though it appeared to be a slum. The building hovered between the lower East Side and Soho, a spot that had once been convenient to merchants and hat manufacturers who could come

104

for an hour to "shvitz out the poisons," as Erwinna's Jewish great-grandfather would have said.

She felt a twinge of guilt because she wasn't buying it for Paul. There was more to running an art gallery, she had told him, than buying a building. She conceded that he had a good eye and had always enjoyed looking at paintings, but he was too young and inexperienced to start a gallery of his own. If he was serious, she told him, he should get a job in someone else's gallery for a year or two and when he had some experience they would see about buying a gallery. She might as well have slapped him. He had sulked off and never mentioned the project again. Nor, as far as she knew, had he sought work in a gallery.

Still unsold, the building hunkered in the middle of its messy, undistinguished street, a few short blocks from the restaurant where she was to meet Paul. Frowning, she studied it a little longer, though the decision was as good as made. She jotted down the name and phone number of the sales agent.

Paul was already there when Erwinna arrived at the restaurant, a small, pretentious, candle-lit, stripped-to-the-brick basement called The Baa-Baa, a name she understood as soon as she walked through the doorway. Men, in couples, sat at every table, some of them holding hands across it. She was the only woman there. How stupid of Paul, she thought, making her way to the table from which he had risen to greet her. Perhaps, she thought hopefully, they would take her for a transvestite.

"Hello, Mother," he said.

"Happy birthday, darling," she said, kissing him, noticing how thin he looked, and how darkly handsome, and how nervous. The table was set for three.

"I've asked a friend to join us," he said. "Someone I want you to meet. I hope you don't mind?"

105

"Lovely," she said, taking a seat and bracing herself. Here it comes, she thought. She must be extremely careful to do and say the right thing. What was the right thing? It was whatever would not alienate Paul, since he already blamed her for so much.

"Any friend of yours, darling," she said. He had not had many friends in his lifetime, never having felt at ease with other boys, except for the occasional stray. He had already ordered wine. He filled her glass and she saw that his hand trembled. Poor Paul. She wanted to cover his hand with her own and tell him that everything would be all right, not to worry. "I only want your happiness," she wanted to say, meaning it. How vulnerable he looked. But before she could reassure him, she saw that he was looking up, his face flushed and alight as though an inner switch had been thrown. She followed his gaze to see striding toward them a tall man, dark like Paul, but strong, larger, older by perhaps ten years. He was smiling at Paul, and then he turned to include Erwinna in his smile. It was a smile of genuine warmth.

"This is Will Kalman, Mother," Paul said shyly.

"How do you do?" Will said, simultaneously taking her offered hand and the empty seat. "Paul has told me so much about you."

Oh God, she thought, checking a primal urge to scream. "And me," she said, "nothing at all about you."

"I'll do that myself," he said charmingly, "as soon as I've negotiated a drink. I need more than wine."

"Oh, so do I!" she said.

A man of princely authority, he motioned and a waiter instantly appeared. Erwinna was impressed. They both ordered Scotch and Paul said he would stay with the wine. Will looked around the room.

"I wouldn't have chosen this place," he said to Paul.

106

"I know," Paul said, blushing. "I knew it was wrong the minute I got here. Someone recommended it. I had no idea."

"The food is probably exceptional," Erwinna said, soothingly, and caught the look that passed between Paul and Will. They were madly in love. She thought despairingly of herself and Marco, then wondered how his meeting with Julius was going. She knew that he had hoped to go to it with a check in hand, and that she had disappointed him. Two hundred thousand was a lot of money to pump into a failing night club, although the Turkish Bath would cost much more than that before she was through with it. She wondered if Marco was worth it, and if she wanted him as much as he wanted that awful place. Men were such idiots. She had never met one she really liked, none of her husbands, not even Marco. But she did want him. She was one of those women who felt incomplete without a man, shameful though she knew this to be, especially since she considered herself to be a feminist.

They studied their menus. They agreed on the rack of lamb. *A point.* Erwinna was not very hungry.

"Will is from Toronto," Paul said. "He's here on business."

"Women's ready-to-wear," Will said. "Paul has designed the fall line for me."

"Paul has done what?"

"I seem to have a flair," Paul said modestly.

"The line is a knockout," Will said. "Paul's a genius."

"He is?"

"You must put Mother's amazement in perspective," Paul said to Will. "There's been no foreshadowing. I never gave any indication."

"You never even seemed to notice. I mean, what could you possibly know about women's clothing?"

"He's a natural," Will said. "His instincts are infallible."

107

"Yes, it's all instinct," Paul said. "Though I couldn't have done it without Will's help and encouragement. He's already taught me so much about the business. Will has a tremendous reputation in the industry. He's very big in Canada, and he's beginning to be known here in New York, too."

"Paul will make me even bigger," Will said, confidently. "He's coming back with me."

"To Canada?"

"Toronto."

"We hope you'll come and visit," Paul said.

"I've never been to Toronto," Erwinna said, stupidly. She felt dazed.

"You'll like it. It's very cosmopolitan."

"You're actually going to live there?" she asked Paul.

"With me," Will said. "I have a house in town. Loads of room. With a garden, though of course in Toronto a garden isn't much use most of the year." His voice changed. "Paul's future is with me," he said. "Paul and I love each other." His face was serene, his deep dark eyes steady. He looked a little the way she imagined Marco might have looked as a young man, but more trustworthy. They might have been father and son.

"I know what a shock this must be for you," Will said. "I want to assure you that I'm not a careless or casual man. Paul's future and his happiness are very important to me."

He was asking her for Paul's hand. Well, perhaps not asking. She turned to Paul. He was blinking back tears.

"I hope you're not too upset, Mother," he said, his voice small, almost a whisper. She looked back at Will and thought, not without envy, how lucky Paul was, what a catch!

"Upset?" she said. She smiled and put her hand over his. "On the contrary. I can hardly wait to buy you a wedding present."

CHAPTER THIRTEEN

Menelaus Talifiero was a woman!

"You're not what I expected," Marco said. Her voice on the telephone was that husky tenor that can so easily belong to either sex. She was a big woman with shoulders, strong neck, coarse black hair cropped short, a full sensuous difficult mouth, dark eyes that flashed like mirrors catching light, sending signals. She wore a mannish gray pinstripe business suit. The nervousness Marco had been feeling vanished.

"Neither are you," she said enigmatically.

"How so?" he asked, surprised that she would have had the imagination to form an expectation. Their phone conversation had been brief and to the point. "What were you expecting?"

"A friend of Tantleman's? Not a gentleman. Someone shorter. Heavier. A different class of person entirely."

"I was expecting a different gender of person. There aren't many women named Menelaus."

"Or men, either," she said.

"Is it an alias?"

"Alias, my ass!" she snorted. "My mother laid the name on me like a curse, a warning, an omen."

"How a warning?" he asked.

"I was her fourth pregnancy, all by different men. Not that she fooled around a lot, she wasn't like that. She was just very trusting."

"So you're part of a large family?"

"No, I'm the only one. She aborted the others. She decided to keep me and give up men. Why am I telling you all this?"

"You were explaining your name, I think."

"Yes. It's not spelled like that Roman."

"Greek. Spartan, actually."

"Whatever. It's spelled like this." She wrote it out in block letters on the back of an envelope. "MEN'LAYUS. "Everyone leaves out the apostrophe."

"Your mother must be an interesting woman."

"Was. Passed away. She was a feminist before her time. A free spirit. Whatever I am, I owe to her."

Marco smiled. "If you don't mind, I'll call you Leah." he said, pronouncing it in French. "You can swap the apostrophe for an aigu."

"No thanks, whatever that is," she said gloomily. "I ought to change it legally, to save all this explaining. On the other hand, you can see how it breaks the ice."

So this was the Mob. The office was strictly business, no frills, like the office of a second string theatrical agent or a fly-by-night entrepreneur, an importer of useless knick-knacks. A scarred desk, a water cooler, a cracked black plastic sofa with brass nail heads, a wooden swivel chair, a soot-encrusted window. The only note of frivolity hung on the far wall, a half dozen black-framed photos of men unsmiling beneath Borasalinos, fat cigars jamming their mouths, signed "To Menny" from Moe, Joe, Vito, etc.

"So enough of this chitchat. Apart from changing my name, what can I do for you?" she said, but before he could answer there was a sharp rap on the door. "Come!" she barked. A hood entered, rain dripping from the brim of his fedora. He placed a bulging, soggy manila envelope on the desk. She glanced at it and said, "Okay, Vince. What's the zip on this one?"

"One oh oh oh two."

She scribbled this on the envelope. "Anyone short?"

"Yeah, the Baa Baa, you know, that fag place. They come up with half. I give them till Tuesday."

110

She made a note and said, "Okay, Vince," dismissing him. When he was gone, she dumped the contents of the envelope onto her desk, a hillock of rumpled cash, and rummaged around in it, extracting a sheet of lined notebook paper on which, Marco could see, a primitive hand had penciled lists of figures. "Just a minute," she said to Marco, "while I check this. Jesus, if there's one thing I hate it's damp money." With the expertise of a croupier, she sorted the bills into neat piles, punching buttons on a desk calculator at intervals. "Sixty-four hundred eighty-two," she said, shaking her head. "That's our worst zip. It hardly pays to keep it going."

"So what you run here," Marco said, surprised that his presence was in no way inhibiting, "is a collection agency."

"You knew that," she said, squinting at him. "You said Tantleman sent you."

"Right. I wasn't sure just what your function was."

"I have various functions," she said, leaning back and lighting a cigarillo. "What function can I do for you?"

He gave her his most engaging smile and took a deep breath. "I want to buy Corned Beef & Cabbage," he said.

"That dump? What for?"

"I think I can bring it back. I have a lot of friends. And ideas."

She blew a long stream of vile smelling smoke at him, her face expressionless.

"So why don't you buy it?"

"I haven't been able to come up with the scratch yet," he said. "Though it's only a matter of a few days. But Julius is of the opinion that a few days is too long."

"Right. His deadline is tomorrow noon."

"Deadline?" His voice quavered. "Tomorrow? Noon?"

"Right."

"Well, that's why I'm here. Though in the future I hope to come with happier proposals than the one I'm about to make."

"I don't sleep with men," she said. "Technically, I'm still a virgin."

"Are you sure that's a ... condition you'd like to retain permanently?"

"Who can be sure of anything in this life?" she said, almost coyly. She got up from her desk and walked over to the filthy window and peered out at the rain. In her man-tailored suit it was hard to tell much about her figure, but her walk and stance were athletic; she was not unaware of her body. "Jesus," she said, going back to her desk and pressing buttons on an intercom. "Where the hell is Pete?" she yelled into it. "He should've been here two hours ago." A voice gargled back that he didn't know where the hell Pete was and should he send a scout. She looked at her watch. "I gotta make the bank," she said. "Give it another half hour, maybe the weather's holding him up." She clicked off the machine and turned back to Marco.

"So? What's your proposition?" she said. "Regarding Corned Beef & Cabbage?"

"I don't know how much Tantleman owes you..."

"Plenty."

"In a few months I'm sure I could resume whatever the payments were if you could forgive his debt and let me take it on."

"We don't forgive."

"That way you'd be getting something instead of nothing. Seems like good business to me."

"So what are you? Getting a business for nothing?"

"Half a business. A partnership. Right now you could hardly call it a business. And not for nothing, for my connections. That's pretty much what you folks do, isn't it?"

"What we folks do is our business."

112

"And what we folks do is your business, too?"

"That's the nature of our business."

"Isn't that greedy?"

"Greed is also the nature of our business. What do you think we're running here, a religion? So what connections?"

"I know everyone," Marco said, lowering his eyes modestly. "The minute word gets out that I've bought Corned Beef & Cabbage, the place will be mobbed ... er, I mean overrun."

"If you know everyone, why do you have to come to us, complete strangers, for the financing?"

"Since it's my understanding that I'd be doing business with you anyway, it seems only practical to start right off as partners."

"We don't do business that way. We like a business to be a going proposition before we move in. Risk is against our policy."

"I can understand that. But in this case you'd have nothing to lose, would you, except the dubious pleasure of killing Julius Tantleman."

Her color rose and she scowled at him blackly. He had said the wrong thing, a wrong word. Pleasure?

"Don't ever talk about killing in this room!" she said between her teeth. "Besides, we don't kill for pleasure. We kill for satisfaction. And only when it's absolutely necessary."

"In this case, Leah, I'd hope it wouldn't be necessary."

"Whatever we do about Tantleman would have nothing to do with any deal we might make with you. I said might."

"If you, er, did away with Tantleman, I wouldn't want to make any deal."

"That's your business. How we deal with Tantleman is our business. It's not that we're unreasonable. If we don't enforce, word gets around and then where are we?"

113

"If you and I reach an agreement, Leah, I want it to be as though I'd bought out Julius and all his obligations to you and your people," Marco said firmly. Although his night with Janet had been both exciting and exhausting (could it ever be one without the other?), it was not guilt that impelled him to fight for Julius's life. Janet had assured Marco that Julius not only knew of and accepted her dalliances but, after the first few nights, pleaded to be allowed to be present, a spectator at her sport. He would sit quietly in a dark corner of the room, unintrusive, inconspicuous, and grateful. Since he couldn't himself perform, he could at least be permitted some vicarious participation. How, Janet asked Marco, could she deny him what was, after all, his only pleasure 'along those lines,' after all he'd given her? Marco, repelled by the idea of Julius slobbering in a corner watching Marco make love to his wife, had no intention of ever permitting this to happen, and, while he might fight to save Julius's life under any circumstances, it seemed especially important to do so now when his death would be so convenient. Marco was a gentleman.

Men'layus Talifiero drummed a pencil on the desktop, studying Marco through narrowed eyes, attempting to comprehend his motive.

"You related to Tantleman?" she asked.

"Oh, no!"

"Old friends?"

"Not at all."

"So why do you want us to transfer his liability to you? Do you know what you're doing?"

"Well, Leah, I hadn't precisely meant..."

"You haven't even asked me what the nut is."

"The nut?"

"How much."

"How much, then?"

"Plenty."

"What's plenty?"

"Quarter of a million. And there's the interest rate on top of that. We run a little higher than Master Card. Figure forty percent."

"Not a bagatelle," Marco conceded, shrugging. "But not unmanageable, either." There was always Augusta. If pinch came to shove, after all, between compliance with the unreasonable wishes of a dead man who meant nothing to her, and the murder of her own father, he knew she wouldn't hesitate to save him. Erwinna, too, though he would hate to have to go to her in such desperate circumstances; she would think it unforgivably messy of him.

"Of course I'd need a reasonable amount of time," Marco said. "And I'd also want a cash advance of, say, another hundred thousand." The words were out before he knew he was going to say them, but he instantly knew that they were inspired; chutzpah was what was demanded at this stage of their negotiations. Chutzpah was self-confidence. He saw Talifiero smile, though it was a smile remote from any suggestion of humor. "I'd want to refurbish, spruce the place up. It's looking stale. And I want to put in a kitchen and get a license to serve food. Nothing heavy or elaborate. I have an idea for a sort of strolling antipasto. Food is always good for the bar business." He hoped he sounded as if he knew what he was talking about since he didn't; he was improvising.

"A strolling antipasto?"

"Not on the dance floor, of course. Among the tables."

The intercom crackled and a voice growled, "Pete's here."

"It's about time," Talifiero said. "Send him in."

"I think maybe you better wait till your meeting in there is done," the intercom said.

She frowned. "It's okay, let him come in."

115

The door opened to admit an anthropoid with overlong arms, even wetter than Vince, with shoulders sagging dispiritedly. He spread the hands at the end of his unusual arms palms up to denote their emptiness, and grimaced at Talifiero.

"Again?" she said.

"Yeh."

"The whole thing?"

He nodded. "Someone knows my route. Jumped me right there in the lobby of The Winged Knish, my last stop."

"Christ, Pete, that's the third time since February for you. What the hell's the matter with you?"

"I'm not the only one."

"At least did you get a look this time?"

"Naah. Come up like always from behind." He shook his head. "Gone by the time I pick myself up off of the floor."

"Whoever they are, they know what they're doing," she said grimly. "You think it's the O'Hara bunch?"

"Naah. They got too much respect. These people gotta be amachoors."

"Yeah. You're right. We're just gonna have to send you out in teams for a while. Buddy system. Ten paces apart."

"Yeah."

"I'll call a meeting this week. You can go now, Pete."

When Pete was gone she said to Marco, "As you can see, we got a problem. Our men are getting mugged. Somebody's stealing from us, somebody with inside information." She looked incredulous. "It's just our weekly nickle dime runs, but they're making monkeys out of us. Not that they have all that far to go with that ape Pete." Marco made an effort to look sympathetic, wondering why he, a stranger and an outsider, should be privy to what must surely be confidential, these glimpses of The Mob's inner workings. Talifiero behaved as though they had nothing to hide. She must judge him to be either trustworthy or incredibly stupid. He hoped it wasn't the latter while wondering why it

116

should be the former, and whether it was a good sign or a bad one.

"The buddy system sounds like a good plan," he offered inanely, conspiratorially.

"We don't like to do it because it can be cumbersome. We want our people to be as inconspicuous as possible. With two apes out there there's twice the risk of being noticed." She got up and went over to the window again. "What a filthy day," she said. "Well, March, leave me your phone number and I'll try to have an answer for you in a few days."

At least, Marco thought, that might mean a temporary reprieve for Julius. "What do you think the chances are?" he felt emboldened to ask.

"I don't know. I think you have talent. What I don't understand is why at your age you shouldn't already have it made."

He was startled. It was a question he'd never troubled to ask himself, having always been a believer in luck which, though it affected him, lay outside his control.

"Thank you for your frankness," he said. "Some day when we're better acquainted, I'll tell you the story of my life. And you can tell me yours."

"I look forward to that," she said.

CHAPTER FOURTEEN

The two crewmembers who came aboard in Florida were twins, playfully named Cleo and Patrick, almost identical except for their sex. They were faun-like, extremely beautiful, and could not have been more than eighteen years old, but Avery Packer assured Augusta that they were experienced sailors, very good at their jobs. Patrick was a navigator and an all-around deckhand and Cleo an engineer.

Marshall instantly fell desperately in love with Cleo but she was cool to him. He took this for a racial slight, although Augusta and Camilla thought not. The twins were inseparable, holding themselves politely aloof not only from Marshall but from everyone. They were a community unto themselves, totally self-sufficient, and seemed, in fact, to come fully alive only in each other's presence. They shared a double cabin and at night Marshall, in the adjoining cabin with Bert, could hear their laughter and, sometimes, music. Cleo played flute and Patrick the violin. They played well and it wrung Marshall's heart. He himself played guitar and sang in a charming, husky baritone from a wide repertory of work, protest, and folk songs, which even Augusta, who had little patience for the simple-minded repetition of most folk music, enjoyed. Since Marshall considered his singing to be a form of proselytism, he was not shy about performing, and had done so several evenings in the lounge off the dining room.

The lounge was equipped with a piano. Augusta was teaching Camilla how to play. She learned quickly and every morning that they were not in port, Camilla diligently practiced. There was also a projection booth and a large movie screen, curtained off when not in use, and, off the lounge a small library and writing room lined with an interesting collection of glass-enclosed books, which Augusta pored over, seeking further clues to Freddy, who must have put them there. His tastes were classical and eclectic, but she found a good choice of relatively contemporary fiction and biography, and a disproportionately large section of poetry from Auden to Yeats, the pages dog-eared and with passages underscored in yellow marking pen. Happily, the margins were free of comment. Augusta, usually annoyed by books defaced by previous readers whose opinions she preferred not to have intrude on her own, was grateful for the yellow markings, which she knew must be Freddy's. She studied them carefully, like a hound on the scent, trying to imagine to what in his life the scored passages spoke.

They had been at sea a little over two weeks and time, far from hanging heavy, flew by. Except for a few hours off Cape Hatteras, and a brief stretch before entering Port Everglades, the voyage had been calm, the Augusta riding smoothly over the sea, rocking gently, making excellent time. The sea gradually changed as they journeyed south, from the cold gray-blue of the north to a greener blue, the clear aquamarine that reflected the changed sky and the soft, slow air. There had been days of trade winds and of watching the silver darts of flying fish set in motion by the churning of the ship.

They stopped for an afternoon in Cartagena, just long enough to wander through the old walled city from the Clocktower Gate to the Plaza Bolivar where the Palace of Inquisition stood. The guidebook informed them that it held the government tourist office as well as an interesting museum of torture instruments. It seemed an odd and unfortunate combination and Camilla and Augusta chose not to go inside.

"The port master couldn't find any record of The Divine Sara's stopping here," Avery Packer told them when they

119

returned to the ship. "Which doesn't mean much. He didn't try too hard. I'm pretty sure there'll be something in Panama."

The following evening, Camilla wrote in her journal:

"The process of traversing a canal was probably inspired by the toilet, but instead of being flushed down, you are flushed up, though I suppose this is reversed on the return. Gatun Lake, which looked from the ship, like an emerald-green paradise, is treacherous, Avery told me, crawling with alligators and snakes and other poisonous things. Avery is our guide. I hope I'm not falling in love with him. Actually, I probably am, but it's no doubt the Mt. Everest syndrome again... because he's there, and seems so unattainable, and such a challenge. Five children. I'd never take a man away from a woman who's borne him one child, much less five. I know just what the group would say and, boring though they are, they'd probably be right. He does seem attracted to me; I could swear I'm getting signals. Should I have a tiny harmless affair with him, just for the length of the trip? I would, if I thought I could keep my feelings out of it, though when have I ever been able to keep my feelings out of anything?

"It's been a happy trip, so far. Everyone seems compatible. No villains, yet. Maybe Bert will turn out to be one, though I don't know why I should think that. Just something familiar there, something that makes me uncomfortable, though I can't put my finger on what it is...not menacing, really, but as though I knew him in another life where I wasn't happy.

"What this trip is costing! Marshall broods about it and we go on talking endlessly about money and luxury, trying to feel miserable with guilt, but failing. Marshall says he can't stand thinking about all the better ways the money could be spent, that this trip is whimsical. Gus says he's right (she's probably sorry she brought him along), but promises that when the trip is over she'll match the cost with

120

a donation to Marshall's favorite cause. No matter what it is? he asked, and she said yes, well maybe, as long as it isn't terrorism, and of course she'll have to know what it is. He agreed and seems much cheered up. But Gus has been quiet and moody, not herself, as though she's under some kind of spell. I've never known her like this and I don't like it. I think she's lost weight, too, though I can't imagine how, Jacques' meals being what they are. I hope it's only that she's missing Ben, but I somehow don't think so."

They were sailing north along the Mexican coast. In two more days they would reach Puerto Vallarta, where they would stop for a few days, then on to San Francisco. From there, they would sail west to Hawaii. That would be the real beginning of the trip. Augusta, on deck, was reading poetry, half listening to Camilla practicing Clementi. The ship was making good time. The engines purred, a sound so soothing that half the time she was unaware of it. How sensuous it was, lying on the cushioned deckchair, the gentle motion of the ship, the smell and feel of the soft pure air and the warm sunlight, all that sea, all that sky, the faint taste of salt on her lips, this world all blue and green and golden. Sunsets were a gaudy irresistible show and nights a dazzle of stars and moonstruck water. Raising her eyes from her book, she looked with pleasure at Patrick at work on the forward deck. They were constantly chipping, caulking, repainting. Nothing, Avery said, was impervious to sea air, and if they didn't keep at it, by the time their journey ended the ship would be fit for the scrapheap. A marvelous skipper, he had thought of everything to make their trip perfect. She was convinced that he had hired Patrick and Cleo as much for their esthetic as their utilitarian value. They were lovely to watch, no matter what they were doing, with their long graceful limbs, their sleepy doe eyes, their sculpted bronze faces, like Greek youths. Augusta, who hadn't touched a cello in five years, thought she might buy one in

San Francisco, and some music, and play with Patrick and Cleo. She tried to remember what was in the literature for flute, violin and cello. Of course, she would have to ask them first; they were strange and skittish and independent, and likely to say no.

Imagine being able to buy a cello as though it were a box of tissues! She remembered what a gift her first real cello had been, and how expensive it had seemed. It frightened her to think of the power of money and the ease with which, in spite of her defensiveness with Marshall, she was growing used to it. She had never thought to bring her cello from home and it seemed madness to buy another, but she knew she would do it, simply because she wanted it. It was a little terrifying to know that, without even having to think twice, she could act on any whim, any desire, anything, that is, that money could buy. She was going to have to be very careful.

She listened to Camilla at the piano. She was making progress, but the piano needed tuning again. Augusta had already tuned it twice. She hoped Camilla wasn't growing too fond of Avery. Camilla was always falling in love with married men and then, feeling responsible to their unknown wives, torturing herself. With five children, Avery was out of the question. He often spoke of them, but had never mentioned his wife, which seemed peculiar. It would all come out in time; the ship was too small and they too much together for serious secrets.

She thought of Uncle Freddy doing this trip alone (oh, really! she must stop thinking of him as 'Uncle'), and wondered how he had managed the solitude. They had checked the canal's records for the year of his voyage and found that the Divine Sara had gone through eight years earlier on the twenty-fifth of June, already days behind their own schedule. He would have had to drop anchor when he slept but they, with their crew, kept going around the clock.

122

Inspecting the rails for paint damage, Patrick had moved closer to where she sat. She called out to him and he turned his head and loped to her side.

"Marshall tells me you and Cleo play flute and violin," she said. "If I were to get a cello, would you let me play with you? I could pick up some music, too. The London trios, and there's a lovely piece by Rorem."

The purity of Patrick's face during her speech remained unmarred by expression. "I'll go and ask Cleo," he said, and bounded off. It must have been a difficult decision; half an hour passed before he was back.

"Cleo says all right," he said. "But it would have to be up to us when we played. You see, we only play when we feel like it and we never know when that will be."

She nodded, disappointed. They couldn't be as good as Marshall claimed if they were so undisciplined. She knew it would require many hours of practice before she approached her own standards after the long neglect. Patrick stood at her side, not quite looking at her, waiting.

"Where did you study?" she asked.

"We're self-taught. We're both naturally musical. It's in our genes."

"Oh, then your parents are musical?"

"Not our mother. We don't know who our father is. But Mother had affairs only with famous conductors."

"Why was that?"

"We aren't sure. She never said. She's a strong woman and we think there aren't many men masterful enough for her. She adores conductors. She goes to concerts the way people go to ballet, with her eyes more than her ears."

This was a long speech for Patrick. Augusta felt flattered.

"Where did you learn about ships?"

"From Mother. She's spent half her life aboard yachts, as a guest, and has almost always made it a condition that we

123

be invited, too, and made to work in some capacity. She didn't like to leave us behind. It's only in the last year that we've been signing on on our own." Another long speech, delivered rapidly in a lilting voice. She had the feeling that he was delighted to be telling her all this. "This trip is very different from the ones we're used to."

"How so?"

"The drinking and the sex. We always felt that yachting trips were carefully arranged prolonged parties designed, you know, to be a sort of total sensual experience for every guest. The great luxury liners try for that, like the grand hotels, with flawless service and haute cuisine and attention to details like fresh fruit and flowers in your room, wonderfully fragrant soaps changed daily, like the linens, silver-wrapped chocolate on the pillow of your turned-down bed at night. But they can't do much about the mix of people. On a yacht the guests are thoughtfully chosen by the host because he finds them attractive or gifted or witty and he expects them to amuse and entertain each other."

Augusta smiled, surprised by his volubility. He sounded like a brochure. "Does it work out that way?" she asked.

"Sometimes. But there's often some incredible antipathy, two people who can't stand each other, or someone who slides into an alcoholic depression and never comes out of it, or a movie star everyone's been looking forward to meeting who turns out to be stupid and boorish."

"Yes, I can see that this trip would be different."

"For one thing, we're all crew, except for you and Miss Stone. And there's something ... well, virginal about this trip."

"We've never done it before."

"It's not just that. I feel the heart of it is in the voyage itself, not in the life on board." He smiled down at her, the brown centers of his beautiful almond-shaped eyes deepen-

124

ing. "In that respect, it's the exact opposite of your usual yachting trip, and purer."

"I hope you and Cleo won't find us too dull," she said.

"Oh, no! We're never bored. There's always so much to think about, isn't there?"

"Cleo, too?"

"Cleo has even more to think about. She has her engines. She absolutely adores machinery, whereas anything more complicated than a can opener is a complete mystery to me."

"Did you and Cleo ever sail with Mr. Nickleby? No, of course, you'd have been too young."

"We did, though. I think we were nine. It was only for a little while, between Naples and Madeira, with stops between at Tangier and Barcelona and Majorca. We saw a bull-fight in Palma and Cleo and I hated it and were sick for two days. Mother was ashamed of us but Mr. Nickleby was so concerned and tender with us you'd have thought he was our father."

"Perhaps he was," Augusta said.

"Oh, no, there was nothing like that between him and Mother. I'm sure of it. He was the kind of man who, if he'd had children, would never have let them out of his sight."

"You liked him?"

"We loved him. We wished we'd been able to know him better. We cried for days after we heard of his death. It's because this was his ship that Cleo and I were so eager to sign on. We like to think we feel his presence."

"I feel it, too," Augusta said, her finger marking the place in the book on her lap, still burning from the underscored lines where it rested, lines from Roethke's "Words for the Wind": "What time's my heart? I care/ I cherish what I have/ Had of the temporal/ I am no longer young/ But the winds and waters are;/ What falls away will fall;/ All things bring me to love."

Patrick went back to work, and Augusta sat on, reading. What time's my heart, how lovely that was. The clock of her own heart kept time while she searched in another book for the lines from Horace she had read that morning.

"Away with desire for the unripe grape! Soon for thee shall many-colored autumn paint the darkening clusters purple. Soon shall she follow thee. For Time courses madly on, and shall add to her the years it takes from thee."

These lines, too, were underscored. He had left clues everywhere, clues and messages, what he thought, feared, dreamed. With each new one, his reality deepened, the reality of his life and, with it, the reality of his death and her own growing sense of loss. She wondered at the bottom of what sea he lay, or rather, his bones, picked clean by fish, his romantic heart carried off in a thousand tiny pieces, for it was beyond her to imagine sharks for him, only flocks of kind little fish with tender mouths nibbling like kisses.

"A dollar for your thoughts," Camilla said. She had finished her practicing and now lay on the deckchair beside Augusta.

"Oh, Camilla," she said, unable to prevent the tears that welled up, "you don't want my thoughts, especially at that inflated price."

Camilla reached for her hand and held it tight. "What is it, Gus?" she asked. "Please, Gus."

"I don't know," she said, her voice at once a sob and a laugh. "It's so weird. I keep thinking about him..."

Camilla smiled. "Then you do miss him."

"Yes. It's so odd."

"It's only natural."

"No, it's completely unnatural. How can you miss someone in retrospect?"

"How else would you miss anyone?"

They turned to look at each other, each slightly annoyed with the other.

126

"But if he was never anything in my life," Augusta said, "What am I missing?"

"How can you say that he was never anything in your life?"

"He never was!"

"That's disgusting. He'd be appalled to hear you say that."

"Not at all. I'm sure he never thought otherwise."

"Augusta! Am I losing my mind?"

Augusta began to laugh, then could not stop. "We've been having two separate conversations, Camilla. You thought it was Ben we were talking about."

"I was certainly talking about Ben."

"Not I."

"Who else?"

"Freddy."

"Who's Freddy?"

"Nickleby."

"Uncle Freddy? What do you mean?"

"Oh, Camilla, it's as though I'm caught in something invisible. I'm becoming obsessed."

"But I don't understand. He's been dead all these years. And he never meant anything to you when he wasn't."

"Yes, but I'm beginning to really know him. And in some odd, impossible way, I think I'm falling in love with him. I think about him all the time."

"That's disgusting!"

"Yes."

"It will pass," Camilla said. Augusta was much too level-headed. She sat in silence for as long as she could bear it.

"Let me tell you about these spiders," she said at length.

"What spiders?"

"I forget what they're called. What's interesting about them is that the female eats the male right after he's impregnated her."

"Not out of anger, I'm sure. Probably to feed her unborn."

"Yes, he's all protein. But apart from that, here is this male spider whose sole function in life is that one grand spilling of his seed in the exact right spot, which is a lot harder for these spiders because of the way they're built."

"Love finds a way."

"Sometimes the male tries to prevent the female from devouring him by first spinning a web around her, but he almost never succeeds. The female, you see, is much larger and stronger."

"Camilla, why are you rattling on like this? It's all very interesting, but I fail to see any relevance."

"I see it as a sort of metaphor," Camilla said darkly. "Though I hope I'm wrong."

CHAPTER FIFTEEN

"Please, Ma, just do this one thing for me," Lynda pleaded.

"This one thing! That one thing! The ones add up, Lynda, and then they aren't ones anymore. Where's your arithmetic?"

Except for her appetite, the only big thing about Natalie Schwart was her voice. Even when she tried to restrain it, as she was doing now because they were dining in a restaurant so awesomely expensive that its patrons accorded it the same hushed respect they brought to funeral parlors, her voice boomed forth, sonorous, plangent, stentorian, so that people, turning to its source, turned again unable to credit her as its instrument. She weighed barely eighty pounds, reaching five feet of height only in high heels. Where within that diminutive frame could lungs powerful enough and resonators important enough to produce that sound reside? She was so tiny that for most of her life she had bought her clothing in children's departments. Only after she was widowed and had sallied forth into the business world, where she discovered her destiny by rapidly turning everything she touched to gold, had she been able to afford dressmakers who could fashion to her childlike figure garments suitable to her years.

Lynda, who had grown up in a more felicitous and vitamin-rich environment, had probably reached her full genetic potential, an average height, but she towered over her mother, even at table.

"This isn't about numbers, Ma," she said, though it was. She was trying to persuade her mother to join her in buying out Ricky. Since she and her mother were two-thirds stock-holders of Marilyn, they could force him to sell. "It's about that I can't stand him any more."

"Six months ago you were crazy mad for him." She sipped her Pouilly Fuisse, then buttered a corner of the single hard roll on her bread and butter plate. She was trying to make the *ris de veau* last. It was delicious and had arrived looking like a work of art, but with too much white of the plate showing, especially for this kind of money. Lynda was going through a French phase. That disgusting movie she had taken her to see, Souffle of the Heart, her own son.

"So I made a mistake, Ma. You've made a few yourself."

It was true. Milt had been a mistake she'd been stuck with for years. A shlemozzle, but how could she have known, such a nice looking young man with good manners. Grebnitz was a small village, not much selection when it came to husbands. And he was ambitious, he was saving up to go to America. But leaving Grebnitz made him timid, frightened. The immigration official at whose desk Milt was stopped for credentials had a prejudice against the final letters of the alphabet. "There's too many Z's coming into the country," he muttered furiously. "Too fuckin' many Z's and Y's and W's and not enough vowels. It's unAmerican. Someday you'll thank me for this, Schwart. And if not you, your children." So they arrived in the new country: Schwart from Grebnit. She never forgave him. "What difference?" he'd said through the years, trying to placate her. "It's the difference between right and wrong," she'd screamed back. "Between black and bla."

"Take pride," he said. "The phone book is wall-to-wall Schwartzes, but we are practically the only Schwart."

"Naturally!" she howled.

"Just because you're not wild about him any more is no reason we have to buy him out. Nowhere is it written that in the world of business, partners have to be in love."

130

She was going to have to tell her mother about Marco. Lynda had inherited her mother's knack for business and they had been working together since Lynda's graduation from high school. She knew that her mother trusted her. She had hoped to be able to persuade her mother without bringing in personal motives. But there was no way.

"There's this other man," she said.

"Aha! That you think you're in love with?"

"Yes."

"I knew it! So?"

"So I want him to have Ricky's share."

"Lynda, are you insane? You can't change business partners like they were dance partners."

"Ma, could you please try to whisper. The whole world doesn't have to hear every single syllable."

"Don't worry, the whole world can't afford to be sitting here eavesdropping in the La Rossignol," she said in what she considered a whisper.

"Le."

"So if you want this man to have Ricky's share of the business, why don't you tell him to buy it?"

"Because, Ma," Lynda said, taking a deep breath, though she was not afraid of her mother, "I want to give it to him and don't shout."

"Give it to him?" her mother shouted. "What kind of a fool am I harboring?"

"Try not to think of this as business, Ma. Think of it as something very important to me. This is it, Ma. I know it in every fiber of my heart."

"Who is he?"

"His name is Marco March."

"Italian?"

"I don't know, Ma. What's the difference? He makes Ricky look like something that crawled out of a swamp."

"He loves you?"

131

"I'm sure of it, Ma."

"You're sure of it? That means you don't know. Has he talked marriage?"

"Not yet. But I know once he's a partner in Marilyn..."

"Not necessarily, let me tell you. And he has no money?"

"I don't know, Ma. For all I know he could be very well-to-do."

"So what do you know? What makes you think he wants a share of the club?"

"That I know. And I want to make him a gift of it. He'll be a terrific asset. Aside from how I feel about him, Ma, it will be the best investment we ever made, take my word."

Mrs. Schwart finished the last of the *ris de veau* but continued to stare at her plate, a mixture of disbelief and disappointment on her face. Only a sprig of parsley remained and in desperation she ate it. She knew she was going to give in to Lynda; she always did. On the whole, Lynda was a blessing as a daughter, devoted, smart, and gorgeous. She was proud of her and, more than that, could not imagine how she and Milt had produced such a perfect tall person.

"What makes you think Ricky can be bought out?"

"I've already sort of approached him and he seemed interested. Of course, we'll have to offer him a little more than book value."

"Such as what did you have in mind?"

"I think a quarter of a million should do it."

"A quarter of a what?"

"Relax, Ma. With Marco there we'll make it back in minutes. Anyway, we have to pay Ricky for his part of the name. We have to keep the name and after all the RI is his."

"How much do you figure we're paying for the RI?"

"Please, Ma, don't be sarcastic."

"Since you're making a gift of a quarter of a million of my dollars to a man I never even met, maybe you should make him a gift of a piece of the name?"

"It's already in there," Lynda said, knowing she had won. She squeezed her mother's hand. "I love you, Ma," she said with real feeling. "A girl couldn't ask for a finer mother."

CHAPTER SIXTEEN

"You be dining home tonight, Mr. March?"

"Aurora, --- it makes me uncomfortable calling you Aurora when you address me as Mr. March."

"Then call me Mz Corcoran."

"All right, Mrs. Corcoran, if that's the way you want it."

"That's the way it's suppose to be. You're the master, I'm the servant."

He saw her eyes twinkle as though she had told a private joke, or as though they were playing some kind of children's game. He had sensed immediately that she was a woman of strong character. At times her speech was more southern than at other times, and it seemed to him that the southern vernacular required a degree of concentration on her part.

"Then, yes, Mrs. Corcoran, I'll be dining at home tonight, and there'll be a guest for dinner. Mrs. Sagendorff." He had invited Erwinna, hoping that in this new ambience she might be more inclined to give him money. Time was growing uncomfortably short. "I leave the menu to you."

"And the wine?"

"I'd like to do that. Is there a key?"

"Pick a red," she said, detaching a key from a huge ring of keys that had been weighing down an apron pocket. "From the Romanee region. And if you be wanting a dessert wine, there's a nice Chateau d'Yquem on the staircase wall just over the light switch."

"Thank you, Aurora. Mrs. Corcoran."

When she was gone, he went to the south window that overlooked the garden, and contemplated the profusion of delights that bloomed there. He had appropriated this third floor suite, which was above Augusta's and almost its twin, bedroom, dressing room, bath, and sitting room. There was a small Louis Quinze escritoire where he liked to think he would be writing checks, paying bills, slicing into the day's mail with that charming cloisonne-handled letter-opener. What a beautiful house it was and how immediately he had felt he belonged in it, had been born to it. Years ago when Freddy was alive, Marco had spent many evenings here, but only in the downstairs rooms. It had not occurred to him, in those days, to envy Freddy. He had been married to that horsey woman then, what was her name, Denise. She and Marco had never hit it off. Later, it was poor Peggy, the drunken poet. He wondered if she was still alive and if so, what had become of her. He had liked Peggy, though she'd made Freddy suffer.

Once again, as he had done dozens of times, Marco wondered about Freddy's will and his own exclusion from it. He had felt so close to Freddy. Why, why, why. He thought again of Talifiero's doubts about him, her stinging question about why, at his age, he was still in effect hustling, and wondered if the two things were in any way connected. He was going to have to invent some sort of story for Talifiero, some explanatory history, what a nuisance. He was not a reflective man; perhaps there was something about himself that he didn't understand. If he weren't always so damn busy he might have time to explore these questions, perhaps try a few sessions with a psychoanalyst.

Through the leafy branches of the young Norway maple, he caught sight of a sun-dappled, slight figure below, bent over the annuals, weeding. He peered down, watching the gardener at work, hands deftly plucking between the marigolds, then sit back on his heels and stretch his arms slowly, luxuriously, and Marco saw that it was a woman, a young tan woman, one of Aurora's "family," no doubt, of whom there seemed to be such an abundant supply. He wondered

135

if they were all on the payroll and made a mental note to question Augusta in his next letter. Not that it mattered, really, since someone had to do the work and the work certainly got done; the house was immaculate, the few meals he'd taken here were exquisite and beautifully served, the silver gleamed, the crystal sparkled, his shirts were laundered perfectly, his suits brushed, his shoes polished, his bed turned down at night.

He would tell Talifiero that he was a graduate of Harvard business school, which was true, and had been on Wall Street, which was not true. He had never in his life held a nine-to-five job. He had sold some insurance, real estate, bought job lots of merchandise at very low prices from firms desperate for cash and found buyers willing to pay cash. He had done whatever came to hand that could be done during hours of his own choosing. He had always been his own man, even during the time he'd worked for Freddy, making deals for plastics. He'd had a few notable coups in those years, the big drug firms he'd persuaded to switch from glass containers. He'd tell Talifiero he'd been a commodities trader (not so far from the truth) and had done well for years. Until Betsy died? Yes. That when Betsy died he'd gone to pieces and lost everything.

"It all mattered so much until she died, and then nothing was important anymore," he rehearsed. "There didn't seem to be any reason to go on, except that I had this lovely little girl."

The young woman in the garden gathered up the weeds and turning, looked up to see him in the window. He smiled down at her. She ducked her head and disappeared into the house.

He had not gone to pieces, although he had loved Betsy, and her death, so sudden and tragic, had shaken him deeply. They had gone swimming one night in Lake George, tipsy after a party, and she, a stronger swimmer than he, had

136

struck out and was far ahead of him when she disappeared. He had called and called, dived and dived, searched for her until the moon disappeared behind clouds and a storm came up. He was exhausted and close to drowning, himself. It was three days before her body washed up. The awful thing was that he would never know if she'd done it intentionally. They had had one of their rare quarrels. Over a woman. He no longer remembered which woman, not that it mattered. Whatever affairs he'd had in those days had nothing to do with Betsy.

But he had never in his life gone to pieces. He had merely gone on, not even grateful for his freedom since he'd never felt he didn't have it. What he had felt above everything was unresolved and angry. Angry because he missed her and because it was terrible for Augusta. Unresolved because he would never be forgiven. For two years after her death he explained and explained and Betsy listened, nodding her head, assuring him that she understood, that he was absolutely right. Then she would tell him that it had been an accident, a cramp, that she had died quickly and peacefully, euphoric after the first struggle. She had never meant any of those things she had shouted at him after the guests had left: that he was a false and hollow man, that he lived only in his nerve endings, that charm was all he knew of character, that if it weren't for Augusta she would leave him, she snapped her fingers, like that.

He sighed. No use dwelling on the past, he told himself, turning his thoughts to the evening ahead. Talifiero just might come through and let him have Corned Beef & Cabbage on consignment, as it were, and his evening with Erwinna would turn out to have been unnecessary. He liked Erwinna and knew that once she was there he would enjoy being with her, but he would have preferred to be with Janet, who was newer. He had told Janet about Talifiero and the deal he was trying to make.

137

"Talifiero's crew mean business," he told her. "Julius is in real danger. I think he ought to go away somewhere."

"Julius has been around people like that all his life," Janet said. "It's you I'm worried about. Keep away from them."

"Oh, I'm much smarter than they are."

"Smart has nothing to do with the way they operate. While you're using your noodle to outsmart them, they're being stupid and shooting off their guns with the silencers. Stay away from them, Marco, please. Promise me."

"Darling," he said, touched by her concern. But he knew that they were in the business of making money, not of killing. They didn't make money off corpses. It was broken promises, unfulfilled contracts that made them violent, and he had every intention of sticking to whatever his word with them would be. Still, he would much prefer to buy the place outright from Julius with Erwinna's money and keep his dealings with The Mob at whatever was the necessary minimum.

Erwinna arrived, cool and handsome in a white silk evening suit, half a dozen gold chains adorning her generous bosom. She had just had her hair cut and it curled softly around her head like a cap of feathers. She looked ten years younger. Earlier, Marco had thought that if she was not going to come through with the money, he might break it off with her, simplifying his life a bit, but as soon as he saw her he changed his mind. Why should life be simple?

"I like your new haircut," he said, handing her a martini. He touched her hair gently. "It makes you look so... vulnerable."

"I am vulnerable, darling," she said, pleased that he had noticed. "You mustn't confuse strength with insensitivity." Her eyes swept over the room while he demurred. It was the smaller drawing room he had brought her into, not as impressive as the other, but so much more intimate. "Well, darling, this is nice. What do you hear from Augusta?"

"I had a card from Mexico today. She quoted her friend Camilla, saying that life at sea suits her right down to the ground."

"Life in her house seems to suit you, Marco, right down to the carpet. You look to the manor born."

"Funny, I was thinking the same thing this morning."

"The place becomes you, Marco."

He smiled at her. "It becomes you, too, Erwinna," he said. She looked absolutely right in the room. Janet somehow would not, nor would Lynda. Perhaps he should marry Erwinna, after all. "Tell me about Paul," he said, politely reciprocating. Two parents. She had told him a little on the phone and now she told it to him in detail.

"He's so young," she concluded, "and I know it's just beginning, but somehow it seems like a happy ending."

"A fairy tale," Marco said, and she looked at him with stern rebuke, though the pun had been unintended.

"And you'll think this odd, but I was envious, Erwinna said. "The way the mother of a nubile daughter must sometimes feel, or a father with a son, something I'd never understood before and certainly never expected to feel with Paul, to envy him in a sexual way."

"I suppose lesbian women might feel that if they had sons," Marco said, nettled.

"But it would be different. What I felt was nostalgia for my own youth. And for Paul's lover. Who, by the way, reminded me of you. He looked the way you must have looked at that age."

"You'd have hated me at that age. I was nothing like the perfect polished gentleman you see before you."

"How happy they were. They were like balloons trying to keep themselves from flying off into the blue sky."

The moment they'd finished their second martini, as though that fact had been telegraphed to the kitchen, the pretty young gardener appeared to announce dinner, dressed now in a serving uniform. The table was beautifully set, an arrangement of freshly cut flowers in a crystal bowl at its center. Candlelight sparkled in the wineglasses, danced in the silverware.

Erwinna shared Marco's enjoyment of food. They gave most of their rapturous attention to the dinner, which merited it. A creamy, chive-flecked vichyssoise was followed by roast duckling, crisp-skinned, its meat tender and succulent and slightly pink, just right, accompanied by tiny roasted new potatoes, slender green asparagus lightly laced with golden hollandaise. The wine was as dry and heady as the air of a perfect spring day.

"Ooh and also aah," Erwinna said. "Who is the diamond in the kitchen?"

"Her name is Aurora Corcoran. She came with the house."

"Instead of that dance joint, why don't you open a restaurant with her in command? You'd clean up."

It was the first mention of the club; he had been admirably restrained. He didn't like her referring to it as a joint. For the briefest moment, his hankering after Corned Beef & Cabbage seemed slightly ridiculous to Marco. If this were his real life, and perhaps it now was, would he want anything more? But then what would he do? He would, in effect, be retired. He would grow old.

The young waitress/gardener, whose name Marco had learned was Star Rising (no mother had bestowed that on her, he was sure), silently cleared away the dishes and brought forth a perfect chocolate souffle and the espresso.

"My compliments to your aunt," Marco told her. "A perfect dinner." The girl bobbed her pretty head and smiled, withdrawing with silent grace.

140

"Speaking of 'that joint,' as you call it," Marco said, bulling ahead, "have you given further thought to my tempting proposition?"

"Has all this been to soften me up, Marco? Is that why you invited me here?"

"How could you suggest such a thing, darling? Though it is on my mind. It's almost always on my mind. And I had hoped that the ambience of this place would lend a certain additional credibility to me."

She laughed. "How charming you can be when you're honest."

"I'm always honest."

"And almost always charming. Oh, Marco, I know it's stupid of me to love you, but I do. I'm so ashamed..."

"Once again, thank you kindly. Erwinna, you don't want to be a headmistress all your life, do you?"

"I'm not headmistress. I've been made dean."

"Whatever it is you do there, darling, it would be so much more convenient to have you in the same county, not fifty miles away."

"Sixty-two," she said, pleased. If he wanted her in the same county, why not in the same house? Might that not come next? "The truth is, Marco, I've been too busy lately to think about anything but school." She was lying. She had bought the old Turkish Bath and was deeply involved with designers and architects and contractors. She was having a wonderful time, but her wish to have Marco there with her, sharing it, was outweighed by her wish to surprise him with the finished product.

"What's been keeping you so busy," he asked, annoyed, "with school almost closed for the summer?"

"Don't look so crestfallen, darling. I promise to give it very serious thought. Give me a little more time."

This was as encouraging as she had yet been, and Marco felt sure she was coming around. "Of course, love," he said, clasping her hand. "I wouldn't want you to feel pressured. Too pressured."

"Show me the rest of the house," she said. "I want to see all of it."

Because she had a knowledgeable eye and was interested in the house and its treasures, it was half an hour before they arrived at the third floor.

"These are my quarters," Marco said. They crossed the threshold into the sitting room where the lamps had been lit. She wandered through his rooms murmuring approval.

"Lovely," she said, and "Perfect. The bed has been turned down for the night."

"Would you care to try it? It's an exceptionally comfortable bed."

"Yes," she said, "I'd adore that."

CHAPTER SEVENTEEN

"That must be him now," Avery Packer said. The engines had been warming up for an hour while they waited at the pier along the Embarcadero in San Francisco for the crewman who was to come aboard. "I was just going to give up on him."

The man running up the pier toward them did not look, from this distance, like a sailor. Instead of a duffle bag slung over his back, two large leather suitcases swung from his hands, bumping against his legs, and he wore a suit and a tie. Except for the luggage, he looked like someone's husband racing for the 6:10 back to Larchmont.

"He looks familiar," Augusta said. She and Camilla and Marshall had just come aboard after an exhausting day of sightseeing and shopping. They had prowled Fisherman's Wharf, taken the #60 cable car over Russian Hill to Victorian Square, lunched in Chinatown, browsed in shops where they bought books and music, and, off Geary Street near the Nihonmachi, Augusta had found a Japanese cello she liked well enough to buy. It rested on the deck at her feet in its tan leather case and, tired though she was, she could hardly wait to tune it up and run through whatever memory returned to her.

"He is familiar," Augusta said as the crewman drew nearer. "He's Ben!"

Camilla, who had known all along that it was going to be Ben, was torn between relief that he had shown up, for surely his presence was what Augusta needed to break the nonsensical spell she was under, and nervousness that the surprise might be unwelcome.

"Is it all right?" she asked.

143

"You knew?"

"He wanted so much to surprise you."

"Of course it's all right," she said uncertainly. But when he had leaped aboard, breathless and radiant with excitement, and had gathered Augusta in his arms, she couldn't help feeling pleased with the solid substance of him. He was so unequivocally present.

"Thanks for not leaving without me," he said, shaking Avery's hand. "I had the wrong pier."

"I guess we won't let you navigate."

"I'd have done better with a compass. Ah, Camilla!" He hugged her and kissed her on both cheeks. "You both look absolutely blooming with health."

"We're exhausted," Camilla said.

They were raising the anchor and Avery hurried off to take charge of their departure from the bay, busy even at this hour with commerce and the white triangles of pleasure craft. It was the last they would be seeing of the continent for a long time. They would be at sea for at least a week before their next stop, Honolulu, 2400 miles to the southwest.

"Okay, Ben," Augusta said, "now tell me all about it."

He was still grinning, his candid freckled face transparent with happiness. "It was all arranged before you even left New York."

"So that's why you were so cheerful our last night together."

"Was I? I was trying to appear devastated. Anyhow, I tied up the loose ends at school, then flew out to Santa Cruz and took care of all the preliminaries there. I've got a marvelous house --- you'll love it. I'm free until mid-September."

"We won't be back by then."

"I'll manage to get back from wherever we are." The setting sun was reflected in his green eyes, turning them amber, and the breeze had uncombed his thick thatch of sandy hair, giving him the rumpled boyish look that initially

144

had made him so appealing to her. But they were still in high school then, and she had probably been amused by how unlike her carefully groomed father he was, yet how much more serious.

"You *are* glad to see me?" he asked, suddenly anxious.

"Yes, Ben."

"I've missed you, too," he said happily. "Though knowing that I'd be seeing you soon and being so busy made it bearable. Look at that bridge! And that must be Alcatraz. What a cluttered seascape. Kronheim, I think, in the earlier years."

"It's not a seascape, Ben. It's the actual sea," Augusta said. When she laughed at him, as she often did, for regarding nature only as the subject in the eye of the artist/beholder, he quoted Hazlitt: "Men at first produce effect by studying nature, and afterwards look at nature only to produce effect."

"That's Sausalito on the north shore," Camilla said.

"Who was Sausalito?" he asked, puzzled. "Oh, Sausalito."

"I'm going to freshen up and then I'm going to get me a tall interesting drink," Camilla said. "It's been a long day."

"I think we can all use a drink," Augusta said.

Marshall, who had helped with the anchor and casting off, came over and picked up the cello.

"I'll take this into the lounge for you," he said, then turned to Ben. "Do you need a hand with your bags?"

"Marshall, this is Ben," Augusta said.

"But we've met, haven't we?" Ben said. "Yes, in your house, Augusta. The guerilla on the top floor?"

"The what?" Marshall said.

"Aurora's nephew, aren't you? One of that band of guerillas on the top floor. That's what we took you for."

"You did?" Marshall scowled and turned to Augusta. "You too?"

145

She put a hand on Marshall's arm and smiled at him, embarrassed. "Not seriously, Marshall."

"You had a definitely military look," Ben said.

"Where do these bags go?" Marshall said gruffly, slinging the cello case by its strap across his shoulders and picking up Ben's suitcases. Augusta hesitated. Ben would expect to share her cabin. She didn't want him there; at least not for the time being.

"Since you're crew," Marshall decided, "I guess you can go in number six."

"Hold on, I'll carry those. Like you just said, I'm crew, not a guest."

"Right." Marshall put the bags down. "A little confused there for a minute. All dem slave years."

"Lead the way, Mate," Ben said cheerfully. He grinned at Augusta. "I'll just slip out of these civies and into some skivvies, if that's the right word."

"With crew like you and Marshall," Augusta said, "we'll be leaning heavily on God."

"Nonsense, I'm going to be very good at this." Ben said, following Marshall inside.

When they reconvened, they were well out of the bay and San Francisco was a distant cluster of stars on the horizon. A stiff breeze had sprung up out of the northeast. The sea rose and fell with it, but the Augusta rode the swells gracefully, forging ahead through the troughs and over the crests with a steady rocking motion that was far more soothing than alarming. After almost three weeks, this was their first rough patch of sea. Camilla, behind the bar, was filling drink orders, while Patrick sat crosslegged at Augusta's feet. She had the cello out of its case and between her knees where it was softly singing.

"It comes back," she said, "though my fingers feel like kindling wood."

146

"It's a fine cello," Patrick said, watching her fingers on the strings, his eyes shining. "It's going to be fun playing with you, Augusta, when you've had a little practice."

She laughed, looking down at his beautiful upturned face. A professional, she was not accustomed to being patronized, and certainly not by an untutored child. He was perfectly serious, his youthful face sweet and guileless. He raised his glance from her hands, for she had ceased playing.

"Thank you, Patrick," she said, resting the bow in her lap, trying not to show her dismay at what she now saw in his eyes. It looked suspiciously like adoration. Since that moment a few days ago on deck when she had broken through his silence, it was as though she had waved a magic wand that had caused the imprisoning walls of his reticence to tumble, and he had hardly shut up since. Although he was amusing and articulate and charming, he was at moments tiresome in the way of a puppy who is constantly frisking at people's feet, being adorable. Once or twice at dinner, Augusta had seen Cleo stare with disbelief at her brother, as though he had become someone she no longer knew. Perhaps he had.

Ben, changed into slacks and a sport shirt, lurched into the room just as the ship dipped into the trough of a huge wave.

"Dandy ship you've got here, Augusta," he said, leaning to kiss her cheek, "though none too steady."

"The ship's steady enough," Patrick said. It's the water beneath it."

"This is Patrick," Augusta said.

Followed by Marshall, Cleo now entered, a grease smudge on her cheek. "And his sister Cleo, our engineer. Meet Ben, our new crewman."

Smiling affably, Ben shook their hands. "I've been excused from duty," he said, "this being my first night." He was to report to the bridge at six in the morning. "Camilla,

147

if you're tending bar, I'd love a vodka and soda with a squeeze of lemon. A goodly squeeze. Have to be wary of scurvy now that we're on the high seas."

"Have you done much sailing?" Patrick asked him politely.

"None at all."

"Oh, then you're a friend of Augusta's, not of Avery's."

"A very good friend of Augusta's," Ben said, grinning at her. "Cleo, I'd like to see the engine room some time, if that's permitted."

"Are you interested in engines?" she asked, "I'd love to show them to you." People, she had noticed, were rarely interested in engines. No one here, not even Marshall, had asked to see them. It was one of life's small mysteries.

Camilla poured a beer for Marshall and a coke for Cleo, which Marshall carried to her, sitting beside her, all solicitude, as though she were an invalid. Camilla watched his face, tender when he looked at Cleo, harden with faint dislike when he turned to Ben, who was telling Cleo about his fascination with the idea of engines. They were the heart of machines on which, though their origin was so relatively recent, mankind had come to depend for so much. Cleo, as engineer, was the physician who kept their ship alive. Marshall observed that along with dependency on engines had come an equal dependency on fuel, the heart's blood, and look what that was doing to the world!

"We'd all be better off if we could return to sails and wind, horses, beasts of burden," Marshall said.

"Back to nature," Patrick said dreamily. "Think of it, the greening of the highways. The unpaving. The death of shopping malls."

"The freedom from welfare for all who've been replaced by machines," Augusta said. "We'll spin cloth, make candles, split wood, maybe even read books."

148

"Lovingly printed on hand presses," Camilla said. "On handmade paper. The world as crafts fair."

"Crafts fairs can be so boring," Ben said. "The same stuff over and over again."

"If the world were like that, "Cleo said shyly, blushing at the sound of her own voice, "then I would have to invent the engine. I think engines are lovely." Marshall smiled at her adoringly, but she wasn't looking at Marshall. He couldn't bear it.

"Yes, we can't blame engines for man's abuses," he said.

"Oscar Wilde said that the Greeks were right, civilization requires slaves," Augusta said. "That unless there are slaves to do the ugly, horrible, uninteresting work, culture and contemplation are impossible. And that, since human slavery is wrong and demoralizing, the future of the world depends on mechanical slavery, the slavery of the machine."

Ben, who had been staring across the room at a painting on the wall, said, "It *is* a Turner. I can't believe it!" He got up to examine it more closely. "Very early, but a Turner all right." He shook his head in disbelief. "On a boat. That's been in drydock for years. Unused. Unseen. I'm surprised no one had the sense to steal it. Augusta, you're going to have to be more careful with your possessions."

"In time. As soon as I know what they are," Augusta said, ashamed that she had not even noticed the painting. It wasn't very large.

"Talk about luxury!" Ben said.

"We have," Camilla said. "Endlessly. Is that your idea of luxury, Ben? A Turner blushing unseen?"

Ben thought for a moment. "My definition of luxury is never having to make your living at something you don't enjoy doing. By my own definition, I've always lived in luxury."

149

"Then so have I," Augusta said, reminding herself once again that her new wealth was accidental, something she would never have pursued for its own sake.

"Shaw said, I forget where, that we have no more right to consume happiness without producing it than to consume wealth without producing it," Patrick said. "But he also said that lack of money is the root of all evil. I suppose he was talking about two different kinds of money?"

"Yes, a lot of it and enough of it," Marshall said.

Camilla had been observing the expressions on their faces and the sound of their voices, fascinated at the subtle changes among them that had been created by the introduction of a single new element, Ben, himself so well-meaning, affable and inoffensive. He had engaged Cleo's interest; Marshall, for some reason, clearly disliked him; Patrick seemed to resent him. It was still too soon to tell about Augusta, but at this moment she was more the old Augusta than she'd been for days, and Camilla attributed this to Ben's presence. The insular society of shipboard life, the forced hothouse associations of closed places where people did not come and go, heightened the dynamics between them as if they would forever be all the world there was. Was it the instinct to pair off, that persistent need for intimacy? She herself, despite her better judgment, felt more and more drawn to Avery Packer, who still had not mentioned his wife, although last night he had shown her photos of his children, all five of them. She had searched the corners of the pictures for some sign of a hovering mother, a hand on a shoulder, a skirt in the background, some clue, but there had been none. The children, ranging in age from seven to sixteen, were posed individually and in groups. Avery, too, was absent from the photos, but this was probably because he had taken them. In one, a shadow lay on the grass between the photographer and the twin girls, their arms linked, smiling identically gap-toothed smiles. The shadow

150

might have been Avery's, but it might also have been his wife's. The children were beautiful; their mother was probably beautiful, too. Why did he never mention her?

Marshall consulted his watch and, rising, announced that it was time for his shift. He was proud to have learned enough to take his place in the rotation with Avery and Bert and Patrick, who were seasoned sailors and could do everything -- read charts, navigate, handle the radio, fix parts, have Cleo machine new ones if necessary, and interpret the weather and seas through which they passed. Once Ben learned the ropes, the length of their shifts would be reduced. Marshall liked the night shifts. While everyone slept, the loneliness of sailing through the dark and silent sea made him feel all-powerful and yet, because they occupied the tiniest corner of the universe, insignificant. Still, in these hours he felt important and responsible, if only for the small ship and its handful of passengers, and this, together with his awareness of the vastness of the earth and of its long history, made him humble, and taught him something about the illusory nature of power.

He liked, too, going from long thoughts in which he counted for so little to the shorter ones, to his immediate concerns, where he was restored to his everyday stature which, at the center of his daily life with its emotional freight, was enormous. He was more and more obsessed with Cleo. Often when he was on duty it was a relief to be away from her so that he could really think about her, undistracted by her presence and the tumult it stirred in him. He had never believed he could fall in love with a white woman, but he had. Here, in the intimacy of their small, shipboard world, he went for days forgetting that he was black and they were white. Rebuffed by Cleo, in the beginning he had blamed their racial difference, out of habit, but the consciousness of it was very likely his, perhaps not hers at all. Just as now, and Marshall could not have said why,

151

Ben made him so aware of his blackness. Because Ben was so blonde and fair and freckled? Because for a brief moment he had thought Ben had called him "that gorilla on the top floor?" Because Cleo hadn't taken her eyes off Ben from the moment they were introduced?

Marshall had exchanged few words with Cleo. In Puerto Vallarta he had asked her to go the beach with him, but she and Patrick wanted to shop for embroidered shirts. They didn't ask him to join them. In San Francisco he had asked her if she would show him the city, but she and Patrick were going to spend the day with an aunt. At meals she was usually silent, speaking only if questioned, when it was absolutely necessary, the good child, seen but not heard. But it was her physical presence that bewitched Marshall. She was magical, a nymph, all fairy grace and quickness. When she was in a room, wherever she sat or stood, a light shone. He was enchanted by her eyes, imagining in them a deep, deep soul, and by her expressive hands that had their own life, as though the shyness that kept her silent had no control over them. He loved to watch her hands, but when he did, he missed her face, and though he knew he was making her more and more uncomfortable, he couldn't bear to take his eyes off her and could do so only by leaving the room. She had begun to inhabit his dreams, too, and even there, if anyone else intruded, his dream-self became irritable and cranky. He wondered if this was what was meant by obsession.

In the dining salon below, they were finishing dinner, another gastronomic triumph provided by the San Francisco markets and Jacques' artistry, oysters, crab bisque, salmon steaks in dilled butter. The waves were mounting and with them the ship's undulations. The coffee in their half-filled cups sloshed about, small mirrors of the sea.

152

"If any of you need a seasick pill, they're here," Avery said. "This isn't going to let up for a while. Bert, you'd better give Marshall a hand."

"Maybe I should," Ben said, reaching for the bottle of pills. "I'm a touch queasy."

"Nothing to be ashamed of," Avery assured him. "You have to get your sea stomach."

They all rose from the table. Tired from the long day ashore and the hours since accommodating themselves to the pitching and shuddering of the ship, they drifted apart after dinner. At the door to her cabin, Augusta saw that Ben was right behind her.

"May I come in?" Ben asked, following her through the doorway. "Wow! This is quite a cabin, though cabin is hardly the word."

"Isn't it sumptuous?" Augusta said. "And I'm already used to it. I walk into it without even thinking about it, or really seeing it, except for a sense of pleasure when I'm here."

"You could fit everyone aboard this ship in that bed," he said gloomily. "And you didn't want to share it with me."

"I've had such an overpowering need to be alone." She sighed. "I don't even know how to explain it."

He put his arms around her and nuzzled her neck, trying to hold steady while the room around them swooped and danced. "Oh, darling, I want you so much," he said. 'Don't go away from me." Groaning, he released her abruptly. He had turned white.

"What, Ben?" she asked, alarmed.

"I'm going to be sick," he croaked, hurling himself from the room.

He was sick all night. At dawn, after cleaning up the last of the Jackson Pollacks from the bathroom floor, he fell into

153

an exhausted sleep. When he failed to report to the bridge at six, Bert came looking for him and saw at once that there was no point trying to rouse him. His first lesson in seamanship would have to wait.

CHAPTER EIGHTEEN

"So you're Tantleman's wife," Talifiero said. "I can't believe it. That toad, if you'll excuse my saying so."

"It was nice of you to meet me here," Janet said. Sooner or later, everyone called Julius a toad; she didn't mind. He was a toad. "I couldn't face the idea of going to your office."

"How come?"

"I don't know. I guess I wanted to meet you on neutral turf."

"Well, even I have to eat. I usually have lunch at my desk, but this is our slow season."

"I'm really glad I was able to persuade you." She smiled at Talifiero, lowering her eyes to half-mast and flashing them, signifying something out of the ordinary, sincerity or warmth, or invitation. She was wearing a beige silk suit, but since it was a warm day she had removed the jacket. The dress beneath, a sleeveless sheath, revealed her shapely, white arms, which somehow looked more naked than bare arms normally look, except in severely orthodox places. She held an unlit cigarette an inch from her mouth, waiting. Talifiero stared at her across the table, then fumbled for the matchbook in the ashtray and leaned to light the cigarette, her hand trembling slightly. Janet registered this with satisfaction.

"What shall we have to drink?"

"I don't drink," Talifiero said.

"Oh, come on, just a little something? I have the feeling this is a ... well,, special occasion, don't you?"

"Now that you mention it," Talifiero said, blushing.

"I'm going to order a Bloody Mary for you," Janet said, signaling for the waiter. "That's hardly a drink at all."

155

"Maybe make it a virgin Mary?" Talifiero said, blushing again, while the waiter stood poised above them.

"One Bloody Mary," Janet said, ignoring her, "and one Beefeater Gibson straight up, please." She turned from the waiter to Talifiero. "Trust me, Men'layus."

"Trusting isn't one of my specialties."

"Yours must be a hard life."

Talifiero sighed.

"I've had a hard life, too," Janet said.

"You don't look it."

"I have, though. I grew up in a coal mining town, the oldest of fourteen kids. My old man had the black lung and couldn't work most of the time. He was so angry at all the mouths he couldn't feed that he was always beating us and my Mom. God, he was stupid. Those babies would have had to come straight out of his prick before he made any connection between it and them. My Mom was so worn out that from the minute I could stand without holding on, I had to help wipe snot from all those faces that always had colds because we couldn't afford heat. It was some life!" She wasn't sure why she was inventing this idiotic history for Talifiero.

"Jesus, I feel for you," Talifiero said, and blushed again. "I was an only kid and my mother loved me."

"So what happened?"

"What do you mean? Nothing happened."

"The day my old man died was the first happy day of my life," Janet said. "It was like a holiday, or the last day of school. Men are shits, aren't they?"

"I never knew my own father," Talifiero said. "My mother probably didn't, either. I wasn't born in wedlock."

"You were lucky."

"I don't know, there were times I'd have liked to have had a father."

156

The waiter brought their drinks. "Name one," Janet said, raising her Gibson in a small salute to Talifiero, who responded in kind.

"Sometimes things got a little heavy with my mother. She leaned on me a lot. She expected me to be all things to her. Say, this is pretty tasty."

"All things? What do you mean, Men'l ... I can't call you that. What do your friends call you?"

"Friends? Well, they usually call me Menny." She took a long swallow of her drink. "And sometimes. Well. One person calls me Léah."

"Léah? That's pretty. May I call you Léah?" Marco had told her about his meeting with Talifiero and how his renaming her had seemed to please her. "Shall we order lunch?"

Talifiero gazed at her empty glass. "I think I'll have another one of these," she said. "You're not in any hurry, are you? Waiter, bring me another one of these."

"Léah?"

"Yes?"

"I feel. I don't know how to say this. I feel as if I've known you all my life. Isn't that weird?"

Talifiero smiled wanly.

"Do you feel that, too, Léah? "

"No."

"What do you feel?"

"I don't know. Something else."

"It's so easy to talk to you. What do you mean, something else?"

"I don't think I can say."

"Something bad?"

"No. I don't think so."

"Then say. Please."

"Later, maybe. Let's change the subject. Why did you want to meet me? Your husband told you about his problems? You want to ask me to go easy on him?"

157

"Julius doesn't tell me his problems. Anyhow, I wouldn't butt in on anything like that. I don't really care what happens to Julius. I mean, I certainly don't want something bad to happen to him, you know what I mean? I mean our marriage isn't what you would call a marriage."

"Why do you stick with him?"

"I probably won't much longer, but I wouldn't want to throw a divorce at him right now. He has enough trouble. See, I feel sorry for him. He's always been very good to me, you know what I mean?"

Talifiero's eyes hardened. Words like "good and "sorry" made her nervous."So tell me the reason you wanted to meet me."

"The reason," Janet said. "Well, there are two reasons. Number one. You may not believe this, but it's true. In high school there was a girl, she was older than me, her name was Mary Polka. She was a really strong, attractive person and for a couple of years I had, well, a kind of crush on her, you know what I mean? It was like a sickness. I mooned about her all the time. Then she got killed. She was knifed in a roadhouse."

"Who did it?"

"Who did it? They never found out," Janet said, irritated by the irrelevant question. It was at this point that she had meant to have tears come to her eyes, but that was now unmanageable; she had lost the thread. Instead, she sighed and her lower lip quivered. "I never got over it," she said. "I still have dreams about her."

"Excuse me," Talifiero said, waving to the waiter and pointing at her glass. "There's nothing to these drinks, is there? They're all ice cubes. So you were saying?"

"Well. When Julius first went to see you he was so surprised that you were a woman that he told me about you. I don't know why, but my interest was aroused. Something psychic, I'm sure. I asked him a lot of questions about how

158

you looked and what you wore and your gestures and every-thing, and you know what? Whatever he said about you could have been said about Mary Polka." She leaned across the table and placed a pale hand with its long blood-red nails on Talifiero's square hand with its fingernails filed down to the quick. "You're younger than Mary Polka would have been but not young enough to be her reincarnation."

"Her reincarnation?"

"I believe in that. I'm not a Hindu or anything, but I do feel that the human soul goes on, no matter what happens to the body, don't you?"

"No. It's a horrible thought. The people I know."

"Poor Léah. What a terrible life you must have."

"If I thought it was so terrible I'd change it," she said gruffly. "So you're convinced now that you've met me that I'm not Mary Polka?"

"I knew that before I met you. Not her reincarnation. But you're so much like her that you could be her double. I believe in doubles. I guess that's why I have this feeling that I've known you forever, you know what I mean?"

Talifiero smiled happily, her eyes almost crossing. "What was number two?" she said. She had an orderly memory.

"Number two? Oh, yes. There's a man who wants to buy Julius's disco. What was his name? Well, it will come to me. Anyhow, he said if I could talk Julius into selling it to him, he'd give me a piece of it. Not sell it exactly, because I don't think he has the money, but agree to let him have it and pay off a percentage, like a mortgage."

"Why do you want a piece of it?"

"It's funny, I was never interested in the place while Julius was running it. Julius is such a slob, he really should go back to being a butcher. But this man, what's his name, Polo? Marco Polo? Well, Marco something. He has style. And he seems to know all the right people. I think we could

159

make a go of it. And if I leave Julius, I'm going to have to do something."

"You like this man?"

"What man? Polo? What has like got to do with it?" She withdrew her hand from Talifiero's and sat back. "I'll tell you the honest truth, Léah. I don't much like men. Do you?"

Talifiero shrugged.

"Tell me what you didn't want to tell me before, Léah."

Shyly, Talifiero tossed back her current drink. "What I felt. Feel." She was having trouble getting her mouth around the words. "What I feel. Is that you exploded into my life. Like a bomb."

"Oh, Léah."

"I'd really prefer it if you called me Menny."

"Oh, Menny."

"Like a bomb."

"Truly, Menny?"

"A Goddamn bomb. Waiter!"

"Do you think we're falling in love, Menny?" Janet's voice was a whisper.

"Falling in what?"

"Don't be scared, Menny. Trust me. Say my name, Menny. You have never yet said my name."

"Janet Tantleman."

"Just Janet."

"Just Janet."

***

At the other end of town, somewhat northeast of Janet and Talifiero, Marco arrived for a luncheon date with Lynda. It was his intention to terminate their affair as gently as possible. Lynda was becoming too serious.

160

"One of your party is already here, Monsieur March," the maître de said, leading him into the dining room.

"One? But I reserved only for two, Charles."

"Mademoiselle altered zat. Ah, here we are."

The table was set for three. Lynda smiled radiantly up at him, her genuine happiness at seeing him making her lovely face as incandescent as a child's. Being loved so openly never failed to move him. He bent to kiss her.

"Who's the third?" he asked, sitting down.

"I asked Mother to join us. She's late, as usual."

"Mother?" he said, annoyed. "I didn't know you had a mother."

"Yes you did, Marco. I've mentioned her lots of times. Why are you so surprised? A lot of people have mothers."

"I'm not expected to have lunch with a lot of people's mothers."

"Marco, don't be grumpy. I thought it would be a treat for her."

"What have you told her about me?" he asked darkly, feeling walls closing in.

"Oh, no, Marco, nothing like that, if that's what you mean. Marriage," she lied, "is the furthest thing from my mind. You should know that. It's just, I think you're so wonderful I want to show you off a little." Glowing happily, she leaned to kiss him on the cheek. "*Mon homme adorable.*"

Although her mother was not yet visible, Lynda could hear the tolling of her voice. "She's here," she said.

"Where?"

Charles was approaching, but not until he was almost upon them did Marco see that he was escorting a child in extremely high heels. No, it wasn't a child. It was a small woman, close to his own age. He rose.

"Ma," Lynda said, "this is him. He. Marco."

161

"How do you do, Mrs..." What the hell was Lynda's last name!

"Call me Natalie," the woman boomed, climbing onto the chair Charles held for her. "So this is ... him."

"Marco," Marco said. "Call me Marco."

"Waiter! I'm starving," she called to Charles. "Could we get a little something, pretzels maybe, to tide us over until we order?"

"Ma, that's not the waiter. And they don't have pretzels in a place like this."

"Anything, then. Bread and butter. So, Marco, tell me about yourself. Nothing makes me hungrier than shopping, except jogging. When Saks has a sale it's really a sale. Not that they ever have anything in my size, but what I found for you, Lyndala! Where's the menus?" A waiter stood at Marco's elbow, asking if they would care for something to drink.

"Absolutely," Marco said. "A double martini for me. What about you? Natalie? Lynda?"

"A martini for me, too." Lynda said.

"A banana daiqueri," Natalie said. "Though hungry like this I'll probably slide under the table."

"You can bring the menus," Marco instructed the waiter, who instantly produced three enormous crimson flocked folders that matched the wallpaper. Natalie disappeared behind hers. They heard her groan.

"Another one of your fancy French places, Lynda!" she said accusingly. "With the tippytoe food."

"This is country French," Lynda said. "Not nouvelle. You'll like it."

A busboy brought a basket of rolls and a vat of whipped sweet butter. Lynda's mother cheered up, tore into a roll and, chewing, turned her attention to Marco.

162

"So. Let me look at you," she said, squinting at him. "I expected someone younger. Lynda, you never mentioned that he's old enough to be your father."

"Ma!"

"As a matter of fact, my daughter Augusta is a few years older than Lynda."

"Lynda, you hear that?"

"I knew it, Ma. Marco has told me all about his daughter. She's a composer. What are you going to have, Ma?"

"What do you suggest, Mr. Marco?"

"Umm, let's see. I know the *ris de veau* here is uncommonly good."

"That's sweetbreads? I had that the last time. Of music?"

"Electronic music. The duck is excellent, too."

"Duck is too greasy. You mean with machines?"

"Yes, synthetic sound. It's not greasy here. What about the *poulet bonne femme*, then? Or the *rognons*. "

"Musical instruments aren't good enough? What's rognons? They were good enough for Beethoven, Mozart, Bach, those fellas."

"I couldn't agree more. Kidneys."

"For centuries it was art to make instruments that sound beautiful. Phagh! Kidneys are for processing urine, not to put in a person's mouth. And musicians who practice six hours a day so they can make beautiful music on the beautiful instruments. Not one but two arts."

"What about the calves liver, Ma?"

"So why throw away two arts and replace them with technology, a noise machine? All right, the chicken. Some day there won't be any more concert halls if they keep this up. We'll all have to go to arcades and listen to Pac-Man instead. I hope I don't live to see it."

"So you're a music lover, Natalie."

"You bet. A subscriber."

"I strongly doubt that electronic music will ever replace instrumental music. Thank you, waiter. Yes, Madame will have the *poulet*..."

"First the whatever this is," she said, her finger pointing at the menu.

"*Coquilles de Fruits de Mer Monblason*," the waiter said.

"Whatever. Then the onion soup."

"Mother has a terrific appetite. She can eat and eat and she never gains an ounce."

"So why do it?" she asked when Marco was through ordering. "Who really likes it, if they told the truth? Waiter, come back! Instead of the *poulet*, bring me the riss de view."

"*Ris de veau*, Ma."

"Sweetbreads. I'm not the one going to school so I can eat in French. It took me enough years to learn to eat in English. You can't hum it. You can't even tap your foot to it. And you can't remember it after it's over. There's only the relief that it stopped."

"I'm glad you two have found something in common. I knew you'd hit it off."

"When Augusta returns, I'll bring you two together. She can defend her music better than I can."

"Returns from where?"

"She's on a trip around the world."

"Around the world? One of those cruises? The Royal Viking?"

"Her own yacht."

"She made a good marriage?"

"She's not married."

"Not married? How does an electronic composer have the wherewithal to go around the world on her own yacht?"

"She had an unexpected inheritance."

Natalie looked meaningfully at Lynda. The wordless message was: "We should give a quarter of a million dollars to a man whose unmarried daughter can afford to go around

164

the world in her own yacht? Are you crazy?" Lynda's unspoken reply was: "Yes." Meanwhile, Marco was thinking about money, too. He had stumbled on a large amount of it a few hours earlier when he had gone down to the wine cellar to choose the dinner wines. He had pulled a few bottles out of the rack when he noticed, standing upright behind where they had been, a huge dusty amber bottle, a methuselah. Curious to know what wine it contained, he had pulled it forth into the light. It was stuffed with money --- bills, none of them smaller than a fifty. There must have been, he reckoned, pulling a few of the bills out of the neck of the bottle, at least ten thousand dollars.

"That's mine."

He wheeled to see Aurora standing behind him. He hadn't heard footsteps and she had startled him.

"That my money. My life savings."

"This is no place to keep your life's savings, Aurora. It's not safe. Why don't you put it in a bank?"

"Can't trust those banks. They make too many mistakes."

Marco stuffed the bills back into the bottle and gave it to Aurora, but he was troubled by the incident. If the money came from her wages, why would it all be in cash, bills that had obviously passed through a few hands before finding their way into Nickleby's ... no, Augusta's, wine cellar? There was something fishy going on.

"Why is she going around the world? For pleasure?"

"She's looking for a man."

"There aren't enough men right here in the states?"

"I mean a particular man. The man who left her the money. He's dead, of course, but I think she wants to find out, if she can, where and how he died. You see, he was sailing around the world in his other yacht ..."

"Two yachts yet!"

"... when he disappeared. He was a family friend, sort of an uncle to her, or at least I imagine that's what he felt."

165

"That's so romantic. Lynda, isn't that romantic?"

"It's very romantic."

"What do you do, Mr. Marco, if I may inquire?"

"Marco. My surname is March. I'm an entrepreneur."

"That's French," Lynda said. "It means between to take."

"A middleman?"

"In a way. I bring people together who need each other in a business way, a sort of financial matchmaker."

"Mother's a business person, too, Marco."

"Is that so?"

"I have fingers in several pots."

"Pies, Ma."

"What pies? Ladies' undergarments is my main source. The Lynda shops, you've heard of them? I started in corsets and girdles but you know what happened to those. Even brassieres took a nosedive thanks to the women's freedom movement, but I'm happy to say they're making a comeback. Women's bodies weren't designed for freedom."

"Liberation, Ma. That's so unfeminist of you!"

"Ah, food at last. That must be my cockle."

"*Coquille*, Ma."

"Creamed fish," she said, poking at it with a fork. "Listen, Lynda, you're getting boring with all this correcting. If you don't care for my pronunciation, how's about once in a while we dine American?"

CHAPTER NINETEEN

"What in the world is a blit train?" Camilla asked.

Avery laughed. "The bullet train," he translated as their taxi pulled up in front of the station. "It goes like a bullet, fast and straight to the point."

It did. It was a miracle of clean, quiet efficiency, and they had to be quick getting off when they reached Kyoto since the doors operated with split-second precision, waiting for no one, whatever his nationality. Ben and Augusta shot through one pair of doors and Camilla and Avery out of those at the other end of the car, laughing as they linked up again on the platform. They were impressed and, thinking about the New York City subway system, they were humbled.

"The Japanese didn't lose the war," Ben said, shaking his head. It was good to see him on his feet and with some color in his face. He'd been seasick all the way to Honolulu, emerging only for the day they'd spent there, but as soon as they set out for Japan, the rough seas sent him straight back to bed. He had been weak and sick and embarrassed. Everyone dropped into his room to try to cheer him up, but he was adamant in his misery. Augusta ministered to him tenderly, but she confessed to Camilla that having him laid up was a relief, in a way, since it delayed the moment when she would have to tell him that she didn't want to sleep with him.

"I don't know why," she told Camilla. "I'm sure I still love him, but anything physical between us no longer feels right or natural." She looked almost as if she were in a trance, her gaze turned inward, the way Camilla felt when she was working on a piece of sculpture, or was deep in a

167

novel whose world and people had become more real to her than the one she physically inhabited.

"It's that web again, isn't it?" Camilla said, but Augusta merely shrugged.

Cleo, too, spent every moment she could spare at Ben's bedside, pleading to be allowed to fetch him something, or to read to him, undaunted by his pallor and helplessness and the pathetic blankness in his eyes, or his wish to be alone and to sleep. When he had refused everything, she nonetheless laid cool washcloths across his brow and sat simply and quietly at his side, not fidgeting, and after a while she slipped away. He spoke of flying home from Japan, but Cleo had bought a new seasick remedy, a patch that went behind the ear, that she swore would be effective. He promised to give it a try as far as Hong Kong.

They had docked at dawn that morning in Kobe in the wake of a large cruise ship that was being accorded a royal welcome by a band assembled on the pier, forty Japanese musicians in scarlet uniforms with gold braid, which, with their horns and trumpets, gleamed in the rising sun. Led by a tiny, spry, jumping-jack with a white baton the size of a yardstick, they played Marching Through Georgia and The Washington Post and Hands Across the Sea with esprit and no trace of a Japanese accent, while overhead, helicopters circled and dipped, noisily percussive. They all came out on deck to share in the welcome, Augusta adding an hour of tape to her mounting collection. Although she was looking forward to the day ahead, she could hardly wait for it to be over so that she could replay the tape and hear what she'd collected. She had recorded the approach and the departure of the bullet train, and she hoped the temples they were going to visit would provide sounds that had nothing to do with transportation, but would suggest another era and spirit entirely.

And she hoped that there would be a letter. Soon after their arrival that morning, Avery had seen the port master and asked him to search through his files for some record of The Divine Sara's passage. If it had been here, there might be a letter. It seemed a long time to have been without one and she was impatient for more of Freddy, exactly as she might have been in any burgeoning affair.

Ben and Avery, having negotiated a car and driver, ushered Augusta and Camilla into it. Settled and on their way, Camilla again took up the subject she had introduced in the train: sexual dimorphism.

"Among jelly fish and sea urchins, for example," she said, "males and females look so much alike that it's nearly impossible to tell them apart. I'm not talking about the hermaphrodites, which *are* the same."

"Camilla, it's another century out there," Augusta said. "That's Kyoto. We've never been to Kyoto. Look at it."

"I am looking at it." It was a jewel set in a ring of purple mountains. "It's where a division of sexual labor begins that you get sexual differentiation," she persisted." Which seems to go without saying, doesn't it?"

"Then why are you saying it?" Ben asked. "And so soon after breakfast?"

"I'm trying to make some sense of this feeling I have about Patrick and Cleo. Ahh, look at that, how beautiful they are." A flock of young women with elaborate coiffeurs and downcast eyes were fluttering along the sidewalk, color-ful in kimonos and bright obis. "Like butterflies. Not the heliconians, though."

"Why not the heliconians, Camilla?"

"Because among some species, the female is much dowdier than the male. If you were more receptive, I'd tell you why. Also, I think they're the ones that smell and taste awful, which protects them from predators."

169

"Patrick and Cleo don't smell awful," Ben said, "and I don't imagine they would taste much different than anyone else."

"They're both bright and beautiful," Avery said.

"Camilla, you're too quick to anthropomorphize," Augusta said.

"I think it's rather poetic, though," Avery said, smiling fondly at Camilla. "She thinks metaphorically."

"Thank you, Avery."   They had not become lovers, at least not yet, though they had come close on several occasions. Whenever he was free, he sought her out. In Honolulu he had taken her to Pearl Harbor and to the Bishop Museum and to see the long undulating view from Pali. Then they had gone to the Pacific National Memorial Cemetery in Punchbowl, so solemn and stirring with its infinite neat geometry of white crosses and high marble columns engraved with the much-too-long lists of the names of the dead. She had thought it frivolous to put a cemetery in a place called Punchbowl, as though they'd all died on Christmas eve at a party, and she wept when she read the names. So many of them sounded familiar, names of boys she might have gone to school with. Their names made them real and vulnerable, young men who had not meant to die, whose parents not so many years before had happily talked about what to name the baby if it was a boy. Avery, serious and attentive, had whisked her off to Waikiki where they swam and lay in the sun, not talking, recovering.

Now here they were among the enemy, the descendants of the young men who had killed those young men and been killed by them. It was infuriating and unforgivable, the stupid and unnecessary waste of all those lives that could have been spared to ride the blit train if only time had been taken, the time that had anyway eventually solved their differences and soothed their passions. Just thinking about it made her want to weep again, this time with rage. There was nothing in the subhuman world to compare with it, at least nothing that she knew of. There the purpose, almost the only reason for life, was to create life, to perpetuate one's species, not to destroy it.

The car crossed a moat and drew to a halt in the cobbled courtyard of a sprawling gray stone castle, crowded with tourists.

"Nijo Castle," Avery announced. Although this was his first visit to Japan, as it was theirs, he had assumed the role of guide. He knew exactly what they must see, and why, and even how. He was the kind of man, Camilla saw, who did his homework so that he could always feel in control, the captain, born to command. He would be that as a lover, too, Camilla guessed, considerate, attentive to details, masterful.

They removed their shoes at the entrance to the castle, leaving them in cubby holes already crammed with every kind and size of footwear. Being a tourist was not what you were led to expect from travel films and brochures, where the view is unobstructed and the step unimpeded, and what you've come to see uncluttered and purely what it is.

"At any given moment, I suppose," Camilla said, "everything in the world worth seeing, every garden, temple, painting, ancient ruin, is being seen, surrounded and penetrated by tourists."

"You can rely on it," Ben said.

Many of the tourists came in motley groups with plastic identifications pinned over their hearts, led by guides who spoke in many tongues, with the huge buses that had brought them panting in the wings.

In the castle, the floorboards had been designed at intervals to make the sound of a nightingale's song when stepped on, to warn the emperor of the approach of assassins, but it was difficult to hear above the din, though Augusta turned on her recorder anyway. Children ran and slid in their socks, their parents imploring them in a dozen

171

languages to cut it out; a middle-aged couple with head colds never stopped sneezing or blowing their noses, and a party of Germans, slung with elaborate photographic equipment, were relentlessly jovial. Others were distracting in less noisy ways: three youthful Soviet sailors with rosy cheeks and suspicious eyes; a tall, incredibly thin man wearing a hunting cap and a hideous green suit made of fabric that looked like blotting paper; a group of stout Swiss in lederhosen and feathered hats. Augusta found it impossible to lose herself in a dream of the emperors and shoguns and the softly chirruping pitty-pattying women who long ago had dwelt here. She and her fellow tourists contrasted too harshly; they were too large, too tall, too incongruously garbed; their hair, their complexions, their eyes, their voices were all wrong.

From there, they proceeded to the SanjuusangendoTemple, dark and drafty, with its 1,001 gilded Buddhas, row on row of them lit spookily by the wavering light of candles, and thence to the Heian Shrine where honeymooners go, and where bridal couples were being photographed in the courtyard, and finally to Kinkakuji, the Golden Pavilion, floating on its lake, its beauty mirrored and doubled in the still water. They stood on the bank of the lake, Camilla and Augusta rapt, although Ben would have preferred to be seeing it in a painting, even a print. He would have chosen to use his limited time browsing in some dusty shop, hoping to unearth some fragile treasure on rice paper. Although he would not avert his eyes from the Taj Mahal, he was not terribly interested in architecture or monuments. When he entered an interior, whether it was that of a home, a cathedral, or a cave, his eyes went first to the walls to see what was there, and then to the ceilings and the floors. It was the afterthoughts, whether for decoration or as historical record, the thoughts, the memories, the impressions, the messages of men and women of their era that most interested him. Architecture, no matter how magnificent and inspiring, seemed to him to stop soon after its initial impact. There it stood, frozen, the work of artisans and craftsmen, but it was the artists who added the gargoyles and the stained glass, the frescos, murals, mosaics, statuary and tapestries, what he considered to be its true life.

Standing beside Augusta, he reached for her hand and held it. He was not unappreciative of what they were seeing today, but he was seeing it primarily to please Augusta, and to be near her. She had not been cold, exactly, but distant, almost aloof. During the two days in Honolulu, when he had been free of the seasickness and feeling himself again, Augusta had put him off with faint, unconvincing excuses, utterly unlike the Augusta he knew. He had tried to talk to her about it but she was either unwilling or unable to explain herself.

Now, at this monument to love, her hand imprisoned and passive in his, he looked at her face and saw that she was lost in some dream. He thought how achingly lovely she was and how far from him. He missed her. Perhaps he would speak to Camilla about her, though it seemed wrong not to hear whatever it was from Augusta herself. He vowed to try once more when they were back on the ship that night. He looked away and saw Avery smile down at Camilla and put his arm around her waist. That the two of them were making a beginning gave him a momentary pang of bitterness, but then he thought fondly how at any moment Camilla would be telling Avery something esoteric and irrelevant about the mating habits of the variable tree frog. He wanted to tell Augusta a little of what he was feeling but he was afraid his voice would come out a moan, and he had done more than enough moaning in his seasickness.

"Augusta," he said, and sighed. She looked up at him questioningly. It had begun to rain lightly, and the sky had turned ominous. The surrounding mountains were black. He felt, all at once, that familiar sense of loss that had nothing to do with Augusta, that had to do with painting. As far back as he could remember, he had wanted to paint. He had begun early to study but it was increasingly apparent that he hadn't the gift, only a small talent. He couldn't get onto canvas what was in his head, and even what was in his head was rarely inspired, surprising, original. He had accepted his limitations early. If he couldn't do it, he could make a career of his appreciation of it. And he had. But every once in a while there was a moment of self-doubt, a feeling of ineffectualness, though those moments, happily, were growing rarer as his reputation as a teacher and critic increased. But now he was having one of those moments.

"It's going to storm," he said. "We'd better go."

"Tomorrow we'll go to Nara to see the sacred deer," Avery said to Camilla, his hand protectively encircling her arm as they trotted back to where their car waited. "Nara is the old imperial capital. And tomorrow night we'll go to Takarazuka for the local equivalent of the Rockettes."

"And tonight?"

"Tonight I want to make love to you."

"You plan ahead, don't you? You have every minute scheduled."

"In this case, it's more wish than plan. Which one depends entirely on you."

Quite late that night, after almost an hour of lovemaking, Camilla lay idly running her fingers over the golden hairs on Avery's chest, following their swirls and dips, thinking that he was probably descended from Vikings. He had indeed been masterful. Her previous lovers had usually been timid or tentative at first. Or like Mark, in a terrible hurry to land his fish before it got away. Or like Jonas, filled with angst: sometimes very good but more often terrible.

174

Avery had been nothing less than perfect, skillfully and surely leading her exactly where she wanted to go, and going there with her. And yet, and yet.

"Avery?" she said.

"It was wonderful," he mumbled. He was almost asleep. Irregular hours had taught him to fall asleep quickly. "Couldn't you tell?"

"Yes, but."

"It was good for you, too, wasn't it?"

"Oh, yes."

"But? You said but?"

She liked some conversation during love. It was so much more intimate than that complete withdrawal into the body, where she sometimes tended to feel lonely. But Avery had been silent.

"You never spoke."

"I just did."

"I mean during."

"I was totally engrossed in you, darling. What did you want to talk about? The dwarf male worm?"

She had told him earlier about dwarf male spiders, who consist almost entirely of their seed pod with its attached ejaculating apparatus and the means to transport it, whose sole function in life is to impregnate the much larger female, and then to die. Poor spiders.

"No."

"You wanted me to tell you that I love you."

"No, I don't mean that."

"When I say it, you'll know it's true."

"I don't think I want that," she said, thinking of his wife and all those children.

"I'm not saying that it isn't quite possibly true now," he said.

"No it isn't, Avery. We hardly know each other."

"Well, what I do know I find entirely to my liking."

175

He was, she reminded herself, older than any of her previous lovers. He was probably fifteen years older than she.

"Although 'like'," he said, folding her in his arms again, "is hardly the word. Now I'm going to surround you with silence again." He covered her mouth with his and proceeded to take her again to that place where they were both delightfully in no hurry to arrive.

"It's been a wonderful day, Gus," Ben said. He had a drink in one hand, a nightcap, and with the other he was fingering the things on her vanity table, the crystal stopper of a perfume jar, the bottles and jars of lotions and creams she didn't need. "It's so good to be feeling normal again."

"It's good to see you feeling normal," she said.

"I walked around all day today not only enjoying Kyoto, but enjoying my body, my sense of well-being, something I almost never think about normally. We just take our equilibrium for granted, don't we? But after all those days of being betrayed by my middle ear, I know what normal means. It isn't just freedom from misery, a negative. I feel it. It's palpable."

"It's too bad that that awareness of comfort in one's body doesn't last," she agreed. She smiled at him through the mirror above the vanity. He came and sat beside her.

"Speaking of bodies," he said, leaning to nuzzle her ear, "couldn't we go to bed? Please?"

She put a hand on his shoulder. He was so big and solid. His mouth, nibbling her earlobe, his warm moist breath, implored her. She felt her heartbeat accelerate, not with arousal but with something like fear.

"Oh Ben I can't," she said. "Sex is the last thing I feel like."

"What's the first thing?"

"I feel ... affection."

"Then couldn't we make a little affection?" His mouth slid from her ear slowly across her cheek to her lips. He held her in a long probing kiss, anything but merely affectionate. He could almost taste her emptiness.

"What is it, Augusta?" he whispered.

"I don't know. Nothing." It was nothing. She felt nothing.

"No, it's something. You're different. You're not really here with me."

"I'm so sorry, Ben."

"Is there something between you and Patrick?"

She smiled at the thought of it. "No, Ben. There may be something with Patrick, but there's nothing between us."

"He's in love with you."

"He may think he is."

"Anyone can see he is."

"He's only a boy. Not even that. A gazelle, a sprite. He's not even real to me."

"You don't seem real to me either, Gus. You're not really here, are you?"

"What do you mean?" she asked, frightened. "I mean you're somewhere else. Gypsies have stolen you away."

There had been a letter. It was waiting for them when they returned to the ship, delivered by the port master with some other papers. It had lain somewhere in the office of this port in Kobe for years, gathering dust, waiting for her. The knowledge that it was still waiting for her to read it had more weight, was more pressing, than the feel of Ben's mouth on hers, or his questions, his needs, his desire for her. How could she be real if she had fallen in love with a ghost?

"Yes," she said, her voice quavering, 'I'm somewhere else."

177

Marshall, leaning against the forward rail, stared out at the lights of downtown Kobe. Red, white, blue. Yellow and orange. It was very late. He had gone to bed, then giving up on sleep, had pulled on jeans and a shirt and, barefoot, come out on deck. It was a warm, starless night and, though it had stopped raining, the air was dense with harbor smells and a rising mist through which the city's lights shone blurred and distorted. He had spent the day with Cleo and Patrick, part of it in Kyoto and part here in Kobe. Though only a few years older, Marshall was much further removed from childhood than either of them. He had, in fact, stopped being a child when he was fifteen. That was the year his father had died of drugs and alcohol and Marshall, deeply affected, quit the gang he'd been hanging out with and started going to school regularly. He knew he was blessed with a good mind and a strong body and he made up his mind to take advantage of his inherent capital. He was determined never to be a victim. It was a serious decision, one that he had worked hard at in the years since.

But today he had felt like a victim. He was a victim now, helpless before his feelings. His day with Cleo had nearly undone him. Although she had seemed at moments abstracted, and Patrick was intermittently broody, the day had been a lark. They were like children, impulsive and delighted, each knowing without asking exactly what they would do next, as though they were Siamese twins joined at the mind. Marshall could only follow where they led, grateful to be allowed that much. Wordlessly, they would dart into a pachinko parlor to play the pinball machines, stopping at almost the same moment to move on. Although there were hundreds of shops along the mile and a half long Sannomiya-Center-gar, wordlessly they would turn into one of them, as if it had magnetized them, and once inside would be drawn to the one woodblock print they must have. Only in one shop did they diverge. Cleo, after silently meditating,

178

bought a pearl necklace. She had held it round her neck and looked inquiringly not at Patrick, who seemed confused and disoriented by what she was doing, but at Marshall. "Oh, yes," Marshall said. "It's perfect for you." He was dying to buy it for her but he knew that he couldn't yet make such a gesture. It was enough that she had asked for his approval; it made him deliriously happy. At lunch they both ordered sashimi and Marshall, to whom the idea of raw fish, which he had never eaten, was repugnant, ordered it too. He wanted to have in his own mouth the exact taste and sensation that Cleo was having in hers, which was as near as he could get to kissing her, and while they ate, although he was clumsy with his chopsticks, he tried to mirror her every move, going from the slice of tuna to the slice of sea bream when she did, watching her mouth as she chewed, imagining that he was inside her mouth (oh, God!) and, since they sat cross-legged on tatami mats before a low table and there was no tabletop to shelter the effect of all this eroticism, he was grateful for the napkin, which was linen and generous.

"Do you think, Marshall," Patrick asked at one point, "that Ben and Augusta are more than just friends?" They both hung on his reply, their chopsticks poised.

"Yes. I think they're engaged," he said, and watched while they both lowered their chopsticks and gazed off in opposite directions, equally despondent. It was a moment that could have been choreographed, and Marshall almost laughed except that he so desperately didn't want Cleo to suffer as he was suffering.

"Show me how to use these," he asked Cleo, distracting her. "It feels all wrong the way I'm doing it." She placed the chopsticks properly between his fingers, lightly touching him.

"The upper one remains steady," she said. "Only the lower one moves." He watched her adorable mouth that was opened and closed by her adorable jaws that held her perfect

179

teeth of which the pearls she had bought were the palest reflection. Cleo, Cleo.

Cleo, Cleo, he thought now, leaning into the railing, his eyes stung with tears, there are no stars, no moon tonight because they're in my hands burning, waiting for me to give them to you, my love, my now and forever love.

Then, as though he had evoked her, he saw a shadow, unmistakably Cleo's, come through the door and stand midship, facing out to sea, away from the city. She moved to the rail and leaned her elbows on it and, her head in her hands, began to heave with silent sobs. It was unbearable. He wanted to go to her, to take her in his arms, to hold her against him and stroke her cropped golden hair, to soothe her with words of love, with the warmth of his body, the heat of his ardor, but in his burgeoning wisdom he stayed silent and motionless where he was, his own face streaming tears of helpless longing.

CHAPTER TWENTY

"What would you say your problem is, Marco?"

Marco? He had set eyes on Dr. Milton for the first time only ten minutes ago. Was this idiot stranger trying to establish a father/son relationship with him?

"Money," Marco said.

The doctor, recommended by a friend Marco trusted, was short and round, probably in his seventies. He had a short round beard that circled the contours of his round face. He sat, almost lost in a plump wing chair, his short legs on a hassock, his round belly looped by a watch chain. He looked like an elf, one of Santa's helpers. He could never be Marco's father. Nobody could, but certainly not this man.

"Money is a problem for you, Marco? It's a problem for most people. How is it a problem for you?"

"I haven't got enough of it," Marco said.

"Many people haven't," the doctor said, "but they don't come to psychiatrists."

"No, you don't understand. I mean it's a problem. It's all I think about.,"

"Hmmm." The doctor was lighting a pipe. It took him half a dozen strong puffs to get the pipe going. "What about sex?" he then said.

"Sex?"

"Don't you ever think about sex?"

"Why would I think about sex? Sex is no problem."

"How often do you have it, Marco?"

"Sex? On an average? Between, let me see, fourteen and twenty-six times a week."The doctor took the pipe from his mouth and stared at Marco.

"I see," he said.

181

CHAPTER TWENTY-ONE

"The sea of my heart's life in exultation moves
    toward you,
Unreachable far land!
You are that land; you are the sea if which I am
    a part
In love and dream.

"Darling Augusta: What long thoughts one has alone at sea. That's Wheelock above, not one of my favorites, but you never know where you'll find the lines that resonate for the moment. I may be" (here the word reduced had been crossed out) "elevated to writing my own, had I talent enough and not merely time. Confession: I wrote poems in my late teens. I suspected, though, that I didn't have the fire in the belly. Emerson said that artists must be sacrificed to their art, that like bees, they must put their lives into the sting they give. I didn't think I had that, so I incinerated my poems. If I hadn't, I wonder if I might find them not as bad as I judged them in my arrogantly uncompromising youth. I was very romantic."

Augusta laughed; as though he were not still.

"If anyone had suggested then that when I grew up I would be a capitalist, much less a manufacturer of plastics, I'd have shot him dead. When I went off to school, I took with me a beloved Himalayan tomcat named Cato, whose silken grace gave me endless pleasure, and for a long time I thought it inspiring to do my homework by candlelight, nearly ruining my eyes, while Cato dozed on the sheet of paper I was trying to write on.. I was a shameless poseur, happily remaking myself from an ordinary youth out of what

182

I considered a most boring and conventional background, into someone with whom I could have a cozy narcissistic affair. I wore an overlong wool scarf loosely looped around my neck and was given to clutching my brow and saying such things as, "Oh Lord, where did I go right?" Mercifully, it was a phase that soon passed, since in those days such behavior automatically branded me as some kind of nut, and probably also what was then called a pansy. It took me a few years to convince not only others but myself that I might turn out all right.

"For a while, I considered becoming a doctor, like my father, but I knew I could never make it through medical school. Once, in high school, I had to skin open a frog and, while I stopped short of fainting, I dreamed about that frog for months. Although the frog had been chloroformed and was either unconscious or technically dead, I forget which, his heart was kept beating with administrations of a saline solution. The frog's interior seemed to me a jewel of neat, complex efficiency, and my invasion of it an unredeemable violation. That pumping heart, so regular, so game, so undauntedly dutiful, was a wonder and a rebuke of such power that it nearly drove me to a monastery. I knew that I could never achieve the cold, sensible objectivity needed for a medical career.

"It wasn't easy to determine what I had the temperament for, so I coasted through a few years of chemistry and humanities, the former as a compromise with my father's ambitions for me, the latter for my soul. Also, that frog led me to a romantic interest in machines, those bloodless bodies we create to serve us in such specific ways. One thing led to another (I won't bore you with the minutiae of my odyssey), and along the way there was considerable luck. Soon I was so involved with the trees of my life that there was never time to stand back and see the forest. I am standing back now. By most standards, my life would be considered a success. We must all do something, impelled by necessity or passion, sometimes by both. By 'necessity' I mean the economic kind, since passion is its own necessity. It was the economic necessity that I was initially driven by, but soon that was beside the point and I went on, propelled not by passion, never by passion, but simply the momentum generated by the original impetus, that chain of cause and effect in the business world that leads either to gigantism or bankruptcy or that boring middle ground of daily sameness, into which I could never have settled.

"My rewards have been threefold: success for its own sake, not the least important. Every new business is a gamble, and I've never minded either the risk or the winning. I've enjoyed making decisions that have proved, within their contexts, to be wise ones. The second reward is money. Nobody is in business except to make money; money is never incidental. For me, however, such a quantity of it was incidental, not something I'd planned on or worked toward. I think I'm being honest about this. I've given away a lot of it over the years, though apparently never enough to have kept it from continuing to accumulate. I know men who take pleasure in money for its own sake, and not entirely out of greed. It gives them pleasure to count it, water it, watch it grow like a garden, the more profuse the better, and they love the power of it. If they could, they would run through it barefoot, preferably in slow motion. I'm not one of those. I don't mind being rewarded in proportion to the value of my contribution to society, but I know I've been rewarded beyond that, that any good artist or scientist deserves what I have far more than I do. But my chief reward and consolation come of having provided employment and livelihoods for thousands of people."

Augusta put aside the letter to wonder why Freddy should have been so defensive about his money. In his society, with its economy and laws and values, he had

184

earned it. She knew why she felt defensive about it: she had neither worked for it nor deserved it and she was puritanical enough to feel that she had no right to it, though she lived in that same society, with that economy, those laws. Obviously, the fault lay there and Freddy must have known that, too, and been defensive because he'd been such a consenting party to it. It was so hard not having him there to talk to, to question, to argue with. Perhaps he had felt the same frustration then, when he was writing his letters to her, when he was imagining her, trying to guess from what he knew of her who and what she would have become when she was reading these letters. Really, in this odd relationship, if you could call it a relationship, she had the advantage. Because she had outlived him, because he was complete, she could know him better than he could ever know her.

It suddenly came to her that if she hadn't already done the things she had done before reading his letters, gone to see his wives, moved into his house, kept Aurora on, decided to embark on this voyage with Avery as skipper, if her decisions hadn't preceded his letters, she might have seen his letters as instructions to her. He was telling her what to do. He was, in fact, as she had thought before, manipulating her. Was he? And why? Perhaps he had some diabolical plan. She supposed that if that were true, the plan would soon reveal itself, and then she told herself that she mustn't begin to imagine even more than she was already imagining. What was real was this ship and the people on it, and the sea beneath it and the sky above, and music. These pages in her hand were real, and the words on them, and the fact that they had been penned years ago by a man who had since died, a man who had once lived, and the meaning these words had was the same as the words in books: they were history, biography, a record of a man's experiences and feelings; they were poetry and fiction and memory; they were a

185

message in a bottle cast upon the sea and tossed by it for years and years. That was quite enough for them to be.

She went on with the letter.

"Apparently, I'm even more anxious than I thought to have you know me, and I make an assumption, perhaps arrogantly, that you have some curiosity about me. But how could you not, since I've forced it on you. How much simpler it would be, and what heaven, to have the give and take of a real conversation with you. But under the circumstances, I can only supply the give and imagine the take.

"I expect to reach Kobe tomorrow. I've been in Tokyo so often on business without ever having time for any real sightseeing, so I look forward to temples and gardens and castles, to Kyoto, to traditional Japan. When I leave, I'll sail slowly through the Inland Sea, beautiful Seto-Naikai, with its emerald waters and hundreds of islands of all shapes and sizes, with their twisted pines and white sand beaches. I'm told that this passage has inspired centuries of Japanese poets and painters. You mustn't miss it, either. I wish we could go on from there to China but of course that's out of the question. Perhaps for you, though, history will have made it possible. I hope so. It's sobering to reflect on the glib, facile ease with which enemies are changed into friends, friends into enemies. How quickly we've learned that the Japanese aren't less than human and that it is even possible to eat their food.

"Augusta, Augusta. It seems so unlikely that you will ever really read these letters that I drop for you along the trail of my wanderings, like Hansel and Gretel's crumbs. There are moments of such excruciating doubt, when I feel that I've woven a madman's fantasy, and yet I cannot let go of it. You are the sea of my heart's life. Life. But if you are reading this, then I am dead. Am I really dead? And who are you in that when? I've diagrammed it so carefully in my mind --- in the beginning as the sort of entertainment all

186

fantasy is, but how it has taken hold of me, how it keeps me company and warms me! Augusta, my beloved, lives in my house, sleeps in my bed, sails on my ship, has at her disposal all of my wealth, my worldly goods. I have made you my Queen, my posthumous wife, my Augusta. Because I have had no other way to love you, I have made over to you my life."

Weeping, she folded the pages back into their envelope. She had been his fantasy, but wasn't he every woman's perfect fantasy? Someone who has always loved her, who surrounds her and keeps her safe in love and money, the perfect father, the ideal husband. Perhaps that was what love always was: fantasy and illusion. If she could write to him, she would send him the lines of Eliot she'd stumbled across this morning, lines she'd known in college but that now were fresh with new meaning:

"The world becomes stranger, the pattern more
    complicated
Of dead and living. Not the intense moment
Isolated, with no before and after.
But a lifetime burning in every moment."

Her sadness at knowing that she could never share these lines with him was assuaged by the near-certainty that he had known them, that they might even appear in his next letter to her, if there was a next letter.

CHAPTER TWENTY-TWO

During the slow movement, Patrick played with his eyes closed, lost in the soaring purity of the music he was caressing from his violin. He was more than good. So was Cleo, who sat cross-legged on the floor, Pan-like, her back ramrod straight, breathing the clear high silvery notes from her flute. They were not only a pleasure to hear, they were beautiful to watch, the grace of their long sun-bronzed hands, their quick fingers, Cleo's head a flower swaying to the music on the slender stem of her neck, her sloe-eyes turned inward in concentration, as though she could hear with them, too. Augusta was delighted. Bach would have been delighted too. Music came as naturally to them as song to the lark. She had only to say, and rarely, a little more glissando here, perhaps not quite so andante in these three bars, and it was done. They had been playing for two hours.

Half an hour earlier, Ben, who had come in to read, had shut his book after a few minutes and listened to them with rapt attention. Now, as they neared the end, the music rose in intensity until, doubt and passion resolved, it arrived at its peacefully triumphant conclusion. Ben rose to his feet, applauding, his face glowing with appreciation.

"Wonderful!" he cried. "You sound as if you've been playing together all your lives."

They were all smiling.

"Patrick and I have," Cleo said shyly.

"We never thought it would go this well, Augusta," Patrick said. "We never played with anyone before. You're awfully good."

"So are you two. You ought to be doing this professionally."

"Oh, we never could," Cleo murmured.

"We're not temperamentally suited," Patrick said.

"To that kind of life," Cleo added.

"The world's loss," Ben said.

"I doubt it," Cleo said. "Good musicians are a dime a dozen. Good engineers are much rarer." She was dismantling the flute, replacing it in its case. "I'm going down now to check the engines. Would you like to come and see them?"

"Yes," Ben said. The patch behind his ear was working, so far, although it was hard to be sure since the sea had remained calm all through the shallow Inland Sea, out through the Hoyo Straits into the open Pacific, and during the two days since. He had been able to begin his instruction as a sailor, standing one watch with Packer and another with Bert. In one more day, if all continued well, he would be ready to take his place in the rotation. He was not overly enamored; there was no sport to it, as there might be with sails. He was obviously not cut out for a life at sea.

When he and Cleo were gone, Patrick watched Augusta put her cello to rest in its coffin. When she had closed the lid on it, he said, "You don't love him."

"What's that, Patrick?"

"Ben. You don't love him."

Fleetingly, she was angered by his brashness; whether or not she loved Ben was none of his business. Then she saw how young and vulnerable he was. She saw that he was frightened and that it had taken all his courage to say what he had said.

"Ben and I have been close friends for a long time," she said.

"But you don't love him, do you?"

"Of course I love him."

"But not that way."

"It's not that simple."

"He doesn't engage your soul."

189

"Oh, Patrick, really. You mustn't fall in love with me."

"Too late."

"No, it isn't too late. You must talk yourself right out of it."

He laughed bitterly. "I never thought that I would be able to love anyone but Cleo," he said. "We are so much one. This is such a relief, such a blessing for me. I adore you. I think about you every minute. You are my first... my first..." He was blushing furiously, unable to go on. There were tears in his eyes. She would have to be gentle. He was so young. He was so vulnerable. He was so beautiful.

"I'm flattered, Patrick, to be your first. But remember, when there is a first, there will be others."

"Never!"

"And you must know, dear Patrick, that I feel old enough to be your mother."

"What nonsense! You're not that much older. We're going to be nineteen at the end of the week."

"Which day?" she said, feeling more than ever like his mother. "We'll have a party."

"They're twin GM 12V-149 gasoline engines with 2:1 reduction gearboxes," Cleo said.

"They look incredibly complicated. And brand new."

"They aren't. Mr. Nickleby ordered them with a special super finish so that the fitters would be especially careful with them. And to make it easier to spot problems like oil leaks."

"The place is immaculate. It doesn't even smell of grease." Cleo's eyes shone with pride. "Did you know Nickleby?" Ben asked. He was growing increasingly curious about Nickleby, who had so changed Augusta's life and, through her, Ben's. He had more than changed her life. Ben was beginning to feel that he had invaded it, that what had happened was, in a way, a rape.

"Yes," Cleo said, "when we were much younger."

"What was he like?"

"We loved him."

"Why?"

"He increased us."

What an odd reply, Ben thought. She looked so solemn, as though she were speaking of something sacred. How lovely she was. She wore jeans and a white T-shirt and dirty sneakers, but it was easy to imagine that she was a young Greek goddess, disguised, or a princess ... no, a woodland nymph or a creature risen from the sea, not Venus, no, Ondine. But talking to her was so difficult. She spoke only in response, and then as briefly as possible. He wondered if that was the way her mind worked.

"How did he increase you?" he persisted.

But she was listening to one of the engines. She took a wrench from a box and tightened a bolt, then listened again and seemed satisfied. Her mouth curled at the corners, dimpling. He realized with surprise that he wanted to kiss her.

"You're not really interested in engines, are you?" she asked, not looking at him.

"Only in the most abstract way," he said. She nodded as though she understood. "The design, the look of them. They're so purely what they are, invented to fill a need, shaped by their own necessity."

"Form following function?"

"Yes, but utterly without artistry. A house has a specific function, too, but look how much latitude architects have in which to express themselves, what vast possibilities there are in the designing of a house, all the choices that can be made to make the house reflect the sensibilities of the architect, or of the owner of the house. But engines are exactly

191

what they are; they have their own integrity." He watched her face while he spoke. She was rapt, interested in a way that was rare even among his best students. "Tell me more about Nickleby."

"He was strong. He was good."

He felt a pang; it wasn't what he wanted to hear. He wanted to hear that Nickleby was diabolical.

"But you were very young," he said.

She looked at him blankly, as if unable to understand what her youth might have to do with her judgment of Nickleby. He felt rebuked.

"How did you learn about engines?" he asked, hoping to rekindle the light in her eyes. She smiled, rewarding him.

"From magazines and books," she said. "And taking things apart and putting them back together. It was like solving puzzles."

"It is solving puzzles," he said. "You never studied?"

"Studied?"

"In school?"

"No."

"You ought to study engineering," he said.

"But I have," she said, and then he remembered how she had taught herself to play the flute. Her mastery of engines was probably as thorough. He felt humbled.

She turned again to the engine and, with her back to him, said so softly that he wasn't sure he had heard, "She doesn't love you."

"I beg your pardon?"

"Augusta."

He saw that she was flushed and still unable to look at him. She made him feel a hundred years old.

"I know," he said.

"But I love you." He could barely hear her.

"Do you, Cleo?"

"Yes."

192

"Who am I?"

She turned, looking at him like a startled fawn. "What do you mean?" she whispered. "I don't know."

"Then how can you love me?"

"I believe I love you. I feel this burning need to find out who you are."

He took the wrench from her hand and put it down. He leaned to kiss the top of her head, a paternal gesture, but she lifted her face and brought her lips to his. He held her in his arms and felt how she trembled, then drawing back from her chaste kiss, said, "Darling Cleo. You're enchanting. But you mustn't love me, you know. I feel old enough to be your father."

"We're not that young," she said. "We're almost nineteen."

"We? You and Patrick, you are always 'we'?"

"Yes. No. Until now. Not now."

"When will you be nineteen?"

"On Thursday."

"We'll have a party," he said, smiling. "A very grown-up party with champagne."

CHAPTER TWENTY-THREE

Choosing a tie one morning in the large closet off his dressing room, Marco overheard voices coming from above. Looking up, he discovered that there had once been a trapdoor in the ceiling that had been sealed and painted over. It was through this that the voices passed. One of the voices was unmistakably Aurora's, her distinctive rich liquid contralto that occasionally descended to a vibrant huskiness. What was different was not her voice but her speech.

"Think," he heard her say. "You've been in this world eighteen years. There must have been something that interested you." There wasn't a trace of that deep southern accent.

"Fuckin'," a voice rumbled. "Fuckin' and money, they interest me."

"What else?"

"Clothes. Cars."

"Come on, Jimmy. Quit jiving."

"I ain't jivin'."

"George Pepperidge says you're a prime candidate for the RBH. He's never been wrong yet."

"That asshole, what he know?"

"You have a high I.Q. Until you were twelve you were an above-average student, especially in English and languages. What languages were you studying?"

"Francaise. Parley-vous?"

"You were a good basketball player."

"Yeah. I'm still a good basketball player."

"You could draw. Until fifth grade you were the class artist."

"I quit that shit."

"Why?"

There was a bitter laugh. "Ain't no way I could've painted at home. My old man was already calling me a faggot on accounta the French."

"Would you do it now if you could?"

"What, paint?" For a moment there was silence. Then in a voice quivering with anger, the boy said, "You don' know nothin.' You sittin' in this fancy house and you don' know shit. How many nigger painters you think they got hangin' in the Metropolitan Museum? The Museum of Modern Art? Even the Whitney? They jes waitin' for me, right, cause when I was eight, nine, I was the class artist in P.S. Garbage. You sure don' know nothin."

"Okay, Jimmy, we've found your passion." Aurora's voice was rich with relief. "You're our first artist, but we do have a connection at the California Institute of Fine Arts and that's where you're going. If you do okay there, maybe we'll be able to send you to Paris when you graduate."

"You crazy?"

"Your tuition and room and board will be paid for. Because of supplies, you'll probably need more than the usual allowance. Most of our people find some kind of part time work to supplement that, but we'll work it out. Naturally, we'll pay your fare. How's your wardrobe? You need clothes?"

"Jesus!"

"We expect you to write to us once a month to tell us how you're doing. Don't forget that. You'll be hearing from us as soon as the arrangements are made. Meanwhile, stay out of trouble."

Marco chose his tie and left the closet, closing the door softly behind him. So that's what they were up to, a salvation army, saving not the lost but the not-yet-found. That Aurora! And what a relief it was to know that what they were up to was good works, that they weren't terrorists or revolutionaries. Thoughtfully, he knotted his tie. The

195

longer he thought about what he had overheard, the more moved he was.

"But there's still the question of where the money is coming from," he said a few hours later to Erwinna, to whom he had just narrated the overheard conversation.

"She's quite a woman," Erwinna said with admiration. "And such a great cook."

Erwinna was more or less guiding him as they walked, digesting the dim sum lunch they had just enjoyed. Augusta was in, or somewhere near, Hong Kong and this had inspired their choice.

"Where are we going?" Marco asked. "There's nothing in this neighborhood worth seeing. Eating, yes but not seeing."

"There's a quaint old building I want to show you. It's just a few more blocks."

Their pace was leisurely, a pleasant stroll. It was one of those warm, dry, comfortable summer afternoons when the city seemed empty, almost pastoral.

"Everyone's at the Hamptons frantically drinking white wine and bumping into each other," Erwinna said. "Aren't we lucky to be here?"

Erwinna would normally have been at Bridgehampton and Marco frequently there with her, but she had rented her house for the summer, claiming that she was sick of the frenzy and wanted a year off. Marco had declined numerous weekend invitations from other friends. He loved being in Augusta's house and, of course, there was the business of Corned Beef & Cabbage to resolve. And Lynda. And Janet.

"Aurora gets an exceptionally good salary," Marco said. "But hardly enough for all that."

He had told Erwinna about the money in the wine cellar.

"She can't be stealing it from the estate, can she?"

196

"I don't think so. She has a checking account for household expenses, but I doubt if there's enough for that. There's an accountant who keeps track of it."

"Why don't you ask her?"

"Confront her? Tell her I know?"

They came to a halt before a squat ugly stone building, circa 1860. The building had recently been steamed clean of what the years had layered over it, but it still retained a certain ineffaceable dinginess. The words TURKISH BATH, graven in the stones above the entry, were re-enforced with neon tubing in many different colors, tracing the letters. Two men were installing a canopy from the doorway to the curb.

"What's this supposed to be?" Marco asked.

"It's the building I want to show you," Erwinna said. "Come. We're going inside."

She led him through a doorway of heavy glass encased in iron wrought in a Turkish motif featuring crescents, and into a foyer canopied over with dark silks. She led him through this into a huge room with a gleaming polished hardwood floor, a dance floor, bordered by low, heavily inlaid tables, themselves surrounded by plump gaily colored ottomans hung with silk tassels. The walls were painted in bright Matisse colors with a harem of nude odalisques in various postures of abandon. Overhead, on tall ladders, two men were working on lights.

"What is it?" Marco asked.

"Do you like it?" Erwinna beamed. "It's ours."

"Erwinna !"

"You really like it?"

"This is a rare moment: I'm speechless."

Erwinna smiled broadly. It was indeed one of life's better moments. "Now you know. This is what I've been so busy with."

197

Marco extracted a handkerchief from his pocket and blew his nose. "Excuse me," he said. He was crying. "Oh Erwinna. I'm so moved."

"Kiss me."

He complied with such fervor that he nearly smothered her. She laughed gaily.

"Now come and see the bar. The kitchen. The control room."

The bar, in an antechamber, was long and ornate, inlaid with fake jewels and ivory and overhung with narghilas and hookahs and scimitars and gay murals of solemn Turks with elaborately down-turned moustaches, garbed in pantaloons and fezzes, leaping about on the walls.

"I've engaged a Turkish bartender who matches the wallpaper. He's inventing cocktails with names like The Constantinople and The Halivah. I mean I've engaged him subject to your approval, darling, of course."

The control room was a technological marvel whose components Erwinna could only vaguely explain. It would require the services of the sound and light engineer who had installed it.

"Oh my Erwinna," Marco crooned.

"Wait, there's more," she said.

"What more can there be? It's already overwhelmingly complete."

She reached for his hand and led him back to the foyer and up a wide curving staircase. At the top of the stairs, she drew him through a small, elegantly furnished sitting room into a large tiled chamber in which, situated at random and surrounded by potted lemon trees, sat a dozen large ceramic vats. A rainbow of huge Turkish towels hung along the tiled walls.

"What's this?" Marco asked, puzzled.

"Hot tubs," Erwinna said, triumphantly. This, she felt, was the piece de resistance. "They haven't been filled yet."

"Hot tubs? In a nightclub?"

"Don't you think it's a divine way to end an evening of dancing and drinking? It's sure to catch on."

Marco considered for the briefest moment. "Erwinna, you're a genius."

"It was either pave over the name on the building, or this. The name was the inspiration."

"What a gimmick! It's sensational, darling. I knew you were cut out for this sort of thing."

"I did it for you, Marco. It seemed so much more exciting to do it from scratch instead of taking over that dreary defunct Corned Beef & Cabbage."

"It must have cost the earth."

"There's a bank loan, of course; I didn't put down all cash. And Paul and Will helped design it and wouldn't hear of being paid. Eventually, if things should happen not to work out between Paul and Will, I thought I'd turn my share over to Paul. I don't expect it to happen, but you wouldn't mind that, would you?"

"Of course not, love. Oh, Erwinna, you don't know how happy and excited I am."

"Yes I do."

He smiled at her, clasping her hands between his own. For the first time, it occurred to him how aptly she was named: she was a winner. What a handsome, intelligent, inventive, generous, strong woman she was. She was undoubtedly exactly what he needed, after all, the perfect woman for him.

"Is the plumbing working?" he asked.

"Yes."

"Shall we fill one of the tubs?"

They smiled wickedly at one another.

"Let's," she said.

While the steaming water rushed to fill the tub, they slowly and carefully removed their clothing, and then, naked, stood facing each other, their eyes radiant, Adam and Eve in the garden she had created for them.

CHAPTER TWENTY-FOUR

"If everyone here is selling quartz watches, who is left to buy them? Augusta asked. She and Camilla were walking along Nathan Road in Kowloon with its infinity of shops and, off it, the arcades and alleys and byways, all of them crammed with more shops. Indeed, except for restaurants and the hotels, the latter also packed with shops, Kowloon was one vast emporium bursting with watches, calculators, telephones, cameras, binoculars, audio equipment, tape recorders and similar electronic technological necessities of life. "There are enough quartz watches here for every wrist on earth."

She had bought a watch for Marco that did everything but tell the news. Advised to bargain, she did so reluctantly at first, but with a fascination that grew as the price diminished. She couldn't help feeling that if she went on haggling, eventually the merchant would pay her to take the watch. As it was, he behaved as though she were stealing it from him. "With such customers as you, Miss," he complained, "I might as well close my doors and emigrate." Augusta might have felt sorry for him, but she felt that the mandatory bargaining procedure was an outrageous admission of some fundamental dishonesty and that it had made them adversaries.

Their arrival the previous evening through Lei Yue Mun Pass had been spectacular, Kowloon Peninsula to the right, Victoria to the left, its peak towering over Hong Kong center's skyscrapers, the bay a beehive of junks, ferries, sampans, freighters and cruise ships, all light and color and motion, the most crowded place in the world, these four hundred square miles in the South China Sea where, as

201

Avery pointed out, East and West did meet, if only to sell each other watches.

They were walking off their dim sum lunch. Waitresses had circulated with trays of tidbits, an endless variety of steamed and fried dumplings, crisp spring rolls, succulent morsels of squid with red peppers, tiny spare ribs in black bean sauce, crab claws, bean curd and green pepper and mushrooms all stuffed with subtly seasoned mixtures of chopped fish, pork, water chestnuts, shrimp --- the parade of delicacies kept coming and they resisted nothing, not even the chicken feet or the tripe, eating with a joyful sensual greed, something they usually shared in equal measure. The stack of empty dishes, by which their tab would be computed, mounted shamelessly before them.

"It's hard to believe you can pig out on such delicate morsels," Camilla remarked when they agreed that they had come to an end. "You are what you eat. I'm a stuffed dumpling."

"I'm glad the one thing missing from the luxury liner we call home is a bathroom scale. I'd hate to know the truth." They dined so well at sea, so well in port. "How do the rich stay thin? Have we ever seen anyone fat in the society pages?"

"And the Chinese," Augusta said. "All thin. All that great food."

"I could happily eat nothing but Chinese food for the rest of my life."

Augusta agreed that so could she if she were allowed an occasional corned beef on rye with a fat Jewish pickle and a celery tonic.

"I'm so glad your appetite is back," Camilla said. "Today you're the real Augusta."

"What's the unreal Augusta?"

"Ethereal. A bore and a wimp, actually. I've missed our being silly together and laughing."

"Me too. It's so weird. Maybe this is the first time I've really been in love."

"That's sick, Augusta. You can't really be in love."

"People are always falling in love before they truly know the person they've fallen in love with, and then they spend a lifetime trying to fit that person to their misconceptions. I, on the other hand, have been learning who this man is, with no preconceptions, and have fallen in love with exactly what he's revealed of himself."

They were silent for a while, arrested before a shop window filled with wigs in a range of coiffeurs and colors almost as varied as the dim sum they were struggling to digest. It was hard to be serious for too long on such full stomachs. They contemplated the wigs, imagining how they would look in them, trying to decide which single one they would choose if they were bald and forced to wear it for the rest of their lives.

"Would we have to be laid out in it? Buried in it?" Camilla asked, anxious to get the rules straight.

"Naturally."

"Then it's a much more difficult decision, isn't it?"

"You could choose cremation."

"Lord, when you think of the ways people are always fussing with their secondary sex characteristics. Hair, beards, armpits, bras, falsies, cosmetics."

"Yeah, let's not buy a wig."

The morning fog had lifted and the sun blazed forth. They boarded the Star Ferry for the brief ride across the harbor to Hong Kong Island and, behind the Hilton Hotel on Garden Road, caught the Peak Tram which bore them at a 45 degree angle the thirteen hundred feet up to the Peak Tower restaurant where they debarked and, perched like birds, surveyed the view they had just ascended from, the dramatic panorama of skyscrapers, teeming boats skittering across the bay like waterbugs, the Kowloon Peninsula thrusting into the bay and, beyond it, the countryside stretching to the violet mountains of China rising from the mist. It was breathtaking; the world was breathtaking. More and more they were learning what a miracle it was, almost as much for what men had put on it as for what had been given, though man had also destroyed so much of it and might yet destroy it all.

Augusta had been talking about how, in some way, Freddy was every girl's dream of the perfect father. "He told me something interesting in this last letter," she said, bemused.

"Who?"

"Freddy!" There had, indeed, been lines from T. S. Eliot in the Hong Kong letter, as she had anticipated, although not her lines from East Coker, but these from Burnt Norton:

"Time present and time past
Are both perhaps present in time future,
And time future contained in time past."

"He told me why he'd excluded Marco from the will. It's because he believed that it's the pursuit of money that keeps Marco alive and ebullient --- ebullient was his word --- but that the actual possession of it would rob him of his raison d'être. He said that Marco's character needs very careful tending, like a garden in poor soil."

"Did you know that about Marco?"

"No. I know he's always adored the idea of money, that he has no trouble spending it, and that in some way he feels himself to be a failure, but I always felt he was rather casual about making money. He's certainly casual about work."

They took the funicular back down and walked around Hong Kong Central, exploring the side alleys with their stalls selling herbs and snakes and dried sea horses. The streets were dense with life, with fruit peelers and fortune tellers and men touting everything imaginable. Everyone had something to sell except the beggars, who had only their hunger, their deformities and mutilations, and their persistence. Augusta's rule was to give away four dollars for every one she spent on herself in port, a goal easily achieved since to give to one beggar meant to be instantly surrounded and pursued by a swarm of others.

If you lifted your eyes, there was China. There were no beggars in China.

"Avery says the hundred-year-old eggs are only three weeks old," Camilla said. "How would he know something like that?"

"Have you fallen in love with Avery?"

"I don't know. Whenever I think so, I tell myself how neurotic and disgusting it would be, and how little I really know about him. He hardly ever talks about himself and he still hasn't mentioned his wife."

"But he talks about his children."

"Yes. He seems perfect on the surface, but he hasn't let me see much that goes on beneath it. Marshall and Patrick are much more real to me."

"Freddy is real to me."

"Honestly, Augusta!"

"He is."

"You don't really know much about him. Do you know what he likes to eat? Pizza? Burgers? In a French restaurant what would he order most often? What's his drink? Scotch? Martinis?

"I'll ask Aurora when we get back. What silly details!"

"Can you hear the sound of his voice?"

"There's a voice I imagine. Maybe I remember it."

"Can he sing? Carry a tune? Do you know how the hair grows on his body?"

"Oh, Camilla!"

"And what about a nice warm body? What about a hand to touch? What about the way that hand would touch you, the special way it would feel?"

Augusta moaned. They were silent for a moment, watching a street barber at work on a customer. The barber was trimming the man's beard. The man was white, tall and thin. Freddy hadn't had a beard but the shape of the head was his. She edged a little closer, trying to see the man's eyes. Would she know Freddy? Her heart began to beat faster.

"Maybe he's not really dead," she whispered to Camilla. "Maybe that man over there is Freddy."

"Christ, Augusta!"

She was no more than a foot away from him, staring down at him. The man looked up questioningly, then winked lewdly at her. He was not Freddy; not at all. Camilla yanked her arm.

"You're getting really scary, Augusta," Camilla said, dragging her off. "Let's go back."

"Wait, I need to get some of this street racket," Augusta said, clicking on the recorder. Of course she hadn't truly thought it was Freddy. They strolled along, not talking, surrounded by a chaos of sound, of singsong voices in many tongues and the cries of street hawkers, of wheels turning and horns blaring, and off somewhere the insistent barking of a dog, and from an open window above a fish shop, a phonograph or radio playing a popular Chinese song, strings twanging monotonously within its half-octave range of microtones. She was not yet sure what her piece would be. Travelbabble.

When she had collected as much as she felt she might need, they took a taxi to the Tiger Balm Gardens, where they wandered in a papier-maché fantasy world among groups of school children.

206

"Freddy obviously knows more about Marco than I do," Augusta said, "and I'm his daughter."

"That's just it: you're his daughter."

"And that blinds me? Or do you mean that he's careful to keep a side of himself hidden from me? Do you think he has something to be ashamed of?"

"Ashamed? Not Marco. And what do you mean, Freddy knows?"

"Knew."

"I'm getting pretty sick of Freddy."

"Then we won't talk about him any more."

"What about Ben?"

"Ben," Augusta said. "You know, I never thought he was dull, but he is a little, isn't he?"

"Oh, Augusta, you only think that because Ben has the disadvantage of being unglamorously alive."

"Cleo's in love with him," Augusta said.

"Poor Marshall."

"Everyone seems to be falling in and out of love."

"Marshall is so handsome and so good."

"Maybe Ben will fall in love with Cleo."

"You wouldn't mind that?"

Augusta's tape recorder was on. She had hoped for sounds of childish glee, but oriental children were much less noisy than American ones; a few high-pitched giggles politely shared was all she'd been able to collect. She switched off the machine.

"This mating business," Camilla said. "You know, in the animal world, and that includes insects, reptiles, amphibians, so many species live solitary lives and come together only to mate."

"I thought they traveled in packs and swarms and flocks and schools and prides," Augusta said.

"But in order to mate, they have to meet."

"Sounds sensible."

207

"They meet in one of two ways. Either the male seeks out the female, or he entices her to him. In the first case, the male finds the female almost always by smell."

"Then couldn't you say she's enticing him? It sounds so sexist to have it all up to him."

"The female chooses. She chooses the best. But when the female is lured to the male, it is never by smell. It's by other senses, chiefly hearing and sight."

"Why are you telling me this, Camilla?"

"Because you can't see Freddy, or smell him, or hear him, or feel him."

"Yes I can. Anyhow, I'm not mating."

"What if we were all to fall in love with the dead? It's conceivable, you know, what with television and old movies. I mean, imagine trying to choose between Gary Cooper and Thomas Jefferson."

Augusta laughed. "There's some interplay, though, between Freddy and me," she said. "He did know me, and I knew him a little. And there are the letters. And there's his house, his boat, and all that money. Camilla, I don't think I like having all that money."

"How can you not like it?"

"It gives me a sense of unreality. Everything suddenly seems so possible, so easy."

"Because it is."

"When things are too easy, who wants them?"

"How perverse you are. What will you do?"

"Give it away. Being able to have anything is not only too easy, it's too hard. It forces you to find out what you really, really want."

"Isn't that better than having to act out of necessity or expedience?"

"I don't know. Take my teaching job. I never knew until now that I don't really like teaching much. Now I don't have to do it and it seems almost pointless since there must

208

be dozens of people as qualified who would be glad to have my job. But having to teach was probably good for me. So many of our values are dictated by necessity."

"My immigrant grandparents on my father's side were so poor that their only value was money --- getting it and hanging onto it. The finer things of life didn't concern them at all because they literally hadn't the time for them."

They walked along, feeling more and more depressed.

"Let's go to Ocean Park," Camilla said, brightening. "Avery says it has an atoll reef with 30,000 tropical fish. Let's go count them and see if he's right."

"Why don't you ask Avery about his wife?"

"Come right out and ask him?"

"Yes. With actual words."

"That's the problem with Avery. He's not the kind of man one feels comfortable asking about his wife."

CHAPTER TWENTY FIVE

Aurora stood, straight and majestic, in the middle of the drawing room waiting for Marco to tell her why he had summoned her.

"May I have a word with you?" he said, causing her to wonder why white people said so many unnecessary things. Did she have the option of saying no, he could not have a word with her? Would he have called her there so that they could be silent together? Did he really want a word and which one would it be? Politeness was often nothing but some kind of nervous tic. This man was a gentleman, and suave, but he wasn't at all like Alfred Nickleby.

"You can have a whole passel of words with me," she assured him.

"Just what is a passel, Aurora?" he asked, distracted. Why had he thought her stout? There was probably not an ounce of fat on her. She was strong .

"I'm not rightly sure. You reckon it could be a parcel?"

"Please sit down, Aurora."

"That sounds serious," she said, sitting in the matching love seat that faced his. "You going to fire me?"

"Aurora, something is going on in this house that I feel doesn't properly belong here."

"What's wrong? Something not to your liking, sir? Le cuisine?"

"Not le cuisine. The meals have been masterpieces," he assured her. "The house is run immaculately. I've no complaints on that score. On the contrary."

"Then to what score you referring, Mr. March, sir?"

"Please stop calling me sir. And I wish you'd drop that southern slave mammy talk with me. I don't know why you do it."

"That what you bring me here to discuss?" she asked. The calculated innocence was gone from her eyes, and with it the softness of her face. She had cheekbones and a jaw. Her dark eyes were fiercely proud. How noble she was! "Is it the vocabulary or the syntax you objects to, Mr. March, or jes the whole mess?"

"It's the whole pose. What's it for? I've heard you talk when you weren't any more Southern mammy than I am."

"To my ears *you* have an accent. Anyhow, must've been somebody else y'all overheard."

"It was you, Aurora. I wish you'd be straight with me. I'm not your enemy. In fact, I feel a close kinship with you, I don't know why. I feel that you're, well, my spiritual sister."

"Do you!" she snorted, amused. "We haven't a thing in the world in common." The accent had slipped away. "We're probably as unalike as it's possible for two people to be."

He was hurt. "Perhaps you misjudge me," he said. "Look, Aurora, I don't want to stop whatever it is you're doing, as long as there's no real danger. I feel responsible, though, to my daughter. I am responsible. She expressly asked me to stay here to look after things."

"Why should you think there's anything happening here to worry about? There's nothing."

"Then why that pose of yours? I think it's a disguise of some sort. And all those people coming and going at all hours upstairs. And that money in the wine cellar. What about all that?"

"The kids? They're family. And I explained about the money."

He sighed. "I wish you'd trust me. You can, you know."

211

"I trust you, Mr. Marco, but there's nothing to trust you about."

"Aurora, I overheard you telling some kid that you're sending him to art school. I wasn't eavesdropping. I couldn't help overhearing."

"Is that a crime, sending a kid to art school?"

"From the sound of it, he's one of many."

"So?"

"Where's the money coming from, Aurora? You can't be doing it on your wages."

"I have... fundraisers."

"Then why so mysterious and secretive? Aurora, what is the R.B.H.? What does that stand for?"

"I guess I can tell you that," Aurora said, and smiled. "It's our little joke. It stands for the Really Black Hand."

"The Really Black Hand?" Marco said, confused. "The Black Hand, he knew, was an underworld organization. Did it have to do with Ireland? No, that was something else.

There was a sudden commotion outside the door, and Star burst in, her eyes wild and red. She was in a state of extreme agitation. Alarmed, Marco leaped to his feet.

"What is it?" he said.

"I've got to talk to you, Aurora," Star said, ignoring him. "Something terrible..."

"Who?"

"Malden."

"Bad?"

"Dead," Star sobbed.

"Oh, my God," Aurora said. "Where is he?"

"I don't know. The police took his bo... him. He had identification. They notified his mother."

"I'll have to go to her," Aurora said, rising.

"Better not," Star said. "Not yet. They'll question you."

"The telephone was ringing. Automatically, Aurora picked it up, though she was weeping. "This the March

212

residence," she sobbed, reverting. "Jes a minute, please." She handed the phone to Marco, getting up to leave. "It for you."

"It's," Marco said as Aurora and Star, their arms around each other, left the room. "Hello?"

"You been beating the help?" a voice boomed. "Or are they just scared of telephones?"

"Who is this?" he said, moving the receiver several inches away from his ear.

"Natalie."

"Who?"

"Natalie Schwart."

"Who?"

"Lynda's mother, for Chrissake, you sound like an owl."

"Sorry. My mind's a million miles away. How are you, Natalie?"

"To exchange health reports is not why I'm calling," she said. "I'm calling to warn you that Lynda is on her way over."

"I'm not expecting her," Marco said, looking at his watch. It was nearly five o'clock. Erwinna would be arriving at seven.

"That's why I'm warning."

"I can't see her. I've got a business appointment. Is there some way I can reach her? Put it off till tomorrow?"

"No. She wants to surprise you."

"Surprise? Is anything wrong? She's not preg..."

"Don't say it, God forbid! Don't even think it. She's coming to make you an offer."

"An offer?" he said, mystified.

"And I just want you to know that as far as I'm concerned it's an offer you can refuse."

"Well, thank you, Natalie," he said doubtfully.

"Don't thank me, it wasn't my idea. And don't tell her I called."

"When do you think she'll be here?"

213

"Toot sweet," she said, and hung up.

Marco stared at the receiver in his hand, then replaced it in its cradle. He hadn't seen Lynda or called her since the luncheon date with her mother almost a week ago. She had called several times and left messages, but he hadn't had time to return her calls, what with Turkish Bath and spending alternate nights with Erwinna and Janet. He had planned to see Lynda in order to break it off with her, but there hadn't been a moment. Also, he felt cowardly about it. He wasn't good at ending affairs and almost never did it. His way was to drive women to do the ending. Giving them that power, making them think it was their own idea, produced fewer unpleasant scenes. He could be aggrieved, mournful, while she, whoever she was, could be angry if she chose, but not as a victim. She could be triumphant. But with Lynda he was going to have to do it, and this would be as good a time as any.

He went downstairs to fetch ice, not wanting to ring for Aurora. He tried to remember which one Malden had been, and wondered how he had been killed, and why Star had stopped Aurora from going to see Malden's mother. The Really Black Hand. Aurora was in the kitchen crying into a piecrust she was rolling out. He looked at her strong, capable, black hands. The Black Hand, hadn't that been some Sicilian organization?

"I don't want to bother you," Marco said, "but a friend is coming by any minute for a drink and I thought I'd get the ice."

"I'll do it," Aurora said, mopping her eyes with a dish-towel. "The show must go on. Is this the woman who's expected for dinner, or yet another?"

"It's Miss Schwart. She'll be gone by dinner time. I'm sorry about Malden. But I think that's exactly what I was trying to talk to you about. Later." He looked nervously at

214

his watch. "Would you send Miss Schwart up to my study, please?"

It would be better to see her up there where he felt more in command, his own bailiwick, and so much cozier than the drawing room. It must be a tender scene; he would hurt her as little as possible. He must pretend that his heart was breaking. After all, they had shared many delightful hours.

Summer sunlight still poured into the room. He adjusted the shades, the curtains, the thermostat that controlled the air conditioning, and sat down at his desk. He picked up a pen and pulled some papers from a drawer. Let her see that he was busy, that she was interrupting him. It would have to be as short a scene as possible. Poised over the desk, he sat thinking of Aurora and Star, feeling disturbed. It was possible that he'd never seen Malden. He had really not paid much attention.

Lynda burst into the room, Aurora right behind her bearing an ice bucket which she put on the small bar in the corner of the study.

"Will there be anything else, sir?"

"No, thank you, Aurora. Lynda! What on earth are you doing here?" he said, feigning surprise.

"This place is gorgeous, Marco," Lynda said, coming over to kiss him when Aurora had gone. "I'd no idea your daughter was this rich."

"She's even richer than this. What, you've never been here?"

"You know I haven't, Marco," she said reproachfully, though her eyes were shining with excitement. He couldn't help smiling at her, she was so fresh and cool and young. And beautiful. What skin she had! He knew a lot of men who would kill for her. It wasn't fair.

"You know we haven't even fucked in over a week, Marco, or hadn't you noticed?"

215

"Naturally I've noticed," he said, shuffling the papers on his desk. "I've been so busy, Lynda, but I'm glad you're here. We must talk."

"What did you think of Natalie?"

"Who's Natalie?"

"My mother. She was crazy about you."

"She's. She's a. She's an unusual woman."

"She certainly is. She has the Midas touch, that woman," she said with pride. "She turns everything to gold." She smiled modestly, shyly, at Marco. "I take after her."

"Do you dear. Lynda, I've been giving a lot of serious thought to ... us..."

"Oh, so have I, darling, constantly. That's why..." She was rummaging in her purse.

"And I've come to the painful conclusion, my sweet, that I'm being horribly unfair to you." Soft honey-colored curls had fallen across her brow. Her skin was opalescent, perfect.

"Voila!" she said triumphantly, drawing from her purse what appeared to be a legal document. Was she serving him with a summons? Whatever for? How could he have breached a promise if he'd never made one?

"The age difference, you see," he persevered, though his voice was weakening. "You deserve so much more than I can give you."

"Mother and I," she announced, looking at him, a tiny smile dimpling the corners of her adorable mouth, her eyes dancing with anticipation, "want you as a partner in our most lucrative enterprise. In fact, except for your signature, it's a fait accompli. We've bought out Ricky and made his share over to you, one third. A gift. Outright."

"What are you talking about? What enterprise? Girdles?"

"Marilyn," she said.

"Marilyn?"

"You do love it there, I know you do."

"You own Marilyn?"

"Of course. I thought you knew."

"How would I have known?"

"Well, what did you think I was doing there?"

"Dancing. Like me."

"And the name?"

"This is certainly a day for names," Marco said, staggered. "What about the name?"

"M-A for my Ma, R-I for Rickey..."

"Stop. I can guess the rest."

She thrust the document at him. Automatically, he took it. "A gift?" he said. "But why?"

"Because we know you'll be a terrific asset, Marco. And also, oh darling, think of it as a premature Valentine from me. Or a late one."

"Lynda, darling, I don't see how I can accept this," he said. His mouth had gone dry, his heart was beating very fast. He held in his hand the RI share of Marilyn, or the MA could as easily now stand for Marco, or even March, as for Mama. His. One third. Absolutely free. Almost. Invisible strings, maybe. Almost surely. Her arms were around his neck, her mouth nibbling his.

"Are you pleased, Marco?" she breathed, her warm sweet breath bathing him, her adorable breasts pressed against him. "Are you happy?" How could he have begun to forget how delicious she was? In spite of himself, he began to rise to the occasion. Glancing over her shoulder at his watch, he saw that it was barely five-thirty. There was just enough time.

CHAPTER TWENTY-SIX

Love is most nearly itself
When here and now cease to matter
Old men ought to be explorers
Here and there does not matter
We must be still and still moving
Into another intensity
For a further union, a deeper communion
Through the dark cold and the empty desolation,
The wave cry, the winds cry, the vast waters
Of the petrel and the porpoise.
In my end is my beginning.

In my end is my beginning; the words had been revolving around Augusta's head all morning. More of Eliot. Would this prove to be the final letter? She felt they were nearing the end, that every letter would be the last. And then what? She would be caught in a closed circle ... left with what? A handful of dust. More and more, she was frightened. She told herself sternly that in the end, the end of this voyage, she would go back and deal with her new life. She would submerge herself in her music, make a symphony out of these mounds of tapes she was gathering. She would come to terms with her money and the boundless possibilities that were now open to her. She would have to deal with Oswald Summerville, from whom, via the ship's radio, there had been numerous messages along the lines of thinking of you with longing, etcetera. She would make up her mind about Ben, once and for all, unless, as she more than half hoped, the need for that was precluded by Cleo. She need never marry. She sometimes thought of having a child. Really, more and more she would like to have a child, and if she had one she might find that she wanted another. But it was no longer entirely necessary to marry to have children, though it would be better, of course, to be married, for there to be a father. Perhaps someone would come along who wouldn't mind fathering her child, even knowing that she didn't love him. She would deal with that. In the end. Her mind was a cat's cradle, a twisted network of unfinished thoughts leading nowhere. In his end, my beginning.

"Nature," Camilla was saying, "programs its creatures to carry out actions whose final results are completely unknown to them. It was centuries before even man made a connection between the sexual act and childbirth . And how did nature manage this magician's trick?" She took a swallow of her drink. Sunglasses hid her eyes. "With desire. Hunger and desire."

They were sitting on deck before lunch, all except Bert and Marshall, enjoying the gentle air of another perfect day, drinking Bloody Marys, talking, talking, talking. She, Augusta, had assembled all these people. At least it was her money that had caused them to be gathered here, contained in this ship like metal filings drawn to a magnet, her money the magnet, money translated into this moment, her money, her power. Were it not for that, Ben would be getting settled in Santa Cruz or bumbling around Florence, Camilla would still be at her desk making teeth, spending weekends on a nearby beach; Marshall would probably be sleeping off who knew what night's work (depending on the time in New York. She had lost track of all the crossed time zones); Avery would be minding his marina. The twins? She had no idea where they would be, what doing. But here they all were, riding the Burma sea, knowing each other, falling in and out of love, having all these emotions. So this is what the rich feel, this is what power is: to alter, to shape not only

219

one's own destiny but that of others. Change, choice, and the titillation of bottomless possibility, the not-yet-known. How dangerous it was.

"The satisfaction of desire is the highest aim of the individual creature," Camilla said, "but for nature it's only a means to a higher end."

"Are you talking about God?" Ben asked. "Are you going to lump us in with the sticklebacks again?"

"Are you suggesting that we're subverting nature?" Avery asked. "Are you going to make a moral point?"

"Morality is beside the point," Camilla said.

"You could see morality, if you like, as another human invention in the service of that higher aim of Nature," Ben said.

"Anyhow, if what you're going to say is..."

"Why not wait until I say it?"

"...that all the trappings humans invent and use are embroidery and embellishment in the service of this higher law..."

"Not only humans. Birds and fish and butterflies do it with color. Crickets fiddle with their legs and frogs croak. Glowworms and fireflies do it with their little lamps."

"Let's do it," Ben sang. "The itch and the scratch."

"What humans do that other animals don't is to evade their biological responsibility. They develop neuroses. Impotence. Frigidity. And variations like onanism and homosexuality. They use prophylactics. They have concepts of chastity and celibacy and they've invented sin. During much of their lives, and sometimes throughout them, they have sex without any concern for procreation."

"So much more creative."

"And a good thing, too, as you'll agree when we get to India," Patrick said.

"Yes, despite our aimless screwing," Avery said, "and war and famine and man-made or natural disasters, we've

220

somehow contrived to overpopulate this earth. We must be doing something right."

"So don't worry about it, Camilla darling."

"I wasn't worrying," Camilla said impatiently, reminding herself of Avery's five children. If each of them followed the family pattern, in one generation they would be twenty five, in two they would be one hundred and twenty-five, and thereafter the numbers would be staggering. "I was simply toying with some ideas about the complexity and variety and endless imaginativeness of what we use for repellants, or for bait."

Hunger and desire, Augusta thought. They would be so painful if we hadn't the means to satisfy them, but knowing that we do have those means makes them, instead, rather pleasant. Because they were hungry there was anticipation of the pleasure they would take in the meal now being brought out to be spread on the outdoor buffet: a salad with goat cheese and tiny black olives, a turbot soufflé, bright moist raspberries, a mound of whipped cream. What would it mean without appetite? But hunger and desire. "Pain wanders through my bones like a lost fire; what burns me now? Desire, desire, desire." Hunger is appetite too long deferred. What she would do when the letters ended was go into mourning and, in time, she hoped, recover. She reminded herself that she was doing exactly what she had set out to do. She had gotten to know Freddy and when his death came she would bury him properly, with grief, with real tears, and then she would miss him. He would have his due.

"Bait seems such a ... cynical word," Cleo, who until now had been silent, said. She was sitting next to Ben, so close that when she leaned forward, as she was doing now, he could feel the imprint of her small breast on his arm. He wondered if she was aware of what she was doing. Bait. "Sometimes all the bait we offer is ourselves."

221

"When I fall in love," Patrick said, his eyes on Augusta, "it's purely with the person, and not with any idea I've had to concoct about her, or with anything she's done to her hair or with eyeliner, or with how much money she has. I fall in love with her essence, with the ways in which she's happy or sad, with the words she speaks and the sound of her voice speaking them, with the way her eyes shine or fill with thought, with her loveliness, her seriousness, her humor." His eyes burned. He seemed unable to stop." With her walk and the things she does with her hands when she's intense about something. With the way she sneezes and the way she chews her food and puts down her knife and fork. With every single detail of her. If that's bait, I'll gladly swallow it along with the hook, line, and sinker."

His eyes had filled with tears. Augusta couldn't help blushing at the earnestness of his declaration. She was shaken by it, and so, apparently, were they all. It was a long minute before anyone spoke.

"Why Patrick," Camilla said, "how beautiful."

"You sound so experienced at falling in love," Ben said with a trace of annoyance. "Has it happened to you often?"

"It only has to happen once for you to be, as you say, experienced at it," Patrick said.

"I guess I'm lucky. Obviously, there are some people it never happens to." It was Ben's turn to redden. He was very angry. Fortunately, Rosetta chose that moment to announce lunch and the circle was broken.

"You see now that it's too late, don't you?" Patrick said, his voice unsteady. Was he afraid of her, or was it the intensity of his feelings that frightened him? She reached to touch his cheek. It was as smooth as silk. She was almost certain that he had never shaved. She was moved by his tawny beauty, his lean grace. He had only just burst free of adolescence, and though you could see the outlines of his

222

manhood, they had not yet given him his adult shape. He was still growing.

"There is nothing I can say to you that will be what you want to hear," she told him gently. "I can't argue with your feelings and I wouldn't want to. I treasure them."

"Then let me love you. You needn't love me back. I'd never want to bind you in any way."

"Come sit here beside me," she said. When he did, she took his hand and held it between hers. It was a strong hand and, she knew by the way he played the violin, a sensitive one. In time he would be a lovely lover. She felt a small pang of regret. "Patrick, tell me what plan you have for your life."

"My life? To give it to you, of course."

"No, no, I mean at your center, that place that was there before you ever knew me and that will always be there, no matter what happens between us. What is your strength? How do you mean to use it?"

He gnawed his lip, thinking how to answer her. "What difficult questions you ask," he said. "I've never asked them of myself. I've never thought about my center or my strengths. Perhaps I haven't any. I've always wanted only to be free, and to live in beauty."

She smiled at him. "Yes, I think that's who you are, and it's enough. At least for now."

"But I could change for you, Augusta," he pleaded.

"I don't want you to change."

"But you're free, too, Augusta."

"No, I'm not, and I don't want to be, not in that way. I want always to be bound, by love, by responsibility, by devotion to my work and to those I love. We're very different, Patrick. If we were to meet in love, it would only be fleetingly, and it would leave you in far more pain than you think you're in now."

"You are arguing with my feelings. I'm in pain, all right, and it feels very real and powerful to me."

Desire, desire, desire. Almost, she was tempted to assuage it, but that would only serve to feed it, not to extinguish it. She knew this; he did not.

"To be free is not the easiest thing," she said. "It takes courage."

He tried to imagine her in an academic setting, the wife of a professor, all those evenings with other professors and their wives. The dullness.

"What would you do, Cleo?" he asked.

"I'd learn to cook for you."

He groaned. What a thing to do to her! "And summers. Those long holidays when you'll want to be sailing or surfing or water-skiing or scuba-diving, and I'll want to spend all the time in stuffy museums and galleries and caves looking at pictures."

"I'll go with you. I'll learn. I don't surf."

"It would be like putting you in a cage. You would wither and die."

"Never."

"Oh, Cleo, it's out of the question."

"You only think that because you don't love me. But you will."

"I'm tempted to love you. Who wouldn't be? But really, Cleo, at bottom I'm a stodgy man. And I'll no doubt go on getting even stodgier."

"Then you need me to keep you from that."

Her face was inches from his, fresh as a peach, her luminous eyes pleaded with him, she smelled like a breeze off the sea, and like lemons, her arms were around his neck. He disengaged them and stepped back from her.

"Cleo, Cleo," he sighed.

"You're still in love with her," she said mournfully.

"I've been in love with her for a long time. I'm not so emotionally nimble."

"Then I'll give you more time."

"At different ages, each has been my favorite," Avery said. "They're all so different. Maude is the dreamer, Ellie the practical one, all common sense. Billy is impetuous, heroic, physical, always breaking bones. His own bones, of course. Jonathan is studious and shy and careful, never breaking anything. Millicent is a nymphet, already breaking hearts. She's going to be trouble."

Camilla smiled, liking the way he talked about his children, but she was beginning to feel the weight of the baggage he carried from his past. She thought of Michael Bell and his computer, and imagined what it would predict if he were to feed it Avery's components and her own. The Mating Compatibility Program. It made her laugh to think of Michael.

It was late afternoon. They were in Avery's bed. They had not yet made love, though that was why they were there. Avery lay on his back, looking up at the ceiling. She watched his face as he talked, answering her questions. The lines of his profile were strong, regular, the bridge of his nose slightly beaked, the chin firm. When he smiled, his cheeks furrowed and the lines raying from the corners of his eyes deepened.

"Which of the children is most like your wife?" Camilla forced herself to ask.

"My wife?" His face clouded. "Millicent, I suppose. And Maude, too, a little."

"You've never talked about your wife, Avery."

"Haven't I?"

She thought he would turn to look at her, but his gaze remained fixed on the ceiling, in his past, in his other life.

"Never," Camilla said. "Not once."

225

"Why would I?" he said evasively.

"Why wouldn't you? What's her name, Avery? I don't even know her name."

She felt him stiffen, and waited for what he would say, her heartbeat quickening.

"Her name was Ann," he said. "She's dead, Camilla. She died soon after Millicent was born."

"Oh," she said, chastened. But in the next breath she felt her anger rise at the enormity of his lie.

"Why didn't you tell me?" she asked.

"I don't like to talk about it."

"Oh, you don't like to talk about it! How profoundly sensitive you must be."

The bed had been rocking gently, but now, as if to match her anger, its motion became erratic. They were entering rough seas. She got out of bed and began to put on her clothes.

"What is it, Camilla?" he asked, lifting himself up on his elbows, his eyes troubled.

"It's because you want women... me... to think you're married and unavailable for anything but this, isn't it? To keep us from getting too serious?"

"Partly, yes. I don't think I could ever marry again. I need to be free."

"Free? With all those children? Who takes care of them?"

"My parents are raising them. There's a housekeeper, too."

"Do you live with them?"

"No. They're in Connecticut. A big house, good schools. I keep an apartment in town. I see them often. Quite a few weekends. And sometimes the older ones come to town and stay with me."

"I see."

226

"I support them, naturally. I help support my parents, too."

"How awfully good of you."

"Stop it, Camilla. You're being unfair." She was fully dressed, prepared to leave. But she was not quite finished with him.

"How did your wife die?" she said.

She saw his eyes go blank, as though shades against feeling had been drawn over them.

"In a car accident," he said.

"Were you with her?"

"I was driving," he said, and caught his lower lip between his teeth.

"Ohhh," she said, understanding. The captain, the skipper. The man in control. "Oh, Avery, I'm sorry."

"It was a long time ago," he said.

She was silent, waiting. The ship heaved and settled with a shudder.

"I had a cut on my wrist. That was all." He began to cry. "And she was... she was."

"It was an accident," she said. "Fate."

"Not fate," he said, his shoulders hunched, tears streaming down his face. She was frightened. She had been at the door, prepared to leave, but now she came back into the room and sat beside him on the bed. "Accidents are always sudden, unexpected," he said, the words coming with difficulty. "There's no time to make a reasoned choice."

"No, of course not," she said soothingly.

"But one does make a choice, a split-second one. I swerved. I swerved to the left." He stopped for a moment, making an effort to get himself back under control. "If I had swerved to the right, I would have taken the full brunt of the impact and she might have lived."

She put her arms around him. "It was an instinctive reaction," she said.

227

"Yes, but why was the instinct to save myself and not to save Ann?"

"Instincts aren't moral decisions, Avery. They have nothing to do with the mind. They're cellular, bred in the muscles."

"I don't believe it," he said. "I as good as murdered her."

She stroked his hair, sighing. People, she thought! You never knew what they trailed after them. She felt the heaviness of his life, the lightness of her own. He, who had always been in such command of himself, his head filled with all the proper data, the pertinent information. The ship creaked and thumped. And yet so near the surface, this other man, this man who cried, believing he had sacrificed his wife to save himself.

"But no one," she said, "could have behaved differently. Don't you see, Avery? That's why the seat next to the driver's is called the death seat, why it's the least safe. You must have loved her very much."

He reached for a handkerchief and blew his nose, then, dry-eyed, looked at her without expression.

"That's the worst part of it," he said. "I didn't love her at all."

She watched his shoes that had been so neatly paired beside the bed, slide across the floor and back again, still perfectly coupled, as though magnetized by each other. She could think of nothing to say. The late afternoon light coming through the portholes was a strange sick shade of green. She felt queasy, hypnotized.

"I've got to go up," Avery said, getting out of bed and pulling on his trousers. "It looks like we're in for a serious storm."

228

CHAPTER TWENTY-SEVEN

"The Really Black Hand!" Marco snorted. He had put two and two together and he was pretty sure he had come up with four. "You should have called yourselves the Robin Hoods."

"What you mean? I mean what do you mean?"

Aurora and Star were in the kitchen. Aurora was stuffing some birds and Star was polishing silver. Janet was expected for dinner.

"Every night a different one," Star had commented to Aurora. "He sure spreads himself around. Nothing selfish about that man."

"I mean you've been robbing hoods," Marco said angrily. "You're mixed up with the Mafia, aren't you?"

"I don't know what you're talking about," Aurora said. Star looked up, her eyes narrowing. "What Mafia?"

"You know very well what I'm talking about, Aurora. After they've made their collections, one of you, Malden, has been jumping them, stealing their take. That's where the money's been coming from. That's how Malden was killed."

The spoons fell from Star's hand and clattered onto the table. "He's one of them," she said, shrinking back.

"How could you know that?" Aurora asked, her dark eyes blazing.

"Good God!" Marco said. "How long did you think you could get away with it?"

"We've been getting away with it for a long time," Aurora said. "Poor Malden."

"But don't you see, Aurora," Star said. "if he's one of them, we're finished. We'll all be killed."

229

"I'm not one of them," Marco said. "And you're damn lucky those hoods are so stupid. If they hadn't killed Malden on the spot they could have followed him back here and blown us all away."

"Malden wouldn't have come back here. Not right away," Aurora said. "We're not that stupid."

"If I had only known," Marco said softly, sitting down at the table next to Star. "I could have prevented this."

"You?" Aurora said.

"I told you, he's one of them," Star said. "Don't talk to him, Aurora."

"I'm not one of them," Marco said. "I was in their office, you see, trying to save a friend of mine who owes them a lot of money. He owns a dance hall and they were going to kill him, or at least break some bones, and I was trying to make a deal with them. It's a long story. But while I was there, one of their men came into the office right after he'd been mugged by one of you and they talked about what they were going to do. Right in front of me. They decided to use a sort of platoon system, a second man trailing the first. When Malden jumped the first man, the second man must have jumped Malden."

They stared at him. "I don't trust him," Star said. "He has to be one of them."

"No, no. If he were, why would he be telling us this?"

"I think they said ten paces behind. I wasn't listening very closely. But you know what you have to do if you're planning to continue this madness."

"Our own platoon system," Aurora said, nodding. "A second man ten paces behind their second man."

"She's right," Marco said, and laughed at the thought of this proliferating line of men in alternating colors stalking one another through the city streets. "When they're on to that, which will be after the first time, they'll simply put two men on the first man's tail. The streets will be littered with

230

fallen bodies, like dominoes. It's ridiculous. And much too dangerous."

"We'll call it off for a while. Let them think it was just Malden, a one-man operation, and that it's over. Then, when they get complacent..."

"No," Marco said. "I'll think of another way. Let me help you."

"You can't help us," Aurora said sullenly. "Your hand ain't black."

Marco smiled. "It ain't particularly white, either."

"There's the doorbell," Star said, going to answer it.

"Must be your dinner guest," Aurora said, glancing at the clock on the wall. "She's early. Your lady friends are always early."

"They can't wait to see me."

"Well, take your time with drinks. This dinner's going to be late."

When he stepped into the drawing room, to which Janet had just been ushered by Star, he saw that she was holding a thick white envelope. Wordlessly, she held it out to him. His heart sank.

"For me?" he said. "What is it?"

"Open it."

But he knew, even before it was out of the envelope, that it was the lease to Corned Beef & Cabbage. In his name.

"All yours," Janet said, her face radiant with triumph. "You'll never know what I've been through to get it for you."

"Why will I never know," he asked dully, "since you're about to tell me?" It was inevitable that Corned Beef & Cabbage would be his. Lucky lucky Marco. He poured drinks and handed her one, then swallowed his at one gulp. "Go ahead. Tell me."

"You haven't even kissed me yet," she said, blind to his dismay.

He kissed her and sank into the sofa. She sat beside him, filling his nostrils with fragrance, something expensive. Her burnished hair was pulled back severely from her white face with its interesting bones, its scarlet mouth, the heavily made-up eyes that were shining with her pleasure at this gift she was bestowing. A tendril of hair had escaped and curled across the delicate curve of her brow. She was bewitching. Even the lines of age that were beginning to show around her eyes intrigued him. With that corner of his mind that was not in despair, he thought about her knowledgeable body as he had last enjoyed it, naked in his arms, and his palms began to tingle with desire.

"I seduced Talifiero," Janet said, smiling wickedly.

"You what? You seduced her?"

"I knew that's what you were planning to do, you dog, but as soon as I met her it was obvious that it would be more productive if I did it."

"Good God, Janet."

"Is that all the thanks I'm going to get?"

"Of course not, darling, but give me a minute for it to sink in. How will you get out of it?"

"Out of what?"

"If seducing her was so effective, maybe she's fallen in love with you. She may be expecting a continuing relationship."

Talifiero had, indeed, fallen ecstatically in love with Janet, though she could not have put what she felt in those terms, even to herself. She had taken nearly a whole package of Tums in the belief that what she was experiencing was a form of nausea, perhaps from those bloody drinks, and that it would soon go away. She had never had a hangover. The hangover did go away, but she was left with this other feeling that made her restless and, at turns, either happy or miserable, with Janet somehow at the center of what she was feeling. She began to suspect that she would feel somewhat better if Janet were to leave Julius and move in with her. If not for Marco, Janet might almost have considered it. Talifiero had been interesting in bed. Unexpectedly and uncharacteristically, Janet now burst into tears.

"What is it, Janet?" Marco asked, alarmed. "What's wrong?"

"You aren't the least bit upset, are you? Or jealous."

"Of course I am. If it were another man I'd be beside myself."

"You think sex between women doesn't really count?"

"How can it?"

"Male chauvinist prick!" She was furious. "You think without your gorgeous dingdong there's no such thing as sex!"

"I've always had this odd feeling that it's played a pretty important role in our lovemaking. Or have I been deluding myself?"

"No, you haven't," Janet sighed, wiping her eyes which were now smudged with mascara. "But that doesn't mean that it's the beginning and the end-all. Actually, sex with Talifiero wasn't bad."

"I'm so glad to hear it. We might as well get what pleasure we can from our little sacrifices."

"Why are we quarreling, Marco? I've brought you Corned Beef & Cabbage on a platter. I thought it was your heart's desire."

"It's wonderful of you, of course, Janet, but I'd just about decided that you were right, we shouldn't get mixed up with that crew." Really, there was no reason he had to go through with it.

"It's too late. We're both mixed up with them. It's done, it's yours, the whole shmear, along with Julius's debt to them. They're not going to do anything to Julius. Those were your terms, Talifiero said. There's also a check on the

233

way to you for $100,000 to do whatever remodeling you had in mind. She said you even had the chutzpah to ask for that."

"She said chutzpah?"

"We're going to do it, Marco, you and me. Together. We're going to make it really swing."

"What about you and Talifiero? What about you and Julius? What about Talifiero and Julius? What about Talifiero and me?"

If Talifiero had done this for Janet, she was capable of killing any one of them if she thought they were preventing her from acquiring Janet. Any one, or any combination, but mostly him, Marco.

"What are you talking about, darling? What about you and me?"

CHAPTER TWENTY-EIGHT

"The present falls, the present falls away/ How pure the motion of the rising day,"

There was nothing pure about the motion of the rising sea except its anger. The chair beneath Augusta threatened to pitch her out of it.

"The white sea widening on a farther shore/ The bird, the beating bird, extending wings/ Thus I endure this last pure stretch of joy/ The dire dimension of a final thing."

It could no longer be ignored. The sounds had been mounting, pushing into her consciousness, driving out the words on these pages. She put the letter aside and, grabbing her tape recorder, ran stumbling out on deck where Cleo and Patrick were hastily gathering up whatever was loose and stowing it away. Bert was on the bridge, Avery bounding up the companionway to relieve him. She raised the microphone to catch the sound of the rising wind and the waves slamming against the sides of the ship. Marshall came running out on deck to help, with Ben, looking grim, as though he was going to be sick again, a few steps behind. The sky was ominous, giving off a sickly greenish light through the black rushing clouds.

The sounds were magnificent. Augusta stood transfixed, in a state close to exaltation, trying to keep the recorder dry, unaware of how soaked she was getting. The ship bucked like a maddened bronco, waves washing over the decks with every plunge, and now the sky opened and the rain fell from it in solid sheets. She clung to the deckhouse, hoping the storm would last long enough for a major piece, perhaps a concerto for storm and orchestra, but not an ordinary orchestra, something to provide a counterpoint to it that would render it, by contrast, even more powerful and dramatic, perhaps gamelangs and strings. She began to orchestrate it in her head. The storm could not be constant. She would modulate it so that at moments it would be dominant, at others recede to the background while the strings soared or the gamelangs played their bell-like percussive melody, sweetly naive, and of course in the end they would win, the gamelangs and strings, as the storm died. Storms always die, don't they?

So rapt was she that she did not see Bert until he had grasped her arm. "Get inside!" he shouted, his voice almost lost in the roaring wind, as he pulled her along with him to the entrance to the salon.

"No," she cried. "Let go of me."

"Inside, damn it!" He pushed her through the doorway. His roughness and anger at her, more than the storm itself, gave her the first real sense of danger. It hadn't yet occurred to her to be afraid. He was quite right to have spoken to her as he had and, inside, while he fastened the door behind them, she turned to apologize, but at that moment, accompanied by a roar of thunder, a great wave lifted the ship and set it down again with such force that they both went sprawling onto the floor. She saw something fly away from Bert and skitter across the carpet to where Camilla, who had just come into the room, was trying to stay upright. Automatically, Camilla bent to field whatever it was that was hurtling toward her, scooping it up. She held it in her hand, staring at it with disbelief, while Bert scrambled to his feet.

"Give me that!" Bert barked, stumbling toward her, his face livid. He looked murderous as he reached for what she held and grabbed it from her and stuffed it back into his mouth.

236

"You're Herbert Kalinsky," Camilla said.

"Of course I am," he said gruffly. "Who did you think I was?"

"I mean, your teeth. I'd know them anywhere." She began to laugh, then seeing his embarrassment said, "I'm sorry. It's that, you see, I made them."

"What do you mean, you made them?"

"Your teeth. Your plate. I made those teeth. That's what I used to do. I was a dental technician."

He stared at her, his eyes hardening again with anger. "Hah!" he said. "They're lousy teeth."

"They are not lousy teeth. They're perfect."

"I hate them," he growled, making for the exit. "I loathe and despise them." He vanished through the companionway, but he was still shouting. "They're not sea-worthy teeth."

Augusta, watching from the floor where she had been lying prone, staggered to her feet, to retrieve the recorder and microphone. They seemed undamaged. In fact, the tape was still advancing. She shut it off.

"I think I captured that scene for posterity," she said. "Though for once a camera would have been better."

"I embarrassed him," Camilla said. "I shouldn't have said anything." She was seized by a paroxysm of laughter that doubled her over. "But I couldn't help it. Imagine traveling halfway round the world to... to..."

Augusta was laughing, too. Another wave almost knocked them down.

"The day I met Avery that first time at the marina, I'd just finished making those teeth. My masterpiece." She stopped laughing and dried her eyes. "The ship looked awfully big then. It seems much smaller now, doesn't it?"

"Much smaller," Augusta agreed. "It's such a large storm."

237

"Do you think it's dangerous?" The windows swirled with sudsy foam; it was as if they were in a laundromat, all the machines spinning.

"I feel safe with Avery. I think. I'm sure he's been through plenty of storms like this."

Camilla thought about Avery. A quarter of an hour earlier she had watched him cry. Now he was at the helm and their lives depended on him, on his skill and judgment. He was once again their captain, but he would never be quite the same to her.

"I think we should sit down on the floor," she said, "before we're knocked down again."

On the bridge, Avery was hard-pressed to outguess the waves. There seemed to be no predictable pattern. Rarely had he encountered a sea so large and tumultuous. It must have been such a storm, perhaps not far from here, that had taken Nickleby and The Divine Sarah. Nickleby was far less experienced, and his ship so much smaller and lighter. Although a God's-eye view might have seen The Augusta as passive, a helpless partner in some crazy dance, Avery was exhilarated, summoning all his skills and more, that cellular intuition born of both experience and something in the genes perhaps from some other incarnation. The ship rolled and pitched and heaved, but it was a good ship with exceptional stability and powerful engines, sensitive and responsive to the throttle and speed controls that he was calling on so imperatively to keep it from broaching.

On deck, the crew had finished stowing away the chains and warps. The hatches and portholes were secured, all the gear and deck furniture had been stowed or lashed down and, wet to the bone, Patrick climbed to the bridge and exploded through the doorway on a burst of wind and rain and spray.

"What orders, Avery?" he shouted.

"Tell them to get the hell inside and below," Avery said, although they were already doing this, clinging to the deck-house rails as they groped toward the entryways. "And tell Cleo to get below to the engine room and see that the engines stay at full power. I don't know what the devil she's doing out there."

Patrick lifted the speaking tube. "All hands inside and below," he said, his voice magnifying throughout the ship. "And Cleo..." At the sound of her name, she turned her face to the bridge and raised a hand to Patrick, her fingers shaping a V SIGN. "Get down to the engine room and keep the engines at full power." They were all thoroughly soaked and chilled. Cleo's clothes were plastered to her slim body and rivers streamed from her hair. He grinned down at her, but her answering grin was lost in a great wave that washed up and over her. When it receded, Cleo was no longer there. He caught a glimpse of her as she went over the side, caught and held by the wave, her arms flailing wildly.

"Stop!" Patrick screamed. "Stop the ship. Cleo's over-board."

Ben was running after her, after the wave, but when he reached the rail he gripped it and hesitated. Marshall raced past him and, without breaking stride, leaped over the railing into the sea.

"Stop the ship, Avery," Patrick shrieked again. He was tugging at the door but the wind was against it, nailing it shut. "Marshall's in there, too. Goddamn this door."

"Patrick, stay here," Avery ordered, cutting the engines and turning the stern into the wind. "I need you here." They caught glimpses of Marshall bobbing in and out of the waves, diving into them and beneath them, but there was no sign of Cleo; the sea had plucked her off the ship and swallowed her whole.

"Cleoooo," Patrick howled into the speaker, as if the sound of her name could cause her to appear. "Cleoooo!"

"Tell Ben to throw Marshall a line," Avery said, and Patrick shouted into the tube, his voice choked with urgency. They watched Ben unhook one of the life preservers and hold it aloft, prepared to throw it to Marshall, but Marshall was looking the other way, out to sea.

"He can't last long out there in this," Avery said. "See if you can get his attention, Patrick. Tell him to grab the line and hang onto it while we circle. And tell him to keep it taut and clear of the rudder."

Patrick repeated the message three times before Marshall gave any sign of having heard. He was obviously tiring, his arms churning with difficulty. At last he turned toward the ship, his face a mask of pain. When he was in position, Ben tossed out the lifebuoy and Marshall caught it on the first throw. He clung to it with one hand as he turned back to his search. They were all searching, desperately scanning the sea, as Avery tried to hold the ship steady.

"She's a good swimmer," Patrick kept saying. "A marvelous swimmer. She's a fish, a fish." He gripped Avery's powerful binoculars, his knuckles white. "She's got to be there somewhere."

Suddenly, as though mollified, having exacted its sacrifice, the sea's rage abated, the waves began to subside, the wind died, and where the black clouds had sped off, a red sun broke through low on the horizon and a rainbow appeared like a bloody smile, a peace offering. They all drifted out on deck, Camilla, Augusta, Bert, Jacques and Rosetta, and stood mutely at the rail, straining for some sight of Cleo, while Avery slowly circled, combing an ever-widening patch of sea. Augusta looked up at the bridge and, seeing Patrick's ashen, stricken face, ran up to him.

Ben felt the line go slack in his hands. Marshall had let go of the buoy and disappeared into the darkening sea. They held their breath. After what seemed an eternity, he exploded through the surface, holding Cleo's limp body. With what

240

must have been the last of his strength, he grabbed the lifeline and Ben pulled them in. In terrible silence, Ben and Bert leaned to lift first Cleo, then Marshall, onto the deck. Augusta, holding Patrick, felt him tremble throughout his body, then he lurched and broke away from her to hurl himself down to the deck, where Ben was gently turning Cleo onto her stomach and into position for what he vaguely remembered of artificial respiration. He was about to kneel astride her when Marshall raised himself up from the deck and rudely shoved him aside.

"Not that way," he said gruffly. "I'll do it."

He lifted Cleo's limp body as though it were weightless, and grasping her from behind around her waist, locked his fists over her diaphragm and pumped firmly, until water gushed from her mouth. When it seemed that she had expelled all the water blocking her airway, he laid her onto the deck, lifted her neck and stretched back her head, then pulled her mouth open and, sealing it with his own, breathed into her, praying that his lungs held enough life for both of them, trying to count out twelve strong breaths a minute, though there were no longer such divisions to time as minutes, there was only that single moment when Cleo should come alive or he, exhausted, should crumple and die beside her. The others stood and watched, holding their own breath as though not to steal any of the precious air. Patrick, shivering, whispered Cleo's name over and over as though it were a magical incantation. They were all praying, in their way, Augusta to the sea, this monstrous cruel sea that only a little while earlier had been so bountiful and serene. It was the same sea that had turned on Freddy and taken him (and now she could believe for the first time that it had, indeed, taken him). It had risen up to strike, reminding them in their foolish complacency that they were small and insignificant and mortal, nothing, really, in the face of its savage power, and all their concerns, their love, their poems, their money,

241

were even less. Yet, if they survived, she knew that all of it would soon return, restored by the calm, as the sea had been; the mundane concerns, hunger and desire, would creep back to resume their insistencies, their demands, their centrality. Still, she was sure that after today she would never forget what she had always known in that superficial place, her mind, and now indelibly knew in a far deeper place: that in the world, in nature, they were the frailest of candles.

She had no idea how long they had been standing there, waiting, praying, watching while Marshall breathed and breathed into Cleo's lifeless body. Then she heard Marshall gasp. His head was raised, his face lit with hope. He had felt Cleo's chest rise beneath his own. He watched it fall and rise again and then Cleo was retching and vomiting up half the sea while Marshall held her, stroking her hair. Camilla ran to fetch blankets and brandy. In a little while, wrapped in the blankets and breathing regularly, Cleo's eyes fluttered open. They all knelt around her in a circle, waiting, except for Marshall, in whose arms she was still cradled. Her eyes darted wildly, then found Ben's face and rested there, life returning to them.

"Ben," she whispered.

CHAPTER TWENTY-NINE

Marco was in the kitchen, crying. He was seated on a stool at Aurora's worktable, his head hunched into his circled arms, his shoulders heaving, long and anguished sobs, ghastly dry tremolos. He could not have said why he had come into the kitchen to break down, since, as far as he knew, he was alone in the house and could have wept anywhere in private. Was the kitchen where he had gone as a child when in need of comfort? It would have had to have been when he was very young, and it would have been his grandmother he had solicited; his mother had been a terrible cook who used every ruse to stay out of the kitchen. He remembered that when she did prepare a meal, on those occasions when all her tactics failed, everything she cooked turned out gray. He had never been able to figure out how she accomplished this. He remembered little about his early years and this unkind recollection of his mother must have come from some dire need, now, for nurturing. For the first time in his life he was in more trouble than he could cope with.

During the night, an endless one with very little sleep in it, he had tossed on his bed as though it were a stormy sea. Where could he turn for help? His attempt at psychoanalysis had only confirmed his prejudices; it was bunkum. He could hardly turn to God since he never had, and if it turned out that there was a God it was obviously going to be that old testament one meting out justice instead of mercy, a God who had punished his lust for money, for discotheques, in the cruelest way. If Freddy Nickleby were alive, he could talk to him; Freddy would be calm and rational. But, though he knew so many people, he really had no friends, no one to whom he could talk as he once could to Freddy. All his life, his friends, he now saw, had been women, women who were drawn to him because he was so finely tuned to them, so responsive to them. Because he loved them. He did love them, didn't he? Else why would they come to him as they did in droves with their discotheques? It had dawned on him that he owed most of his troubles to the shortness of his emotional attention span. Why, he wondered, was he always most in love with whatever woman he happened to be with at the moment? Was it only her physical presence and the promise of impending gratification that he responded to, and a memory as short as his conscience? Instead of loving women too much, could it be possible that he didn't love them at all?

Aurora, coming in, arms laden with shopping bags, was stopped at the door to the kitchen by the sight of Marco. She stood there for a while, watching him cry and listening to the long horrible sounds he made. She was startled; he had never struck her as a man with enough character for this kind of behavior. She put the shopping bags down and put a hand on his shoulder.

"You want to talk about it?" she asked.

"Oh, Aurora," he wailed, looking up at her with tear-stained eyes. "I'm in such trouble. I'm going to have to kill myself. There's no other way."

She knew he was a man who would never kill himself. She smiled and said, "There, there. Blow your nose," and sat down at the table across from him. He looked imploringly at her through his tears. How was it possible that he had never noticed what an unusually handsome woman she was. That stalwart, matronly bosom, not unlike Erwinna's but somehow more welcoming than aggressive. He longed to lay his head there. He pulled a handkerchief from his pocket and blew his nose. With tremendous effort, he brought his sobs under control, gasping for breath.

244

"Have you been losing weight, Aurora?" he asked.

"I don't think so. Why?"

"You look, I don't know, somehow different." He was beginning to feel a little better, recovered. "More svelte."

"Svelte, my ass," she guffawed.

"I've never broken down like this," Marco said. "I'm so ashamed." Then, in an outpouring of verbiage as torrential as his weeping had been, he told her about Erwinna and Turkish Bath, Lynda and Marilyn, and now Janet and Corned Beef & Cabbage. By the time he was through, she was hooting with laughter.

"It's not funny," he said.

"Three discos," she said. "Man, you are in trouble. Discos aren't even in any more."

He looked at her sharply. "Where did you get that idea?"

"I read it in W.W.D."

"What's that?"

"Women's Wear Daily, man. Don't you know anything?"

"What are you doing reading that?"

"I read lots of things. My tastes are eclectic. Also, it doesn't hurt to know what's trendy, what's fashionable, what's chic, what's hip. That's where the money's flowing."

In spite of his agony, Marco laughed. 'You're a remarkable woman, Aurora," he said. "Do you think it's true about discos?"

"Don't matter," she said. "Something else come along and take their place."

"It does matter. To me. I'm stuck with not one, not two, but three discos." He groaned. "If I were a moralist, which thank God I'm not, I'd be tempted to believe that I got what I deserve."

"Yeah, too much of a good thing. If you were a moralist, honey, you wouldn't be in this predicament. It's not just the discos, remember, you're stuck with the women who go with them. They're the complicating factor."

"It's your hair. You've done something different with it, haven't you?"

"Not since I took it out of a handkerchief."

"Isn't it odd, I feel so much calmer," Marco said. "I wonder why."

"Because I'm here," she said matter-of-factly. "You think I can save you."

"Yes," he said, bewitched. "I feel that."

CHAPTER THIRTY

"But it was Marshall who saved you," Patrick said, exasperated. "He almost died doing it."

He had told her the story so many times already, at her insistence. If he omitted any part of it in the retelling, she would stop him and make him go back and put it in. She was like a child with a favorite book that she herself cannot yet read. She now knew every detail exactly as Patrick had perceived it. She believed she had died and come back, though she had no memory of that exaltation described by those who have returned from death, no echoing sublime chorale, no glorious light at the end of the dark. Perhaps she had not gone far enough into death. She remembered only that for a long time she had fought to stay afloat and not to panic, but that finally she had been overpowered.

"Not in a million years would Ben have gone into that water to save you," Patrick said.

"He's probably not a very good swimmer. He probably knew it would be useless."

"You're impossible, Cleo! Even if Marshall couldn't swim a stroke, nothing would have kept him from leaping in after you. Obviously he loves you more than his life. And then, exhausted and almost drowned himself, how he wouldn't let Ben even attempt to revive you, but had to do it himself, as though only he could give you back your life. Because he wanted it, needed it ... your life ... more than anyone else."

"Because he thought Ben didn't know how. Ben wouldn't know those things." She turned her face to the wall and was silent, listening to Patrick's breathing, which was heavy with unspent exasperation. After a while, she sighed.

247

"I can't help it, Patrick," I can't help my feelings any more than you can help yours. What can I do?"

It was Patrick's turn to sigh. He was seated cross-legged on the cabin's other bed, his bed. He was so thankful that she was alive, yet here he was berating her for loving the wrong man. Still, it was to Marshall that he would be forever grateful.

"I just wish you'd give Marshall a chance. I'd trust him so much more with you than I ever could Ben."

"That's not fair. Ben is older, more settled. He's already made an important place for himself in life." She threw up her hands in a sudden gesture, as though she were tossing something to the winds. "Anyhow, why are we talking about this? Ben doesn't even want me. He wants Augusta."

"But he can't have Augusta," Patrick said firmly. "She doesn't want him."

"You can't have her either. She doesn't want you."

"I know, I know," he said, fidgeting miserably. "Who does she want."

"We don't know. But she knows."

"Maybe it's no one."

"No, it's someone. But he's not here on this ship, whoever he is."

"You're just guessing. You don't know." He sulked for a moment, then said, "What about Camilla? Do you think she'll get Avery?"

"Get?"

"I think she's lost interest in him."

"Love is so arbitrary, so undependable."

"Imagine if everyone fell in love with the absolutely right person, and it was always completely mutual. Imagine how different the world would be."

"Like Noah's ark."

"Perfect couples. There might never be another war."

"Or another book. Or movie. Or much of anything."

248

"Don't be silly. You think if everyone were happily mated they wouldn't need anything else?"

"No, I suppose they'd still have to do other things in order to survive. Freud said love and money, didn't he?"

"No. He said love and work, and that's a very different kettle of fish. It's what you do with... with your center, that place where your strength is, how you use that."

"I doubt that anyone is ever completely satisfied."

"How boring it would be."

"If it were boring, it wouldn't be perfect."

"Still, if it were perfect, how could it not be boring?"

"That's cynical."

"Cynicism comes of living so long, I suppose."

"I think Ben thinks that I don't think. I'm so tongue-tied with him. Brain-tied, too."

"Why?"

"Perhaps because he's so different, so other. And because I'm in love with him."

"Is it because you're in awe of him?"

"I guess so."

"But why are you in awe of him?"

"Because I'm in love with him."

"There's nothing awesome about him that I can see. There is about Marshall. His courage."

"I feel I could learn everything from Ben. And go on learning all my life."

"That's probably because we never had a father."

"I don't care what it's because of."

"Furthermore, it's probably not even true. He could probably learn more from you."

"Only about engines."

"No, Cleo, I think you're very likely wiser in your body and in your intuitions."

249

"I doubt that." She turned away from the wall and smiled at him. "Maybe we should neither of us ever marry anyone. Maybe we should just stay as we are."

He looked at her tenderly. "We get along so well together. We're so much alike. You are almost myself."

"Yes." She sighed. "I suppose that's why we must each find someone else."

"Yes, but it's a pity." He unwound himself from the bed, looking at his wristwatch. "I've got to relieve Marshall. We'll be coming into Bali soon."

"Would you ask him to come see me?" she said. Patrick's eyebrows shot up. It was both question and wish.

"I only want to thank him," she said. "I haven't done that."

She had fallen asleep again when Marshall knocked a few minutes later. She was still so tired and sleep was so good, so sensuous, not at all like death. He knocked again, softly, but through a thin tissue of sleep she heard him.

"Come in," she called, and when she opened her eyes he had closed the door behind him and was standing at the foot of the bed.

"Patrick said..."

"Yes."

He stood stiffly, tall and strong, like a soldier at attention, but his eyes were dark and luminous with love.

"Sit down, Marshall. You must be tired."

He sat uneasily, a transient, on the edge of Patrick's bed. "How do you feel?" he asked.

"I feel wonderful. Tired, but I feel so alive."

"We're all thankful for that."

"Thanks to you. Patrick told me all about it."

"Nothing," he mumbled. "Anyone."

"Not nothing," she said sternly. "And I don't think anyone."

"Well, don't thank me, please. I couldn't help it."

She was suddenly shy with him, but she forced herself to say what she felt needed to be said. "I wish I could love you, Marshall. I mean, I do love you in a way because you are very lovable, but I wish..."

"That's all right. I know."

"I owe you my life. I wish I could give it to you."

"I don't believe in that shit."

"Neither do I. But I wouldn't call it shit."

"It's enough for me now just to know you're alive," he said, his voice choking. "That means everything to me."

"You're so good, Marshall."

"Bull! Anyhow, I have so much to do. For my people. You wouldn't have fit into my life."

"How do you know?"

"Yeah, well."

"I don't know anything about your life, Marshall."

"Only because you never asked. It's political and dangerous and I feel I'm just at the beginning of it."

She looked interested. She was.

"My life," he went on, "has nothing to do with just having fun. That's all I'm going to say because I'm not really sure what lies ahead. But a white woman, you know, would probably be a liability to me."

"Do you mind the color of my skin?" she asked.

"Oh, Cleo!"

"I love yours," she said, looking at his arms, strong and smooth and dark against the white of his T-shirt. "I think it's the right color, the color everyone should be."

He grinned at her. "We've come a long way, baby."

"Is that black talk?"

"It's feminist talk," he said. "Don't you read newspapers?"

"Hardly ever."

"What do you read?"

"Popular Mechanics, mostly. And stuff about electronics."

"You see? We don't really know each other at all."

"Yes."

"We probably have nothing in common."

"No."

"So it's for the best, don't you think?" He got up and stretched. "We're coming into Bali. Padangbay Harbor." It was nearly dusk. "How beautiful it is."

"Describe it to me," she said.

"I'll show it to you," he said. He lifted her easily in his arms and carried her the few steps to where she could look out at the still, blue-glass, L-shaped harbor, volcanic mountains silhouetted against the darkening sky, the shapes of palm trees marching in orderly rows up and down their spines, silhouetted, too, like black paper cutouts. In the west, the sky was shot with the last traces of burnt orange and gold and three shades of pink. As they watched, the still mirror of the water turned from aquamarine to a deep purpling blue.

"This miracle world," she whispered, comfortable in his arms. "I'll never take anything for granted again. I'll never not see everything whole." Her cheek lay against his heartbeat. "I'm so glad to be alive."

He carried her back to bed and laid her gently down.

"Before you go, Marshall."

"Yes?"

"I know it isn't fair to you, but would you please kiss me anyway?"

His eyes wavered, and then he leaned and kissed her. His mouth was soft, his breath surprisingly sweet. Her own breath, she felt, was still acrid and briny. She took his head in her hands, not wanting him to stop just yet. He lay down beside her and went on kissing her.

CHAPTER THIRTY-ONE

Now I adore my life
With the Bird, the abiding Leaf,
With the Fish, the questing Snail
And the Eye altering all;
And I dance with William Blake
For love, for Love's sake.

"My darling:

"Never have I felt closer to you, nor more at peace with myself than here on this tiny chicken-shaped island (you could put Bali into Connecticut twice and still have leftovers), at whose rump you will have docked. If an egg were to fall from it onto the deck of The Augusta, it would be of purest gold. Bali is the morning of the world, paradise. You'll find its beauty for yourself; don't you hate it when someone you're out driving with points out all the sights (i.e. ':Look at that meadow covered with wildflowers,' 'There are the Rocky Mountains at last, rising up out of the plains like a blue mirage.'), as though you hadn't the eyes or the wit to see for yourself?"

They had been three days in Bali before the letter was given to Avery. They had been hot, humid days and balmy nights, with a sense of timelessness that implied that, despite the centuries of the Dutch, efficiency was not an imperative here. They had indeed found the beauty for themselves, in the changing magical landscapes, the volcanic mountains, the rice terraces, the flumes, the palm and banyan trees, the clear mountain lakes, the paddies and salt pans, the wide beaches and the ancient temples crusted mildew-green from eons of tropical humidity, their black *merus* rising into the mysterious mist to touch the gods. It was all so lush and verdant and undulating, filled with lights and darks and vibrant greens, and the people were a match for the beauty of their countryside, so self-possessed, even the children, and full of grace.

"You won't remember, but when you were about fifteen, you played a record you had just discovered and bought. You were excited by its strange sounds and rhythms, looking inward as you do when you're listening to music, or playing it. You laughed aloud. I watched your face, so alive and impishly tickled by what you were hearing. It was the Ketjak Dance."

The monkey dance. When she had first heard it, those years ago, how pagan and exotic it had been. The record jacket depicted a swarm of near-naked brown men seated, their arms raised and fingers splayed, in a temple courtyard hemmed in by jungle. The men were making the record's exotic rhythmic animal sounds, cries, hisses, a monkey army led by the ape Hanuman, helping Rama save the abducted Sita from the evil king Rhawana. Augusta could not have dreamed then that one day she would be present, seeing and hearing it for herself. Yet that was what they had done last night, and even though the ritual had been laid on for them and a handful of other tourists, a commercial performance, she had been thrilled and moved by it, by the animism and energy and the distinctive way in which the Balinese had shaped Buddhism to their own culture, and also by the contemplation of the strange twists of fate that had brought her to this place, this night, this spectacle.

They had also been to the Barong and Legong dance dramas, heard gamelang orchestras, bought ebony garuda birds in Mas, and wonderfully evil and colorful masks. They had feasted on babi guling, which they were assured was roast pig and not dog, and on spicy Indonesian dishes whose fire they quenched with exotic tropical fruits they had

254

never suspected existed, salak and rambutan. Augusta loved the percussive sound of the names of things and places: Klungkung, Kintamani, Denpasar, Lukluk, Besakih. The knock of wood against wood. She had begun work on the piece that, for the time being, she called Global Babble, a collage of voices gathered in streets and bazaars laid against indigenous music, and she could hardly wait to add to it what she was gathering here.

Except for Bert, who went his own way, and occasionally Avery, they went everywhere together, as though the fright of the storm and Cleo's near disaster had impelled them to huddle together protectively. They were now dispersed on a stretch of sandy shore at Sanur Beach fronting the luxurious Bali Beach Hotel, where they had taken rooms for the duration of their stay on the island. After the storm, they were all agreed that they needed a little vacation from the ship.

Camilla floated on her back beyond the gentle breakers. She lay there so effortlessly that she might have been asleep, but she was not; she was thinking hard about her life. Patrick was off somewhere along the shore, collecting shells. Marshall and Cleo sat beside each other at the edge of the water, its lacy fringe lapping their toes, talking and inseparable, as they had been since that moment when, as if she had swallowed a magic potion, Cleo had fallen out of love with Ben and into love with Marshall and, bewitched, had lost all her adolescent shyness and become a young woman. Marshall was transformed by happiness.

In the shade of a palm thatch umbrella, Ben lounged, reading a newspaper. He was bewildered by Cleo's sudden defection, but not pained by it. He was, in fact, relieved, aware that he had been tempted to use her to help heal the wound of Augusta. Joining the ship had been a mistake. He was a man who belonged in cities, preferably European ones where there were enough good paintings to keep him happy

255

every day. He felt deprived on this ship, as he had in most of the places they had stopped, except for Japan. Besides, he had come to be with Augusta and he had lost her. Perhaps if he hadn't come at all she would have missed him and fallen happily into his arms on her return. Instead, he had forced himself on her, been with her daily in a setting that did not flatter him. What he had suspected from his boyhood, an unathletic one, was true; he was not a man of action. He would not be returning to the ship, but would be leaving in the morning for Java, where he would begin the journey back to Santa Cruz. He looked up from his paper at Augusta and felt again this new pain. He was not used to pain. She was reading a letter, her head averted beneath a floppy-brimmed straw hat. There had been a letter for her in almost every port. He could not imagine how anyone would know how to find her so unerringly, since their schedule was so fluid. Nor could he imagine who it was, either, and if the letters were all from the same person, and if that person was a man. He had asked her if there was someone else and she had hesitated and said, "Not really."

"What does that mean?" he'd asked.

"There is and there isn't. More isn't than is. That's not a fair answer, either, is it?"

"No," he'd said, "but it's enough. I'll miss you horribly, Augusta. I miss you already."

"I'll miss you, too, Ben. I hope we'll always be friends."

Friends, always, he thought. The kiss of death.

Augusta, on her lounge chair, went on with Freddy's letter.. An unopened letter from Marco lay on her lap, waiting its turn. She was trying to remember playing the Ketjak record for Freddy and couldn't. Predictably, he went on to explain: "Actually, you were playing the record for some friends, two girls and a boy, and I wandered in and stood in the doorway watching, jealous of your friends who were hardly as entranced as you. Occasionally one would say something and you would hold up a hand in fury and say 'Shhh!, not breaking your concentration. So I listened, too, anxious to hear exactly what you were hearing, and I think I did. I'm sure I did. The boy, bored after a while, began to posture like a monkey, scratching his chest and armpits, and you stopped the record and ordered him to leave. Protesting, but still playing the monkey, he pranced out, accompanied by one of the girls. I felt pleased and in league with you, two adults annoyed by childish capers. You saw me then and smiled, annoyed though you were, and said, "Oh, hello Uncle Freddy, were you listening to this? Isn't it splendid?" Splendid was hardly the apt word but that season it was your word. If anyone asked you how you were, you said, 'Splendid, thank you,' giving the first syllable more than its due. Unless you were not splendid, of course, in which case you were 'a bit under, alas.' Such affectations! Sure though you already were of yourself, you were at that impressionable age when you were still trying on personalities. How I miss you, Augusta, and yearn for you. In my fantasy you are actually reading this letter here on this magic island and I am alive and not far off, waiting for you. In my fantasy I've somehow contrived to bring you here, not by the strength of my will alone but because of a destiny that has touched us both."

Augusta looked up from the letter. Avery was swimming out to Camilla. She wondered what Camilla was thinking about, if she had been thinking about Avery and if her thoughts had summoned him. Actually, Camilla was thinking about Michael Bell and how absolutely right he had been to feed her components into his computer. It was the scientific thing to do and she wondered why she, of all people, should have objected to that. She was completely unaware of Avery's approach until, floating at her side, he said 'hello.' She opened her eyes, aware that she felt interrupted by Avery's presence. She wanted to go on thinking

257

about Michael Bell, and about how charming and funny he was. Later, not now, she would have to think about why she had lost all interest in Avery almost from the moment she had learned that his wife was dead, that he was not, in fact, entirely unavailable. The implications of this would be frightening if she were not now, inexplicably, thinking so hard about Michael Bell, who was even more available than Avery.

Augusta watched Camilla and Avery floating side by side on the turquoise cushion of the sea. They did not seem to be talking, and she envied the intimacy of their shared silence. She looked away from them at Ben, who had folded his newspaper and was staring out at the horizon. Even in this perfect day, there was a sadness. Augusta felt the prick of tears and blinked them away.

"Though it's in none of the guidebooks, there's one sight I want to urge you not to miss. The people have named it 'The Castle of Many Things.' It was built not very long ago by an eccentric anchorite. Though finished, it's never finished; he is constantly embellishing it. And though an anchorite, he is rarely alone. Children come there to play and a small group of natives, Malaysian mountain dwellers, come in the night at the full and half moons and kneel there, praying to it, chanting something strange and wonderful, a paean, happy and triumphant. When you see it in this setting, it may come as a shock, but try to come alone. It's an experience better not shared. I can't really describe it to you except to say that while it's hardly the Taj Mahal, I think the worshippers are quite right, even in its frivolity, to see it as a tribute to life, to the indomitable spirit of man.

"Take the road to Kintamani, up, up, up, as far as it goes, and then leave the car there and look for a footpath. A little way along the path, beside a perfectly round green lake, in the shadow of Mount Batur, you'll find it."

258

The letter ended there, no conclusion, no signature; it simply stopped as though his mind had wandered, as though he'd had absolutely nothing more to say, as though he had died. Yet the letter had been put in its envelope and addressed to her, care of the ship; it had found its way to her.

She would hire a car after lunch. The drive up, she knew, would be beautiful, though she had little desire to see the shrine, or whatever it was. She had seen enough shrines. She wondered how long it would take; distances here were deceptive because of the way the roads wound around themselves. She must be sure to allow enough time. She looked out again at Camilla, wondering if she should take her along, and saw that Avery was no longer beside her. He was swimming back to shore. No, she would do what Freddy advised and go alone. It would be good to get off by herself.

She turned her attention to Marco's letter.

"Darling: Your father's been a very busy man and this is the first minute I've had to write, and what with the vagueness of your itinerary, I'm not even sure this will reach you. You really ought to phone me every chance you have, not only to reassure me of your well-being, but because my affairs have been so complicated that it will take days to catch you up on them. It will have to await your return. Even now, I'm too busy to write more than that all is well here, that I miss you and think of you always, and also that I'm sublimely happy. After all these years, I think I may at last have found the woman I can love completely for the rest of my days, the woman who is absolutely right for me. I won't tell you who she is since I'm not at all sure that she'll have me. She's strong and sensible and I feel with her as if I've come home. She is my safe harbor, which is odd since I never thought I wanted or was looking for one. On the contrary. Still, there it is. What I am to her remains to be seen.

259

"As for my business affairs, I'm on the brink of at last finding myself and making my fortune. I've acquired Corned Beef & Cabbage as well as (you will find this hard to believe) a share of Marilyn and a half share of a new disco called Turkish Bath. I may have to decline my share in Marilyn, since I don't see how I can manage all three places at once. Feast or famine, but that's your father for you. Turkish Bath opened three nights ago to great fanfare, thanks to excellent publicity, and looks to be a smashing success. It draws a large gay crowd, and that means people in the art and fashion worlds. My partner there, Erwinna (you've met her), is having so much fun running the place, and she's so good at it, that she is giving up her academic position. She says she has also given up primal screaming. With Erwinna firmly entrenched there, I will be able to devote most of my time to CB&C, which we're remodeling and renaming Soul. A much better name, I think. We're going to have live music, good jazz and, on dance nights, big band swing, and we'll serve what I can promise you will be some of the best food anywhere. The place, as you know, is on the upper west side, so we expect to draw upper class Harlem as well as the Yuppy crowd. Aurora feels it could well have the success of the old Cotton Club, and I'm sure she's right."

Aurora?

"Well, my darling, continue to have a glorious time, stay well, and call me when you can. I think on your return you'll find your old father blissfully content in both heart and pocket. Meanwhile, I send all my paternal love."

CHAPTER THIRTY-TWO

She left the taxi waiting at the end of the road and walked up the footpath that wound through dense tropical growth around the lake. At this elevation, the air had turned cooler and lighter. Not far along, the jungle abruptly drew back and in a wide clearing there it stood. She stopped dead to stare at it, then couldn't help laughing aloud, it was so wildly fantastic, like an illustration for a fairy tale, yet like nothing she could have conjured up in her wildest imaginings. It was a huge wedding cake, layer upon layer, its facade a frosting of excrescences in every possible color and design, huge bunches of purple and green and red grapes, red apples and golden bananas, and strawberries, all mixed with daisies and nosegays of violets and anemones and balloons, and rabbits sitting at attention, and frogs poised to leap, and clusters of chickadees and robins and parrots. It would require days to take it all in, so cluttered with happy detail was it. Only a madman or an Italian baker could have made it, or someone boundlessly hopeful and free and full of delight.

She took a few steps forward then stopped again, trying to think of what it reminded her, something Camilla had talked about recently. Oh, yes, that jungle bird. The bower bird. Of course.

She had really always known it, hadn't she? Not always. But the knowledge had been growing in her for weeks, an uncertain knowledge, perhaps, but whatever it was it had been larger than hope. She walked along a smaller path made of shells that shone like pearls in the late afternoon sun. She could feel the beating of her heart. She saw him, then, standing in the gaily encrusted doorway, smiling at her, a bearded sunburned man, not the least bit ancient, as she had feared.

"I've been waiting and waiting," he said, walking toward her.

She stopped and looked at him for a long moment, then said, "I came as soon as I could."

The End